Martin Luther and Mahatma Gandhi
A Paradigm for Social Change

Martin Luther and Mahatma Gandhi
A Paradigm for Social Change

M. Christhudhas

2018

Martin Luther and Mahatma Gandhi: *A Paradigm for Social Change* — published by the Rev. Dr. Ashish Amos of the Indian Society for Promoting Christian Knowledge (ISPCK), Post Box 1585, 1654, Madarsa Road, Kashmere Gate, Delhi-110006.

ISBN: 978-81-938241-3-9

Cover credit: Internet sources

Laser typeset by

ISPCK, Post Box 1585, 1654, Madarsa Road, Kashmere Gate, Delhi-110006
• *Tel:* 23866323/22

e-mail: ashish@ispck.org.in • ella@ispck.org.in
website: www.ispck.org.in

Contents

Acknowledgments

I am grateful to God, the Almighty for being with me all through this work and with whose grace I could complete this work successfully.

I am indebted to the Gandhigram Rural Institute, Gandhigram, Tamil Nadu for permitting me to do the research, out of which this book is possible.

With deep sense of gratitude, I acknowledge my guide Dr. M. Mallammal, Professor and Director, Centre for Gandhian Studies, Gandhigram Rural Institute, with whose valuable guidance and effort this work became a great success.

With great honour I extend my heartfelt thanks to The Most Rev. Thomas K. Oommen, the Moderator of Church of South India and the Bishop-in-charge of C.S.I. Kanyakumari Diocese for writing the *Foreword* for this book.

I am grateful to the Rev. Dr. M. Peter Singh, Professor and the Director, Department of Communication Studies, Tamilnadu Theological Seminary, Madurai and the Rev. Dr. M. Justin Moses, the Deputy Registrar, Senate of Serampore College for writing few words about the book.

I offer my gratitude to my friends, Rev. S. Christopher Yesumony, Rev. M. Albert Sutha Gnanadhas , Rev. I. Renjit Vethakumar, Rev. S. Jeyalal, Rev. A. Bright Solomon, Rev. N. Vibin John, Rev. S. Arul Jeba Singh, Rev. C. Gildon Dhayananth, Rev. T. P. Salim Thanka Kumar, Rev. Ramesh D. Dhas, Rev. J. Prakash Nayagam, and Dr. Viju Wilson, for their encouragement and support in completing this work successfully.

I am thankful to my Diocese for mending me in my ministerial journey and enabling me to bring out this book.

I am obliged to my life partner, Mrs. T. Sheela, for her inestimable support and patient for being with me through my life journey, especially, in doing this work and to my children C.S. Bussard and C.S. Bestlin for cheering me up with their love and affection even during this work.

At this moment, I remember my ever-loving gift of God, C.S. Best, my son who lives in memory. I, whole heartedly, dedicate this book to him and for his love.

Author

Foreword

I am delighted to be asked to write foreword to this book. Rev. Dr. M. Christhudhas is serving as the Presbyter in the CSI Church, Payanam, and is also the Secretary of Pastoral Concerns of the CSI Kanyakumari Diocese. He had also served as the Treasurer of the CSI Kanyakumari Diocese during 2012-2015. I appreciate his efforts in bringing out the book, "Martin Luther and Mahatma Gandhi." This book brings out the work and teachings of Martin Luther and Mahatma Gandhi, which may be studied systematically and interrupted rightly by the younger generation.

The book provides an inspiring reading and focuses on the manner in which, both, Martin Luther as well as Mahatma Gandhi, who were from middle class families, strove to obtain social dignity by facing risks cheerfully and underwent sufferings gracefully. The author of the book has strived to bring out the essence of the teachings of these two great historical heroes, Martin Luther "Father of Protestant Reformation" and Mahatma Gandhi "Father of our Nation", who lived in different political and religious contexts.

The effort of the author to bring out this beautiful book is highly appreciable since it is not aimed at the present but future generation too. The book also tries to reveal the hidden ideologies and serves as a guide to involve the readers deeply in the socio-political context which is a great challenge for the generations to come.

The Most Rev. Thomas K. Oommen,
B.A., B.D., M.Th.
The Moderator, Church of South India & Bishop-in-Charge, CSI Kanyakumari Diocese.

Preface

I am delighted to bring out the book *Martin Luther and Mahatma Gandhi: A Paradigm for Social Change*. Martin Luther was the founder of the German reformation in the 16th century. He is one of the figures of the past of whom it may be said that the history of the world was intensely altered by his work. He was the first great and outstanding figure who opposed the Pope and the King and succeeded in his venture. Luther moved men by the power of a reflective religious faith resulting in unmistakable trust in God. His concern with human welfare stood for the religious and social life of the people. In the same way, Mahatma Gandhi was one of the giants of the twentieth century, who left an indelible impact on the social, economic and political scenario of the day. He was a great revolutionary, who, even while he fought for the freedom of his country, was aware of the freedom of all the enslaved people in different parts of the world. Both Martin Luther and Mahatma Gandhi were not only thinkers but also politicians, spiritualists, socialists and reformers of the society and the church. Though a few comparisons of Luther and Gandhi have been attempted, a full-length study is yet to be undertaken. In this book an attempt is made to study the life history of Luther and Gandhi systematically and to compare their ideology and their role in bringing life to the deprived people of Germany and India.

The main objectives of the book are: (i) to study the life and work of Martin Luther and Mahatma Gandhi and their roles in the freedom struggle; (ii) to trace the social and political philosophy of Luther and Gandhi; (iii) to analyze the economic, religious and educational philosophy of Luther and Gandhi; and (iv) to find out the similarities by comparing their life, work and ideology. They will be placed in their historical setting. By adopting the methodology of comparative analysis the book serves its purpose. This book covers a wide range of comparative events in all spheres of life. It is also concerned with philosophical ideas. Thus, this study is bound to be selective. This study has been arranged in twelve chapters.

In the concluding part Martin Luther and Mahatma Gandhi were brought forth as powerful and dynamic leaders of Germany and modern India. They were men of the masses. Though they came from different environments, their devotion and dedication to social progress in all spheres and their selfless service to the poor brought them close to each other. Their lives were unique examples of unity of thought, word and action. They would not lay down one policy for the leaders and another for the masses. Their principles and approaches were people centered and are highly pertinent to the 21st century.

Further studies could be undertaken by comparing their key concepts, life styles, and their literary contributions, etc. I hope this book will be useful to Gandhian scholars, Gandhian activists, Social scientists and Social workers. I hope it will also be beneficial to the younger generation to draw inspiration from the lives and the works of Luther and Gandhi.

The Rev. Dr. M. Christudhas
Presbyter & Secretary of Pastoral Concerns,
Church of South India, Kanyakumari Diocese,
Tamil Nadu, South India.

Introduction

The history of mankind shows how great men have always struggled and fought against prevailing social evils and human suffering. Martin Luther and Mahatma Gandhi were exceptional strategists and they created history. A number of researches have been done on the life and work of Luther and Gandhi. But the researcher could not find any comparative work on these two great personalities, who lived in the 16th century in Germany and early 20th century in India respectively. Martin Luther was an extraordinary person in the Christendom and reformed the religious practices. He questioned the hierarchy that was predominant in the society and in the church. Mahatma Gandhi stood for Indian freedom and was able to bring about constructive reforms in both Indian society and Indian religion. Since a comparative study of the two heroes of different ages, particularly their contributions, has not been done, the present writing is justified.

It is enormously exciting to read or write about Martin Luther, a remarkable religious reformer, who marks a new era in the history of the Christian Church. He was one of the rare and remarkable men of history. He inspired and led successfully the reformation who lived in the 16th century in Germany. He stood for eradicating the evil forces that prevailed in both the religion and the society, particularly in Christian religion. The religious, social and political context of that century also pushed Luther into the storm of reform. Luther stood up and challenged boldly the highest constituted powers of heaven and earth, Pope and Emperor. He discovered the true evangelical faith and truth. He began to fight for the truth which was taught by Jesus and the Apostles. He challenged the authority of the church in matters of faith, doctrine and practices. Luther shook the very foundation of the Roman Church. He was condemned as a 'heretic' by the Roman church and also declared an 'outlaw' by the Holy Roman Emperor. Yet, he became a successful reformer and champion of evangelical faith.

Luther said salvation should not be viewed as something earned or bought by prayers and money; and there should not be a sense of the mechanical about the very life of the church. He did the maximum to the church and the society. He was the man behind the right changes in the teachings and practices of the church. Martin Luther is remembered as an ecumenical person and also a hero for the founding of a new church called Protestantism. He brought freedom to the people in worship. Hierarchy in the structure of worship was highly condemned and the word of God was given prominence in the services. He stood for the religious and political liberation of the German people. Hegel described the nature of the great man: "The great man of the age is the one who can put into words the will of his age, tell his age what its will is, and accomplish it. What he does is the heart and essence of his age, he actualizes his age" (G.W.F. Hegel, *Philosophy of Right*, 295).

Gandhi's ideas and deeds permeated the entire humanity. He was the greatest of the humanists that India presented to the world in modern times. He was a great revolutionary who, even while fighting for the freedom of his country, was aware of the freedom of all the enslaved people in different parts of the world. He was a multifaceted genius, a thinker, a politician, a spiritualist and a social reformer whose thoughts covered all walks of life. Born at Porbandar in Gujarat in a Vaishya clan, educated in India and England, Gandhi went to South Africa to try his fortunes. There he emerged as a Satyagrahi, a mass leader against political suppression and social inequality.

Satyagraha signifies his theory and practice of non-violent resistance. Gandhi was to describe himself pre-eminently as a votary or seeker of Satya (Truth), which could not be in any way attained other than through Ahimsa (Non-violence) and Brahmacharya. In South Africa, he used Satyagraha in the struggle of the Indians to claim their rights and independence. After his return to India in 1915, Gandhi, with his new weapon of Satyagraha, effected a great change in the Indian National

Congress, by transforming it into a mass-based organization with the aim of uplifting rural folk and uprooting the British Raj. His social, economic and political ideas exemplify a deep and abiding interest in a fundamental reformation of the Indian society. He was a charismatic leader with a mass appeal. He symbolized a new trend in the Indian context of an individual wielding immense power and influence on millions without occupying any formal position of power and authority.

Mahatma Gandhi is no more in our midst to-day. His powerful personality has left an indelible influence on every aspect of our individual and national life. He embodied in his own person all those great and lofty principles which have throughout the ages governed and given sustenance to the life and thought of the millions of this country. The inspiration of his leadership has helped many a perplexed soul to find the path of peace and truth. In the early 19th century slavery and bondage prevailed in many parts of the country. People were suffering from different kinds of epidemics and medical facilities were not accessible to all. Economically, religiously and politically high-class people enjoyed all the privileges. In this context he stood for the freedom of the people from the British domination and freed the nation from the yoke of the white race. He worked for the people by responding to the issues of the people. He stood with the ordinary people and fought for political freedom.

The hierarchy of the British management kept the Indians as slaves and they were not able to raise their voice for the betterment of the country. Gandhi was able to realize the need for freedom. Therefore, he stood for the unity of the nation by bringing Indians under one umbrella. He respected all religions and was friendly with people of all castes. He lived as a model figure of his age. The speciality in him was that he lived for the people. He loved the country, wanted to see the country without any division in the name of caste, colour and creed. The spirit of nationalism was deeply rooted in him. He called upon the people to use things made by the people of our country.

The people of our country suffered from various common and contagious diseases. Outbreaks of epidemic became regular and seasonal. Health care and education were areas in which Gandhi involved himself to lift the neglected people from their depressing condition. He knew very well that through education and health care he would be able to save the life of the people. He served the country as a nation builder, emancipator and educationist to free the people from the yoke of white race. He stood as a role model of leadership and also showed a way of life for India to survive as a free nation. Martin Luther and Mahatma Gandhi's message, however, is not only for India but for the entire world. They expected that man could live in peace with his fellowman and promote one another's welfare.

Chapter 1
Life and Work of Martin Luther

Amidst the tens of thousands of names of Christian leaders that crowd the columns of Christian global history with their saintly characters and magnanimities as well as with their dynamic leadership and thoughts, the name of Martin Luther shines like a bright star. He was a man of mystery who created history. Living men of Christendom cannot forget but must cherish his memory and his magnificent contribution to the Christian Church and society. He is, therefore, honoured by Christians from all over the world. He is acclaimed as one of the greatest reformers in world history. The story of Martin Luther is the story of the birth of Protestantism which was the outcome of the Reformation, one of the greatest events of Church history that occurred in the sixteenth century during the time of the Holy Roman Empire in Germany. Marin Luther is best known as a renowned reformer who, as an Augustinian monk and Professor of the university at Wittenberg, inspired and led the Protestant Reformation and who, through that, inaugurated a new era in the history of the Christian Church and society.

The most eminent Church historian, K.S. Latoruette, describes Luther, quite rightly so, as 'The chief pioneer of Protestantism.'[1] A great scholar and famous biographer of Luther, Roland Baintaon, presents him as 'The inaugurator of reform.'[2] Another noted biographer, Henry

Jacobs, praises Luther as 'The Hero of the Reformation.'[3] The words of great Church historian, Williston Walker, 'Martin Luther .... is one of the few men of whom it may be said that the history of the world was profoundly altered by his work'[4]

The medieval society faced enormous political, social, economic and religious upheaval. It was an age of adversity and flux. Moral crisis and corruption were rampant which eventually demanded a Reformation.[5] Martin Luther was a social being and also religious person from the beginning to the end and he was never willing to compromise with the evils that prevailed in the name of religion. He was against social, political, economic, religious and educational deprivation of the poor living in Germany. He was a man of strong faith, will and conviction. He was a man of high intelligence and principles too.

Luther is also best known as a man of tremendous courage and boldness. He stood boldly and courageously against the corruption of the Church. He risked his life and sacrificed all worldly pleasures to work untiringly for the reformation of the Church of Christ. He challenged the power and authority of Rome over the Christian Church. He really shook the mighty Church of Rome, especially the Papacy, which claimed the keys of the Kingdom of Heaven. To understand the real significance of the life and mission of Martin Luther, it is good to see the social context in which he lived and what he said, wrote and did. It was the social as well as religious situations that forced him to be the reformer of his age. This chapter describes the religious, political and social situations of Germany and Europe, along with the early life of and influences on Martin Luther.

Religious context

Due to the temporal supremacy in the pagan Roman Empire, religion was completely subservient to the state. A person, by assuming the office of Emperor, also acquired divinity. Divinity was, thus, a by-product of absolute political power. But, in the medieval period, the Papacy reversed this situation. It asserted its universal standing and extended its supremacy over the secular power too. George P. Fisher says that the King was to the Pope as the moon is to the sun, that is, a lower luminary shining with borrowed light.[6] Roland H. Bainton states that the Pope often could not make up his own mind whether he was the successor of Peter or of Caesar.[7] The Church of the middle ages, thus, was secularized and became the political power. Alister McGrath says that the Papacy reached the height of political power which was unknown previously.[8] Nonetheless, the political success of the Church had its negative effects. The political success forced the Church to participate in the feudal organization.[9] As a result the Church appeared as a legal, judicial, financial, administrative and diplomatic machine rather than the visible embodiment of Christ upon the earth.[10] G.W. Searle says that political success had weakened the Church. As its bishops obtained wealth and position, as the monasteries accumulated the feudal power and as the Friars spread amongst the population, as the Church became identified with the established order of the state, its leaders were no longer seen in spiritual or in pastoral terms and they came to represent the authoritarian aspect of medieval society which came to be so much resented.[11]

The piety of the medieval Church was at a low ebb because it contrasted with primitive Christianity in many ways. Despite the flourishing spiritual movements and the manifestation of the Renaissance, from the point of view of religion of sixteenth century is regarded as an age of instability, of division and resolution, and the age when Europe saw the end of united Christendom.[12] Gerhard Ritter says that the sacred acts of the medieval Church could no longer satisfy the religious needs of the German soul.[13] The piety of the Church left all administration in the hands of priests who were considered a superior class and indispensable almoners of divine grace. The ecclesiastical administration was avaricious and corrupt. Bernard M.G. Reardon says that even secular princes did not surpass it.[14] Worldliness, venality, and rift among the Church's official representatives were predominant. Widespread abuses in the financial exactions by the authorities of all ranks were also prevalent. The Church officials collected money from the people by way of dispensations and the most profitable source of income arose from the granting of dispensations. The following observation confirms the above mentioned idea. A Papal official quoted by A.G. Dickens remarked that the Lord desired not the death of the sinner, but rather that he should pay and live.[15]

In Europe, especially in Germany, there were innumerable Churches. Almost every tiny village had its chapel and every town had its chapel and every town had several churches. Besides, pilgrimage to various shrines was predominant.[16] Nonetheless, piety during the middle ages very much declined. Stern preachers like Geile Keysersberg and Berthold of Regensburg denounced pilgrimages and said that the pilgrimages created more sins than they yielded pardons.[17] The Pope, as the successor of Peter and Vicar of Christ, regarded himself as being on the top of the hierarchical order and as the one authorized by Christ to determine everyone else's place in it. George P. Fisher alludes to the secular spirit of the Popes. As temporal rulers, they were immersed in political contests and schemes of ambition.[18]

Roland H. Bainton says that the Pope did not even hesitate to make alliance with the unbelieving Turks against the believing monarchs.[19] Popes were in a sense wholly committed to a system of military and diplomatic alliances and adventures. They were also worldly members and very interested persons.[20] Richard Kroner too affirms that the display of artistic beauty, the enormous luxury of the buildings, the frivolous life of the Cardinals and the eye of the Pope himself aroused the anger and indignation of devout and the visitors to Rome.[21] The moral life of the Popes was also very degraded. Concubinage was common among them and Pope Alexander publicly acknowledged his own bastards.[22] The Popes were also money-minded and they levied various kinds of taxes. Dispensations for marriage within the prohibited degrees and for acquiring unjust gains in trades were granted on payment. This demoralizing and unwanted collection of money in the name of religion made the Papal treasury richer. The venality and rapacity increased when the Popes sold the offices in the Papal court.[23]

The Bishops too acted as feudal overlords and as political advisers rather than as spiritual leaders. A.G. Dickens says that the Bishops became feudal lords and they continued their secular labours ever after their elevation to bishoprics.[24] In certain parts of Europe, Germany in particular, these Bishops became princes in their own right and nearly one third of Germany was in the hands of these prince-Bishops.[25] In some cases bishoprics were bought and kept in the hands of a particular family.[26] The Bishops were too money-minded and, therefore, they spent most of their time in business and other profitable affairs rather than in spiritual activities. G.W. Searle states that so much of the bishop's time was devoted to the service of the state or the business of administering extensive lands, that little was left either for the close supervision of the ordinary clergy, or for their own participation in pastoral duties. It was not that the majority were not able men, or that they were self seeking and more corrupt than other great landlords or officers of state.[27]

The moral lives of the religious leaders were not satisfactory. Concubinage was common among them. One Bishop flippantly remarked that as a Bishop he was celibate, but as a baron he was married and father of a numerous family.[28] The clergy constantly maintained their superiority over the laity as divinely appointed superiors. Furthermore, they created a universal belief that the mediation of priests was essential for salvation. Though the clergy claimed supremacy, their education was poor and some of them were uneducated.[29] Consequently, they were ignorant of the Church dogmas and doctrines.[30] Their moral life was also not up to the mark. Many priests failed to observe the law of celibacy. Bainton says that on the eve of the Reformation, clerical concubinage was a recognized system condoned by the laity and taxes by the Church.[31] Kingston D. Ian Siggins declares that concubine was made as a source of revenue in the cradle tax.[32]

The clerical dues were regarded as belonging to one system, of intolerable oppression. Hans Bernhard Meyer quoted by Carter Lindberg says that before the Reformation there was hardly a testament which did not include considerable sums for the holding of masses and other services.[33] Besides, the rapacity of churchmen went far beyond the exaction of the tithes. A Spaniard quoted by Thomas M. Lindsay says that we can scarcely get anything from Christ's ministers but for money. They will ring no bell without money, no burial in the Church without money; so that it seemed the paradise is shut up from them that have no money.[34] The cleavage between the clergy and the laity was so glaring that the body of Christians was divided into two groups as clergy and laity. The clergyman always maintained the superiority by virtue of their prerogative power to celebrate the sacraments. For no layman was permitted to administer the sacraments. Roland H. Bainton says that due to this prerogative power the meanest priest claimed himself greater that the loftiest emperor.[35]

In the medieval Church, it was considered less holy to work in the spheres of commerce or administration than to do work that was especially Christian.[36] As a result, monasteries were regarded with high esteem. The monastery was of course somewhat better that the other institutions because of the reformatory movements commonly emanating from the monasteries. Nonetheless, the monks too were subject to all temptations. They were very much concerned with their own petty works and merits rather than with the words of Christ.[37] Above all, the level of educational and spiritual attainment in most monasteries was shockingly low. When the monasteries became wealthy the monks acted as the greatest landowners,[38] which eventually drew them away from their spiritual activities. Popular piety had a huge admixture of superstition in it. The veneration of relics, pilgrimages, and the elaboration of the cult of the saints reached a point higher than at any previous period in Christian history.[39] The most lucrative system was indulgences. Thomas M. Lindsay says that downtrodden people from poor houses gathered round the practice of indulgences.[40] This was the system through which the Popes constantly exploited the ordinary people.

The theology of the medieval Church also misled the people. The Church was paganised to a degree. The mythological, religious and philosophical ideas were not in agreement with the biblical vision of God. Superstitious elements encroaching upon the cult surrounded Christian shrines and faith as well. With regard to man's salvation, the Church insisted on man's own effort. Man could be justified in the eyes of God partially through his own actions and partially through God's grace. When salvation was purely a gratuitous act flowing from the mercy of God, the Church connected it with human merit. The Roman Church also superseded the authority of the scripture and declared itself the sole authority to interpret the doctrines of the Church. Religion was thus converted into an external ordinance and the superstitious elements encroached upon the minds of the common people. Kingston D. Ian Siggins declares that the forms of popular piety had no theological basis but were based on superstition.[41] The medieval scholastic was a philosophical speculation rigorously controlled by logical analysis. It was tightly bound to the traditional belief based on the dogma of the Church Fathers.

Political Context

The sixteenth century was a time of violence. Political tension, intrigue and war were prevalent. It witnessed a long series of wars.[42] Politically, Germany was not in a stable condition. It was divided into many territories and the governmental authority of the territorial states was comparatively weak. Thomas M. Lindsay rightly says that the country was cut into sections and slices, and was hopelessly divided.[43] Although a strong popular sentiment for unity had arisen in the German-speaking portions, no progress was made to make Germany into a united nation. The only authorities who could create unity were the Emperor and the princes. But due to the difference of opinion between the two, the expected unity never materialized. The princes on the one hand resolved to keep their independence and their policy for unity was always oligarchy. But the Emperor preferred to be autocratic because he did not want to be controlled by an oligarchy of German princes.[44] The shift from centralized power to territorial power in the German Empire led to a struggle for freedom within the estates. They exercised a great influence in the affairs of the Empire and sought from the Emperor some of independent civil government.[45] They did not like the centralization of power and the central authority. On the contrary, the Emperor sought to assert control of his vast Empire since the estates wanted to escape from his control and to enhance their power within the Empire. As a result, political tension as well as political instability prevailed.

Social Context

At the beginning of the sixteenth century, a restless social condition prevailed in Germany. The condition of Europe and of Germany in particular was one of seething discontent and full of bitter class hatreds, the great capitalists against the 'guilds',[46] the poor against the wealthy and the knights against the princes. The picture of this class hatred was abundantly manifested in the folk songs of this period.[47] During the middle ages the land was the only economic basis of wealth and this was largely true in Germany. In society all relations rested on land.[48] But the sixteenth century witnessed the rise of capitalism. James Atkinson says that it was the first time that 'money talked'.[49] Currency rather than goods was now taking pre-eminence. As a result, great banking houses arose along with trading companies with all the machinery of capitalism. The rise of capitalism on the one hand helped the rich to become richer but on the other hand it created a proletariat class.[50] Roland H. Bainton says that the rise of capitalism simultaneously developed banking and fostered big business.[51]

Another evil was the inception of usury. Due to the new moneyed class usury became a common practice, which ultimately suppressed the financial growth of the poor masses. The constant rise in prices too eventually aggravated the social situation, whose results were painfully manifest in the crowds of sturdy beggars who thronged the roads the refuse of all classes in society, from the broken noble and the disbanded mercenary soldier to the earned peasant, the workman out of employment, the begging friar and the wandering student.[52] Owing to the monopoly of the merchants and the manufactures the old spreading classes were being ousted and, therefore, there were divisions among the people. The confrontations were of the poor against the rich, of debtors against creditors and of men who had scanty legal rights or none against those who had the protection of the existing laws. The knights and the peasants' revolts were indications of deep strains of the medieval society. The future of the people of the low orders was bleak and on the whole open to exploitation. Therefore, they violently and desperately tried to attain some kind of influence in the government in order to elevate their social position, which eventually created an explosive atmosphere with revolutionary ideas.

In the above said religious, political and social context, Martin Luther stood up for the deprived community for bringing about equality at every level in the structure and practice in both the Church and society. To eradicate the prevailing evils in the society Luther spoke, wrote and endeavoured. In conclusion, the medieval Church was both positively and negatively ripe for the Reformation.

Birth and Early Years of Martin Luther

Martin Luther was a man of unique character and complex personality. He was a Professor, Pastor, Philosopher, Poet, Musician, Monk, Theologian, Educator, Economist, Politician and a successful Reformer. Most important of all, Luther was God's instrument for the restoration of the pure doctrine of the Holy Scripture. He was a man who rediscovered and fought for the truth which Jesus Christ and His Apostles once taught. He was also responsible for the restoration of Christian liberty in general and the freedom of the laity in particular. Indeed, he was a true follower of Christ as well as the true reformer of the Church and the society. It is interesting to note that such a great man of unique character and dynamic personality had to begin his earthly life in a humble way like many other great men of history.

Luther's Parents

The story of Martin Luther begins in a poor peasant's home in Germany. His father, Hans Luther, was a peasant by birth. His grandfather, Anns Luther, was also a peasant. They all lived in an obscure village called Moehra. It was a beautiful hilly place situated at the edge of the Thuringian Forest. Hans Luther was called 'Big Hans' so as to distinguish him from his brother 'Little Hans', who was a notorious person. Young Hans Luther, while still residing at Moehra, married a young lady of the neighbourhood, Margaret Liegler. She belonged to a respectable Christian family of the middle class of Neustadt, in the district of Wurzburg. Hans did not inherit any ancestral property. He had to depend totally on his daily labour for their daily bread. At times they had to face many hurdles and hardships. Young Margaret did not expect such sufferings. At the beginning of her married life, however, she faced these difficult times with courage and faith. Hans Luther was a man of vision and action. Knowing pretty well the barrenness of his land and the helplessness of his condition, Hans decided to move to some other place to find a better means of livelihood. He realized, perhaps, he would have to face more problems and difficulties when his family would grow, if he continued to stay there. He probably could think of Eisleben, the place where the mining industry was thriving. It attracted him for he could think of better prospects there. Finally he shifted to Eisleben with his young wife Margaret.[53]

Luther's home had a religious atmosphere. It was the providence of God which brought them to Eisleben, in the Province of Saxony, Eastern Germany. It was on a calm and cold winter midnight, when the darkness fully covered the land, when the stars began to shine in full gloom, a new soul entered the world crying and thus breaking the silence of the night. That was Martin Luther, our great hero of the Reformation. He was born on Monday November 10, 1483, between 11 p.m. and 12 p.m. If the memory of the Margaret was correct that was the golden day in the history of the Church and society. Who knew at that time that this child would be the future Reformer, the champion of the evangelical faith? It was quite obvious that both Hans and Margaret were extremely happy when God blessed them with a male child. They both were brought up in the Catholic faith. Quite naturally they decided to dedicate the child to God. Next day, Tuesday, early in the morning, Hans carried the little child, with gratitude and joy, to St. Peter's and St. Paul's Church in Eisleben as per the custom of the day.

The child was baptized at the font of this Church by the parish priest, Bartholomew Rennebcher. The child was given the name Martin in honour of the saint remembered that day according to the calendar of the Church. Because of high infant mortality (heaven must be full of little children, Luther later commented) babies were baptized as early as possible. Hence, following the tradition, Luther was christened the very next day. Significantly, it was an auspicious day, the day of the Feast of St. Martin of Tours, a charitable Roman soldier turned monk - bishop, who took an axe to pagan shrines and who happened to be one of the founders of Monasticism. It was quite obvious the name of this saint was given to Luther. But neither his parents not the pastor, at that time, realized that this child would become more famous than the saint. Thus, Martin Luther's humble birth took place in a humble way in a humble family. He never forgot his origin. He always remembered his poor peasant's home. He, in fact, took pride in saying at his Table Talk: "I am a peasant's son. My father and grand-father were all peasants."[54]

Once again the poverty of the family struck Hans. His expectation of getting better prospects in Eisleben looked miserable. It was becoming difficult for him to support his family with his meagre income. Eventually, in the summer of 1484, Hans and Margaret moved to Mansfield, six miles from Eisleben, the capital of the rich mining district, where the prospects looked more promising, for he could work in the mines, the industry which was thriving in that town. He had, hopes of not only getting a better job but of getting a degree of independence. When they moved to Mansfield, Martin was just eight months old, still an infant in arms. It was in this town of Mansfield that Hans and his family finally and permanently settled and gradually flourished. It was in this town Luther spent his childhood. That is why Luther is more associated with this town than the place of his birth.

Luther's Childhood

It would be quite interesting to know the childhood experiences of Luther at home. This would help us to understand his parents as well. His reminiscences of his childhood were, however, not those of sunshine and rainbows. His childhood was spent in poverty. He grew up amid the poor, coarse surroundings of the German peasant life. His home was, undoubtedly, a real peasant's home, in its strict sense of the word. He remembered those sad days throughout his life. His father was so busy with the metals that the son hardly enjoyed the affection or love of his father. His mother was very active and busy with her work. Nevertheless, Luther loved them. He appreciated their efforts and hard work they put in bringing up their children. But at times, he also regretted the harshness and the severity with which his parents treated their children and which perhaps, clouded the memory of his early years. Severe punishments were given to the children for doing wrong or for not doing the work assigned to them. Luther seems to have said at one of his Table Talks, "My Parents dealt with me so severely that I became completely timid."[55]

"The apple", said Luther, "should always lie beside the rod"[56] While speaking about punishment from his mother, he said, "My mother hangs me for stealing a nut until the blood came."[57] On another occasion for a similar misdeed, said Luther, "My father once whipped me so that he ran away from him and felt ugly toward him until he was of pains to win me back."[58] This shows that parents of Luther were of very strict discipline. But, this does not mean that Luther's parents were bad or inhuman or cruel or they did not have any love for children. Remember what King Solomon had said "He that spare his rod, hate his son, but he that loves him chaste him bad times."[59] These words are true to Luther and his parents too. They did love their children even when they punished them. Luther realized this while he himself said, 'at heart they meant it well.'[60] Quite right someone has said, "what is to become great, should begin small and if children are brought up too delicately and with too much kindness from their youth, they are injured for life."

In fact, both Hans and Margaret were very good, gracious and God-fearing people. They were strict because they wanted their children to be obedient, God-fearing as they must learn the will of God. Hans was an upright man. He was ambitious and industrious. He was known for his integrity and independent spirit. He was frank and firm in his decisions. It was happened to bend him or break him. He was like a metal. But he was diligent in business. Melanchthon, the friend and biographer of Luther, describes him as 'a man of purity in character and conduct.' To some extent Hans Luther can be called a chip of the old block.' Martin Luther described his father as a 'tough Saxon of peasant's stock'. Margaret possessed all the good qualities of a good woman. She was known for her purity and piety of life. She was very simple but very strict. She was very humble but a little harsh in her treatment of her children. She was very quiet but quite hard-working woman. Melanchthon spoke of her as 'worthy of woman.' As it was pointed out, "Margaret possessed all the virtues that can adorn a good and pious woman. Her modesty, her fear of God and her prayerful spirit were particularly remarked. She was looked upon by the matrons of the neighbourhood as a model whom they should strive to imitate."[61] Luther's friend and Court preacher, Spalatin, spoke of her 'rare qualities'. If the portraits of Cranach are reliable, Martin grew to resemble his father in frame and his mother in eyes and mouth.

As the years passed his family grew in number and the needs of the family also increased. A big family with seven children, four sons and three daughters, caused constant anxiety and worry to Hans and Margaret for their maintenance and education. Hence, both had to work hard to support and maintain them. They had to make a lot of sacrifices for their children's sake. Acknowledging this in later years the Reformer said, "My parents were very poor. My father was a poor wood-cutter and my mother has often carried wood upon her back that she might procure the means of bringing up their children. They endured the severest labour for our sakes."[62] Perhaps Luther accompanied his mother to the forest to gather wood to get his daily food. This may have given Luther an opportunity to accustom himself so early in his life to hard labour and frugality.

As little Martin was growing spiritually the big Hans was growing materially. As young Martin was growing, gradually, in strength and knowledge, Hans was growing in status in the society and his financial condition was gradually improving. People of Mansfeld appreciated his hard work, his independent spirit, his integrity, his spotless life and good sense. They elected him as one of the four members of the Mansfield Town Council. So, in 1491, within a short space of seven years, Hans became a town Councilor. By 1511 he also became part owner of six shafts and two foundries. He was soon able to rent out several furnaces. This improved his economic condition tremendously. This was a great boost for him to think of giving a proper education to Martin. Both of his advances, the honourable position in the society and economic prosperity, were the fruits of Hans's hard work and hardships.[63]

As stated earlier, Hans and Margaret were staunch Roman Catholic Christians of the middle ages. Luther was brought up strictly in that faith by his parents. His parents were regular attendants at mass. True and genuine piety prevailed in their home. He was early taught a few simple prayers and hymns at his mother's knee. He was taught the Ten Commandments, the Creed and the Lord's Prayer. Luther's early image of Christ derives from a painting he saw behind the altar in a Church window. It showed the saviour, stern of face, sword in hand, sitting on a rainbow in the world. This picture of Christ as a stern judge stayed in the mind of young Luther. He was always affected by the fear and terror of Christ. He began to pray desperately to the saints. He began to rely helplessly upon the saints for protection. Whenever he saw the picture of Christ his eyes cast down with fear and he would immediately pray, "Dear Mary, pray to your son for me and till his anger."[64] Thus he grew up to fear God. He believed in the reality of heaven, hell, angels, saints, the devil and demons. St. Anne was a popular and patron saint of the miners and that is why in times of trouble Luther would cry out to her.[65]

Apart from the fear of parents and fear of Christ he also had one more fear. They lived just at the edge of the forest which was full of darkness and superstitions and fears. He carried his fears like welts across his back. He could not overcome those fears. People, including his mother, believed strongly in all kinds of spirits and superstitions. Whenever he asked for any information, the old wives shrieked horribly into their cooking pots about the devil. Every tree was a devil, ready to seize the first poor soul who wandered too far from his hut. At times his mother terrified him with her superstitious stories until his heart quaked. Thus Luther grew as a young boy in all kinds of fears that made him always not only to be watchful and cautious but also to throw him totally to the mercy of St. Mary and other saints.[66] Now with such a father and mother and such a religious background, it was certain that Luther was bound to take life seriously and seize every opportunity for advancement which will be described in this study.

Luther's Education

Luther's education began at home. However, the real foundation was laid at schools in Mansfield, at Magdeburg and at Eisenach. These schools played a vital role in the life of Luther, especially in moulding his personality and character. He remembered those days spent in these schools throughout his life. Of course, his experience was of both light and shade. Little Martin was taken to school at quite an early age. Normally, children were admitted to school at the age of seven. But, when Hans carried his little son Martin for admission to school he was just four and a half years old. It was on March 12, 1488 that Luther was admitted to the Latin School at Mansfield, where he learned the international language of scholarship, government and the Church. Since he was too young he was carried in his father's arms. Quite strangely, in those days, there were no holidays. It will be interesting to know what little Luther really learnt at this school in Mansfield. He did, however, learn four things: reading, writing, singing and Latin. He learnt the rudiments of Latin and the elements of music. Learning of Latin language and music connected with religious instruction were all part and parcel of the school curriculum at that time. The boys were taught music so that they could sing in the Church. They were taught Latin because Latin was necessary to learn music. If the children were trained in music, later, they could earn and learn by singing in the Church services. Many poor boys sang and supported themselves in this way in education.[67]

As a beginner, little Martin of Mansfield learned Latin, which was largely a memorization of elementary forms and contents of Fibel, or the Latin Primer. He learned the Benedicite, the prayer before meals, and the Gratias, the giving of thanks after the meals. Besides, he learned the Confiteor or the Confession of Sins, the Creed, the Lord's Prayer, the Ten Commandments, and the Hail Mary. These little youngsters were taught hymns, vesicles, responses and psalms and given an explanation of Epistle and Gospel readings. Music, in fact, always played a significant role in the curriculum of the Latin school. Quite early the boys were introduced to musical techniques. They were taught the Catholic liturgy. They were required to learn the psalms, notes and the rules of harmony. The curriculum was designed in such a way that by the completion of the sixth grade, the students became very familiar with most parts of the Catholic Church services and mastered the elementary grammar of the Latin language.[68]

The methods of the school, as Jacob writes, were 'crude and mechanical.'[69] Young Luther was treated in this school with harshness and even with violence. It was quite obvious, as he later spoke of schools as 'prisons and hell' on earth and of schoolmasters as 'tyrants and executioners'.[70] Luther spoke, from time to time, very critically on the harshness and unreasonableness of the pedagogy of the rod. He had been whipped, Luther tells us, fifteen times one morning, for any fault of his own, having been called on to repeat what he had never been taught.[71] In spite of such bad and bitter experiences in the school, Luther could still think of the benefits that he gained there. As Atkinson writes, Luther gained an uncommon mastery of the Latin language and developed into a highly competent musician.[72]

Luther studied at Mansfeld Latin School till he was fourteen years old. Then his father thought of shifting him to a better place, perhaps for better education. The place he chose was Magdeburg, a bustling commercial town, 40 miles north on the Elbe river. It was around Easter 1497 that Luther was sent to a school here in the company of John Reineck, the son of a neighbour and business associate of Hans. The two boys seem to have been close friends and their friendship continued throughout their lives. The reason for changing the school for Martin is not clear. However, two biographers say something about it. While Melanchthon speaks of the "blossoming schools of the Saxon lands", Mathesius claims that the school in Magdeburg had a reputation "far above many others".[73] Besides, as Schwiebert suggests, it may also be possible that the German custom of attending a number of schools to obtain a diversified education and atmosphere was a factor influencing Luther and his friend John Reinicke.[74] Moreover, in the meantime, the financial condition of Luther's father had improved and so, he could well think of giving the best possible education in the best schools available at that time. Though it was difficult for the parents to send their son away from home, they prepared to do it in the interest and for the wellbeing of their promising son.

It was indeed an adventure on the part of this young lad to leave his parent's house and go altogether into a new and strange atmosphere. Magdeburg was the largest city of the region. It had, probably, 30,000 inhabitants. It was a centre of trade and commerce. Being the seat of an archbishop, the city filled was with churches, chapels and clerics. Here was a beautiful cathedral noted for its richly decorated altars and its store of relics. Hence the city was called "miniature Rome". The palace of the archbishop, the cathedral and other religious buildings were the ornaments of the place. Luther saw this as his first experience and contact with city life. There were many parochial schools in Magdeburg. So, we cannot say definitely which of the schools young Martin attended. However, after a quarter of a century, Luther himself mentioned that he was at school "with the Null-Brethren" (literally, Zero Brothers), that is, members of the Brethren of the Common Life. It was an order founded by Gerhard Groote of Deventer; they belonged to a late medieval pious movement, the Deyotio Moderna, who emphasized Bible reading and the return to simple life. They were a semi-monastic brotherhood of pious clergymen and laymen who dedicated themselves, without taking any vows, 'to promote among themselves the salvation of their souls and the practising of a godly life and to labour at the same time for the moral and social welfare of the people by preaching the Word of God, by instruction and by spiritual ministration'. Perhaps they took a special interest in the education of the young. These brethren were able to make some deep impression on this young boy through their 'Simple Christianity" and inward piety'.[75]

During his stay at Magdeburg young Martin may have stayed in one of the homes of this brotherhood. Quite early in his life he began to taste the hardships of a student's life. His father's help was not sufficient to meet his boarding, lodging, school fees and other expenses. So, he had to find other means to support himself. Like other school-boys of the days he begged his bread by singing hymns at the doors and windows of the wealthy citizens in company with children poorer than himself. Mathesius observes with regard to Luther's year at Magdeburg: "Like many a child of respected and wealthy parents, this boy also shouted in the streets (Panem propter Deum - Give us bread for God's sake)."[76] In those days, perhaps, begging was not considered something low or disgraceful but rather one of the recognized means by which a poor student could get help for his education. Moreover, the giving of alms was considered to be a meritorious act. Once, during Christmas time, he went to sing Christmas carols in neighbouring villages. There he had a very wonderful experience which he recollected later in his life and said: "We stopped before a peasant's house that stood by itself at the extremity of the village. The farmer came out with some victuals which he intended to give us, and called out in a high voice and with a harsh tone, "Boys, where are you (rascals)!. Frightened at these words, we ran off as fast as our legs could carry us. We had no reason to be alarmed, for the farmer offered us assistance with great kindness; but our hearts, no doubt, were rendered timorous by the menaces and tyranny with which the teachers were then accustomed to rule over their pupils, so that a sudden panic seized us. At last, however, we stopped, forgot any fears, ran back to him, and received from his hands the food intended for us. It is thus, adds Luther, "That we are accustomed to tremble and flee, when our conscience is guilty and alarmed. In such a case we are afraid of the assistance that is offered us and of those who are our friends, and who would willingly do us every good."[77]

There happened another incident at Magdeburg which is reported only by Ratzeberger and which, perhaps, he may have heard from the lips of Luther. Since he was a physician he has reported it with special interest. Once Luther was lying sick with a burning fever and he was tormented by thirst. He wanted to have some drink but he was refused. So, one Friday, when the people of the house had gone to church and left him alone, he, no longer able to endure the thirst, crawled on hands and legs to the kitchen, where he drank off with great avidity a jug of cold water. He went back to his room and fell into a deep sleep and on waking the fever had left him.[78]

Added to these incidents and memories there was one person who stood out most clearly in his memory. He was Prince William of Anhalt, who had forsaken the halls of the nobility to become a begging friar and walk in the streets carrying the sack of the mendicant. Like any other brother, he did the manual work of the cloister. "With my own eyes I saw him", said Luther. "I was fourteen years old at Magdeburg, I saw him carrying a sack like a donkey. He was so worn himself down by fasting and vigil that he looked like a death's head, mere bone and skin. No one could come upon him without feeling ashamed of his own life."[79] Another picture, as Lefever informs us, Luther retained in his mind was that of a painting of a great ship, representing the Church. The pilot was the Holy Ghost, the passengers were the Pope, cardinals and a company of bishops, and the crew were priests and monks. There were no laymen on board; they were to be seen, rather struggling in the water, their only chance of survival depending upon whether they were able to hook themselves on to the ecclesiastical Ark of Salvation. 'How secure', reflected young Luther, 'are the clergy compared with the laity'.[80] One year's stay of young Martin at Magdeburg was a memorable one. However, one cannot say definitely how far the Brethren of the Common Life, Prince William of Anhalt and the painting of a great ship influenced and inspired Luther later in turning his attention towards becoming a monk himself.

Luther's Higher Education

After a year of study at Magdeburg, Luther's parents decided to send him to a school in Eisenach. The reason for this quick change, again, is not known. Perhaps, Luther's mother had some relatives there who, they thought, might be of some help to him. Eisenach was one of the four principal cities of Thuringia. It was not big but a beautiful city and somewhat smaller than his home town, Eisleben. It had about 420 houses and a population of about 2,100. This city was called "nest of priests' for it was filled with priests.[81] It was said that every tenth person was a priest. However, in this 'nest of priests', Luther spent four years, necessary to complete his preparation for the university. In Eisenach, Luther was admitted to the Franciscan School, dedicated to St. George the Dragon Killer. Here, his studies were chiefly grammatical and classical. As for his progress in his study, Meelanchthon tells, "Here he rounded out his Latin studies; and since he had a penetrating mind and rich gift of expression, he soon outstripped his companions in eloquence, languages, and poetic verse." The teachers of Eisenach school were quite different from those of the school of Mansfield. In its curriculum this school was very much similar to those Luther had previously attended. But the art of teaching was so good that it won Luther's lifelong appreciation. Luther acquired thorough knowledge of Latin which was then the chief preparation for university study. He learned to write it, not only in prose but also in verse. Luther was fortunate to have that high quality of preparatory education at Eisenach before his entry into Erfurt University.[82]

Young Martin's overall development was, not confined to the classroom of the school. What happened outside the school also made a significant contribution to his development. When Luther was sent to Eisenach, perhaps, his parents thought that their relatives there would help their young Martin. But, unfortunately, they were so poor that they were not able to render any material assistance to the boy. So, as in Magdeburg, Luther remained a 'crumb seeker' in Eisenach as well. Mathesius says. "... There (in Eisenach) he, for a while also sang for his bread from door to door".[83] Luther himself wrote in his sermon on the duty of sending children to school (1530): "It is true, as is sometimes said, that the Pope was once a student; therefore do not despise the boys who beg from door to door, 'a little bread for the love of God'; and when the groups of poor pupils sing before your house'. I have myself been such a beggar pupil, and have eaten bread before houses, especially in the dear town of Eisenach, though afterwards my beloved father supported me at the University of Erfurt with all love and self-sacrifice, and by the sweat of his face helped me to the position I now occupy; but still I was for a time a poverty student, and according to this Psalm, I have risen by the pen to a position which I would not exchange for that of the Turkish Sultan, taking his wealth and giving up my learning."[84]

Luther's singing and begging, however, brought him the care and protection of two distinguished Christian families at Eisenach. One of them was that of Frau Cotta. She was the wife of one of the most distinguished and influential citizens of the town, who sprang from a noble Italian family and who had acquired a lot of wealth by business. She lived in a several storeyed building. The sweetness of Martin's singing and the earnestness of his praying in the Church captured the attention of this kind lady. She had also seen him singing at the door of her house. She had sympathy towards this sweet young boy and received him in her house and extended hospitality to him at her table. She was like a second mother to Martin. Ursula Cotta was a member of another distinguished family of Eisenach, the Schalbes. She was also attracted by Luther. She also took him into her house and helped him. In return, says Atkinson, Luther took her little son, Henry Schalbe, to school and helped him in his homework. Thus Luther remained grateful to her in coaching and teaching her little son by sitting alongside the little boy in that Christian home. Luther was quite at home in that family circle. Ratzeberger, the family biographer, tells us that Luther lived with the Cottas and ate his meals with the Schalbes. "In this Cotta and Schalbe circle", writes Schwiebert, "the young Luther had every advantage that a young student could desire. Here was a congenial, comfortable atmosphere dominated by strong religious conviction and often at the scene of stimulating conversations with distinguished guests."[85] Luther never forgot the love, affection, kindness and protection that he enjoyed with these godly women. He so said later, "Nothing on earth is dearer than woman's love if one can win it."[86] The Cottas and the Schalbes were known not only for their wealth and prosperity, but also for their deep piety, which inspired and motivated Luther in his studies.

Another godly man whose intimate contact Luther established and whose close friendship he enjoyed and continued even after he left Eisenach was John Brown, one of the numerous vicars of the Cathedral Church of our Lady. Luther was influenced and inspired by this priest. He continued correspondence with him and he also invited this friend for this first mass. In one of his letters Luther wrote of him: "A pious man, my dearest friend."[87] It may be possible that some seeds planted by this friend and others, both at Magdeburg and Eisenach, in the fertile mind of the young student may have germinated at Erfurt and contributed to Luther's decision to enter the Augustinian Monasteries at Eisenach and to regard this period as one of the happiest periods of his life since he proudly spoke of Eisenach as "My beloved town." Luther did his college education at Erfurt University, obtained the Master of Arts degree and got an appointment as a Professor of Philosophy in the same university. He was able to develop the religious experience in the time being. In the University Library he saw the New Testament and studied the passages thoroughly. When he compared the life style of the Pope and monks with the scriptures he understood the falsehood in Papacy and in the monastery. The different views about the life after death and also the fear about the future life forced him to think of his personal salvation. To save himself from the sin he thought that the best place would be the monastery and he joined the monastic life on 17. 07.1505. As a monk he was not satisfied and the seeking for salvation from sin did not vanish from his mind. The life of the senior monks was not at all pleasing to God. The life of the Pope was not an exemplary one to the people. Martin Luther started to question the attitudes of the religious leaders and the Pope. The transformed behavior of Luther was later known to the world as the religious reformer or the one who questioned the wrong notions of the Papacy.[88]

Luther's Reform

In 1505 Luther entered the monastic life. He associated himself with the Augustinian hermit at Erfurt. He observed the life of poverty for obtaining salvation and also to free himself from sin, which may lead the individual to eternal life. He left the family and followed very strictly the monastery rules. He was not satisfied with the monastic life. He was in the monastery and was ordained as a priest in 1507. In 1508 he became a Professor of Wittenberg University. In the teaching profession he was able to discover three Biblical passages (Romans 1:16, 17, psalm Chapter 31, and Galatians). The Pauline writing of the Bible empowered him to rediscover the concept of 'justification by faith alone'.[89]

From October 31, 1517, he started to attack the practice of the indulgences and also condemned the attitude of the bishops and the Pope and said that those who have true repentance are already forgiven. He was called to withdraw his statements by the Pope but he never compromised or went back from his sayings. He was placed before 'Diet of warm' and his answer was "until and unless I am convinced by the Holy Scripture and plain reason, I shall not recant. My conscience is thrilled to the word of God; it is neither safe nor honest to act against one's conscience." He based his teachings and work on the word of God. It was his guide at every step. In fact he gave primacy to the word of God, and stood by the word of God. He declared, 'here I stand".[90]

Luther broke away from the forced celibacy system which prevailed in the religious structure. In 1522 he elaborated on monastic vows in a treatise concerning married life. He declared that marriage depended upon the option of the individuals. Many monks and priests went in for family life. Martin Luther married on 13th July 1525. He married a former nun Katherine Von Bora.[91] Martin Luther never blended his reform with religious colour. To achieve the reform he educated the people in all levels of life. Therefore his reformation became contextual and ethical.

Luther's Death

On 17th February 1546, while eating supper with his colleagues, Luther complained of chest pain. As he lay dying, Luther repeated again and again 'God so loved the world that He gave His begotten son, that whoever believes in Him shall have everlasting life' (John 3:16). Then he prayed three times: "Into your hands I commend my spirit. You have redeemed me, true God. Indeed God has loved the world". [92] To affirm his peaceful death, Luther's family members called Michael Zolius, the Mansfield Court preacher and he asked, "honored father do you die in the faith in Christ and in the teachings that you preached in His name?" This question was necessary so that his opponents would not be able to say that Martin Luther recanted on his deathbed. Luther answered clearly with the last word of his life "YES".[93] He was very strong in his reforming zeal from the beginning to the end.

The early life, education, exemplary hard work of the parents, fear about the life after death, monastery experiences as a monk, close association and friendship with different families, discovery of the word of God, unwanted elements that prevailed in the religious practices, enabled him to fight for the right. He raised his voice for the poor who were deprived in the society and the Church. His reformation was contextual. The prevailing socio, economic, political, religious and educational context of Germany in the 16th century pushed him to get involved in the reformatory endeavour. He lived in an age that was largely seeking an escape from the binding restrictions, exploitation and oppressions of the authorities.

Endnotes

[1] K.S. Latourette, *History of Christianity*, p.703.

[2] Roland H. Bainton, *The Reformation of the Sixteenth Century*, p.22.

[3] H.E.Jacobs, *The Hero of the Reformation*, p. 4.

[4] Walker, W.A, *A history of the Christian Church*, p.302.

[5] Timothy George, *Theology of the Reformers*, p.33.

[6] George P. Fisher, *The Reformation*, pp.29-30.

[7] Roland H. Bainton, *The Reformation of the Sixteenth Century*, p.15.

[8] Alister E. McGrath, *Luther's Theology of the Cross*, p.7.

[9] Haje Holborn, "*The Social Basis of the German Reformation*", Church History No: 5, p.10.

[10] Alister E. Mc Grath, *Op. cit*, p.7.

[11] G.W. Searle, *The Counter Reformation*, p.25.

[12] A.G. Dickens. *Reformation and Society in Sixteenth Century Europe*, p.9.

[13] Gerhard Ritter, '*Why the Reformation occurred in Germany*', *Reformation Material or Spiritual*, p.71.

[14] Lewis W. Spitz, (ed.,) *Spiritual Lexington*, p.71.

[15] A. G. Dickens, *Op.cit*, p.37.

[16] Tomas m. Lindsay, *A History of Reformation*, p.136.

[17] *Ibid*, p.136.

[18] George P. Fisher, *Op.cit*, p.50.

[19] Roland H. Bainton, *Op.cit*, p.4.

[20] George P. Fisher, *Op.cit*, 47.

[21] Richard Kroner, *The Meaning of the Reformation Today*, Lutheran Quarterly, p.34.

[22] Ian D. Kingston Siggins, *Luther*, p.6.

[23] A.G. Dickens. *Op.cit*, p.35.

[24] *Ibid*, p.36.

[25] G.W. Searle, *Op.cit*, p.17.

[26] Roland H. Bainton, *Op.cit*, p.14.

[27] G.w. Searle, The Counter Reformatin, p.17.

[28] Roland H. Bainton. *Op.cit*, p.7.

[29] Aliter E. Mcgrath, *Lutrher's Theology of the Cross*, p.8

[30] M.G. Bernard Reardon, *Religious Thought in the Reformation*, p.1.

[31] Roland H. Bainton, *Op.cit*, p.15.

[32] Ian d. Kingston Siggins, *Op.cit*, p.6.

[33] Carter Lindberg. *Beyond Charity: Reformation Initiatives for the Poor*, p.95.

[34] Thomas M. Lindsay, *Op.cit*, p.97.

[35] Roland H. Bainton, *Op.cit*, p.10.

[36] Ulrich Duchrow, *Two Kingdoms: The use and Misuse of a Lutheran Theological Concept*, p.8.

[37] James Atkinson, *Martin Luther and the Birth of Protestantism*, p.98.

[38] G.W. Searle, *Op.cit*, p.18.

[39] Ian D. Kingston Siggins, *Op.cit*, p.6.

[40] Thomas M. Lindsay, *Op.cit*, p.223.

[41] Ian D. Kingston Siggins, *Op.cit*, p.6.

[42] James Atkinson, *Op.cit*, p.27.

[43] Thomas M. Lindsay, *Op.cit*, p.35.

[44] *Ibid*, p.37.

[45] James Atkinson, *Op.cit*, p.28.

[46] 'guilds' = the associations of workmen was commonly called 'guilds.'

[47] Thomas M. Lindsay, *Op.cit*, p.112.

[48] Roland H. Bainton, *Op.cit*, p.9.

[49] James Atkinson, *Op.cit*, p. 30.

[50] Thomas M. Lindsay, *Op.cit*, p. 89.

[51] Roland H. Bainton. *Op.cit*, p.3.

[52] Thomas M. Lindsay, *Op.cit*, p.112.

[53] Harold J Grimm, the Reformation Era, p.90

[54] H.E, Jacobs, *Op.cit*, p.4.

[55] M.J.H. D' Aubigne, *History of the Reformation of the Sixteenth Century*, p.49.

[56] H.E.Jacobs, *Op.cit*, p.8.

[57] R.H. Bainton., *Here I Stand*, p.23.

[58] *Ibid*, p.23.

[59] *Holy Bible, Proverbs* 13:23

[60] H.E. Jacobs, *Op.cit*, p.8.

[61] M.J.H.D' Aubigne, *Op.cit*, p.51.

[62] *Ibid*, p.50.

[63] *Ibid*, p.51.

[64] A G.Dickens, *Op.cit*, p.3.

[65] *Ibid*, p.8.

[66] *Ibid*, p.11

[67] Harold J Grimm, *Op.cit*, p.91.

[68] *Ibid*, p.92.

[69] H.E. Jacobs, *Op. cit*, p.10.

[70] J.Koestlin, Life *of Luther*, p.13.

[71] *Ibid*, p.13.

[72] James Atkinson, *Op.cit*, p.23.

[73] E.G.Schwiebert, *Luther and His time*, p.117.

[74] *Ibid*, p.118.

[75] S.D.L. Alagodi, *God Help Me : A life and work of Martin Luther*, p.10

[76] E.G.Schwiebert, *Op.cit*, p.127.

[77] M.J.H.D' Aubigne, *Op.cit*, p.52.

[78] J.Koestlin, *Op.cit*, p.14.

[79] R.H. Bainton, *Op.cit*, p.33.

[80] H.C. Lefever, *The History of the Reformation*, p.54.

[81] R.H. Fife, *The Revolt of Martin Luther*, p.25.

[82] E.G. Scwhiebert, *Op.cit*, p.125.

[83] M.J.H. D' *Op.cit*, p.52.

[84] *Ibid*, p.53.

[85] E.G.Schwiebert, *Op.cit*, pp.127-128

[86] R.H. Fife, *Op.cit*, p.27.

[87] *Ibid*, p.28.

[88] S.D.L. Alagodi, *Op. cit*, p. 32.

[89] J.R.Narchison, *The Image of Martin Luther Among roman Catholics, Martin Luther's Obedience to God Glory*, The Indian Lutheran, Vol. III, p.18.

[90] *Ibid*, p.19.

[91] Robert Kolf, Luther's Way of Thinking, p.30.

[92] *Ibid*, p.3.

[93] Hans Schwartz, *True Faith in the True God*, p.34.

Chapter 2

Life and Work of Mahatma Gandhi

Mahatma Gandhi was one of the giants of the twentieth century, who left an indelible impact on the social, political, economic, religious and educational scenario of the day. He was a great revolutionary who, even while he fought for the freedom of his country, was aware of the freedom of all the enslaved people in different parts of the world. History clearly shows how great men have always struggled and fought against the prevailing social evils and human suffering. In this chapter, the intention is to dwell on the impact of his early life and of the continents of Asia, Europe and Africa directly on young Gandhi. The indirect influence of the continent of America and the sub-continent of Russia on Gandhi will also be dealt with in this chapter. It is an extraordinary coincidence that Gandhi had direct and intimate contact with three continents and indirect contact with another continent.

The impact of the first mentioned continents on Gandhi was slow and steady and continuous and enduring. By the impact of a continent is meant the contact and intimacy of men, women and events; the impact of the culture and civilization of that continent on Gandhi by firsthand experience and through literature. Asia is one of the five continents. It is noted for the oldest and outstanding civilizations of countries like India, China and Japan. As a student, Gandhi learned about the history and geography of Asia in general and India in particular. In elementary school and high school he learned English, Sanskrit, Gujarati, Mathematics and other common subjects. The influence of heredity and environment on Gandhi was not ordinary.

Early Life

Mohandas Karamchand Gandhi was born on 2nd October 1869 at Porbandar, Kathiawad, Gujarat. His parents were Karamchand alias Kaba Gandhi and Putlibai. His father and grandfather served as diwans of various principalities of the Kathiawad region of Gujarat. They belonged to the Modh Bania caste of the Vaishya Varna and seem to have been originally grocers.[1] Porbandar, one of the Kathiawad districts, is a coastal city on the west coast of Gujarat. Dwaraka, a place of pilgrimage for Hindus, is situated in this province. The place had been tremendously influenced by Jainism and Vaishnavism with their principles of non-violence and strict vegetarianism. Islam and Hinduism co-existed well in this region and Christianity had its influence.[2]

Gandhi's grandfather, Uttamchand Gandhi, who was honest, spiritual and a man of principles, took the office of the Diwan of the Porbandar State. His father Karamchand Gandhi known as Kaba Gandhi married four times as he lost his first three wives in quick succession. His last wife Putlibai gave birth to a daughter and three sons. The youngest son was Mohandas. At the age of twenty five, Kaba Gandhi succeeded to the Diwanship of Porbandar on his father's retirement. He was truthful, brave, honest and a man of principles. He never had any ambition to accumulate wealth and left his family very little property.[3]

His mother Putlibai was a saintly and religious woman. She used to fast and observe continence, and abstain from taking food on certain days in keeping with her religious faith and piety. His mother's influence saved him from many sinful actions. Gandhi's father used to invite religious scholars of different denominations and initiate debate on religious matters. As a result, scholars well versed in Jainism and Hinduism frequently visited Gandhi's house. As a child he used to gaze at their discussions and deliberations. As a boy, Gandhi accompanied his mother to the Jain temple as well as the Hindu temple. The habit of his father and his mother in giving equal respect to different religions, inculcated a feeling of equality and unity of religions in Gandhi from childhood. This feeling became a full-fledged ideal in times to come.[4] The religious faith of the family was Vaishnavism and this too created an atmosphere round young Gandhi and clung to him through life. In childhood, Gandhi was influenced by his father, mother, brothers and sisters, two other women and a few teachers. The general non-violent environment in Gujarat had its impact on young Gandhi. As a boy, he understood that India was a subject nation. He thought and felt about Indian slavery to British yoke. From his friends and teachers and by direct observation he understood that the British were strong and sturdy. He took into his head their physical superiority on account of British meat-eating and non-vegetarian habits. He felt that Indians were conquered by the British owing to the vegetarian dietary habits of Indians.

Gandhi thought about ways and means to free India (Here we see a glimpse of his early political philosophy). He hit upon a plan. Gandhi, with his personal friend Mehtab, privately resorted to eating meat to become strong. In order to make money for this unethical purpose, Gandhi stole a part of his brother's golden bracelet and sold it. This was due to the influence of the above said Muslim friend. Gandhi's spontaneous veracity prompted him to brood over the above illegality and make a clean breast of his misdemeanour. As a result, he made a confession to his father about the meat eating and the theft. He wrote his misdeeds on a paper and submitted it to his father. His father read it and wept silently. In his autobiography, Gandhi says: "Those pearl drops of tears cleansed my heart and washed my sin".[5]

Although Kaba Gandhi visited temples sometimes in the early days and attended religious discourses, in his later life he recited verses during his prayer time at home. Gandhi's mother, Putlibai, stood for religious faith and devotion. As a traditional Vaishnavite, she had a deep faith in religion and never took her food without daily prayers. She observed strict vows, religious fasts and would not miss going to temples. She had a strong common sense and she had wide knowledge about the affairs of the state. To quote Pyarelal, "He gave respect to his father, but his mother he adored ... his father to him was the embodiment of uprightness, his mother of piety ... His mother became the core of his inner being. Her affection continued to protect and influence him even when physically she was away and even ceased to be."[6]

School Life

The general climate and conditions in India during Gandhi's school days were of much importance. The Indian Renaissance movement was in full swing. Raja Ram Saraswathi had established the Aryasamaj. Gopala Krishna Gokhale, a living institution by himself, was a Professor in the Fergusson College, Poona. Ramakrishna Paramahamsa had paved a new way in the religious life of India. This general awakening throughout India has its reverberations in Gujarat. Gandhi was in Gujarat till the age of eighteen.

Gandhi was not only faithful to his parents but also a genuine and truthful student in his school life. Gandhi had his primary and high school education at Rajkot. At the age of twelve, he was shifted to the Alfred High School. He was a mediocre student, shy and timid. His books and lessons were his only companions. From his school records none could forecast his future greatness. But he showed all the signs of inborn quality especially towards truth, love and service. During his school days, he never told a lie to his teachers or others. There was an incident which was significant. A British school inspector, Mr. Giles, had come to examine the school. He set a spelling test. One of the words was 'kettle'. Gandhi misspelt the word. The teacher asked him to copy the correct spelling from his neighbor's slate. But he refused to do so.[7]

From the very beginning of life, his young mind was experiencing a kind of spiritual bewilderment and groping which led him to try to read and understand Manusmiriti[8] which was among his father's collections. During his school days, he was greatly influenced by an ancient play *'Shravana Pitribhakti Nataka'* portraying the boundless love of Shravana for his old parents. He went through the book with keen interest again and again. He was amazed to know how Shravana carried his blind parents on a pilgrimage, by means of slings fitted for his shoulders. This play left an indelible impression on his mind.[9] The other play that captured his heart was *Harischandra*. He read the book many times. Referring to this play, Gandhi wrote: "This play Harischandra captured my heart ... Why should not all be truthful like Harischandra was the question I asked myself day and night. To follow truth and to go through all the ordeals Harischandra went through was the one ideal it inspired me".[10]

Both Shravana and Harischandra became living realities to him and he decided to serve with devotion like Shravana and to follow truth as Harischandra did inspite of many ordeals. According to the custom of his time, Gandhi was married while he was in the high school, at the age of thirteen, to Kasturba.[11] She was also of the same age. She was the daughter of a Porbandar merchant, a friend of Gandhi's family. By nature, Kasturba was quiet and self-possessed. Gandhi was fond of his wife though he attempted to dominate her like all traditional Hindu husbands. Three years after his marriage, while his father was on his death bed, Gandhi's sexual desire prevented him from nursing his father.[12] The young Gandhi was afraid of thieves, ghosts and serpents. He never had courage to go out at night. Darkness was a terror to him. He felt ashamed when he saw that his wife was more courageous. He shared his fear with his dear nurse Rambha, an old servant of his family whom he held in great esteem. She suggested a remedy for his fear through the repetition of 'Ramanama'. His faith in Rambha prompted him to take up this remedy to drive away ghosts and spirits. Later on, his mysticism centered on 'Ramanama'.[13]

Gandhi was empowered with the power of non-violence, self-sufficiency, selfless love and active service from his parents. He practised these in everyday life. Gandhi believed that non-violence was the law of the human race.[14] After passing his matriculation, Gandhi joined the Samaldas College in Bhavnagar. During this time his father died in

1885. In the meantime, a family friend, MavjiDave, advised Gandhi's widowed mother to send Gandhi to England to become a barrister. Gandhi's brother took the initiative for sending Gandhi to London. The traditionalists in the Baniya caste of Gandhi opposed Gandhi's crossing the sea. Gandhi did not like this superstition and disobeyed their dictate, so he was threatened with excommunication. But he was not scared. This incident shows that, as an adolescent, Gandhi was bold enough to take the risk and resist even elders on reasonable grounds. [15] Mahatma Gandhi wanted to become a physician since he thought that was an effective way to serve people. Encouraged by his brother and a Jain monk named Becharji Swami, he decided to go to England for legal studies. His mother's objection to his going abroad was overcome by the son's solemn vows not to touch wine, women and meat. The vows were never violated. He went to Bombay to sail for England on September 4, 1888, a few months after his first son Harilal was born.

London Phase (1888 - 1893)

On 4th September, 1888, Gandhi sailed for England to become a barrister. The continent of Europe is supposed to be the cradle of modern civilization. It was true in the nineteenth century also. Gandhi reached London in October 1888. At first, he endeavored to be like a European. After his enrolment for the study of law, he caused wasteful expenditure to study dance and music. His habit of keeping correct accounts opened his eyes to the reality. He thought about his family and realized his folly. He cut short unnecessary expenses and said good-bye to useless extra-curricular activities. He began to live a far more religious life, cooking most of his own food, and living as simply and as economically as possible. He says that this change harmonized his inward and outward conduct. All the same, Gandhi voluntarily studied elements of natural science, physical science, rudiments of history and geography and a bit of Greek and Latin prescribed for the London Matriculation examination. This widened his mental horizon. It also improved his scientific temperament and logical approach. Gandhi had taken a pledge in keeping with his mother's wish. He had promised to eschew wine, women and meat eating. It was very difficult to live in England as a vegetarian in those days. So, Gandhi was practically starving. Fortunately, he came across a vegetarian restaurant and a Vegetarian Society. He became a member of the society. Somebody from the vegetarian boarding house gave him a Bible. He read it. The New Testament in the Bible attracted him. He says "the New Testament was more interesting and the Sermon on the Mount went straight to my heart".[16]

Contemporaneous with this he got acquainted with two remarkable women. They were moral geniuses. One was Madam Blavatsky and the other was Annie Beasant. The latter was destined to be his co-worker in India after a quarter century. Madam Blavatsky was a scholarly woman from Russia. Both of them were theosophists. The friendship with these two women enabled Gandhi to learn more about India and India's religious heritage. It was from these theosophists that Gandhi learned that the Bhagavad Gita was a classic second to no other work in the world. He read the 'Song Celestial', a translation of the Gita by Edwin Arnold. Gandhi also read the book *Light of Asia*, by the same author, about Buddha and Buddhism. Thus he got grounding in Christianity, Hinduism and Buddhism during his study of law in England. The influence of theosophists helped Gandhi to compare, contrast, assess and evaluate Christianity, Hinduism and Buddhism dispassionately. He also came across Bradlaugh, an atheist. This type of reading gave Gandhi an insight into theism, skepticism and other philosophies. Gandhi used to go to the British Museum and sit on the chair in which Karl Marx used to sit in the library during his exile in England. This means that Gandhi had some idea in this formative period about Marx, Marxism and its greatness. Continental countries like France and Italy wielded an indirect influence on Gandhi. He mingled with students from these countries who came to study in England during this period. During this interaction he kept his vows and lived an honest life. E. Stanly Jones says, "Gandhi was deeply influenced by the west. Had Mahatma Gandhi not been educated in large measure in the West, he would never have had the world influence he has had".[17]

He was very bold in convincing people and he never discouraged anyone with any kind of false sayings. One can notice this in the false engagement described in Chapter 19 of Part 1 of his Autobiography. It appears under the legend 'The Canker of Untruth'. It shows that Gandhi, even as a youngster, never wanted to deviate from the path of truth. The substance of that episode is that he became a family friend of a widow. He came across her in Brighton. She gave him her London address. Gandhi was accustomed to receiving her hospitality on Sundays and holidays. It was his first year in England. The widow introduced a young woman staying with her to Gandhi. The old lady went on spreading her net wider every day. Gandhi felt a great prick of conscience, for he was passing off and acting to be a bachelor as most Indian students of those days were accustomed to pretend. It was a fashion of Indian Students in England, in the 19th century. Gandhi was a married man and father of a son. He wanted to make a clean breast of the real state of affairs. He wrote a long letter to the old lady explaining the fact of his early marriage and the fact of his having a son. He specifically asked her to pardon his untruthful behaviour. The land lady sent an amusing reply. She invited Gandhi again to brief her about his child marriage in order to laugh at his expense. In his autobiography, Gandhi says that he felt relieved of the 'Canker of Untruth' with his written confession. Thereafter he had never hid the fact of his married state.[18]

He was very truthful in England. One day he happened to see a vegetarian restaurant in Farringdon Street. From this restaurant he bought a copy of Salt's *Plea for Vegetarianism* and was greatly impressed by it. After reading this book he became a vegetarian by choice. He read some more books on vegetarianism like Howard William's *The Ethics of Diet*. In this book he saw that all philosophers and prophets of the world were vegetarians. Henceforward he made it his mission to spread vegetarianism. Later on he was elected as an executive member of the vegetarian society. He contributed eight articles to the journal *Vegetarianism*. His involvement with the vegetarians made him more sociable and popular.[19] He attempted to become an English gentleman by wearing costly English clothes and by learning dance, music and

elocution at a heavy cost. But soon he realized that he had come to
England for studies and not for becoming a gentleman. He said to
himself, "If my character made a gentleman of me so much the better.
Otherwise I should forego the ambition."[20] With self-determination he
studied Latin, French and Chemistry privately besides law. He failed
in the London Matriculation Examination in December 1889, which
was of a very high standard. Then he passed it in June 1890. After
much hard work and strenuous efforts, he passed the bar examination
in 1891. His life in London changed him in many ways and drew him
out of his shell.

During his stay in London, Gandhi's first spiritual illumination
took place. According to Gandhi the central theme of the Gita was
that a balanced state of mind can be achieved by killing all passions
and by renouncing desires rather than objects. He believed that the
Gita advocated the supremacy of moral power over physical force.[21]
In England Gandhi was persuaded by a Christian friend to read The
Bible and took great interest in the New Testament, particularly "The
Sermon on the Mount". He was attracted by the teaching of Buddha
through Edwin Arnold's *The Light of Asia*. He tried to discover the
unity of the visions of Krishna, Buddha and Jesus. Tolstoy's The
Kingdom of God is within You stirred him. Carlyle's *Heroes and Hero
Worship*, especially its last chapter, 'Hero as a Prophet' afforded him a
knowledge of a prophet's greatness and bravery and austere living. His
quest for religion that started in London led to his own philosophy
"Truth is God".[22]

After finishing his legal education and enrolment as a barrister in
England, Gandhi set sail for India on 12th June, 1891. His examination
results were declared on 10th June. He enrolled on 11th June as a
barrister. He set sail for India on the next day. These three events
show how he had imbibed the principle of conscientization. When
he reached India, he was given a warm welcome in Bombay by his
kith and kin. He searched for his mother. Gandhi wanted to tell her
that he had kept his vows intact. But the news greeted him that his
mother had passed away a few weeks before. This incident hardened

his attitude and life. Gandhi went to Bombay and hired an office to practise in the High Court. His brother, who was a country pleader, was always ready to help him in legal matters. But Gandhi did not compromise with principles. He got some cases on account of the reputation of his father. He stood up to argue his first case. He was unable to argue due to buck fever. The endeavour was a total failure. Without much delay he returned to Rajkot from Bombay. He started preparing plaints and writing petitions and thereby made a living. He was able to make an income of between rupees two hundred and rupees three hundred per month. The experience in Bombay as a barrister and the experience in Rajkot as an advocate were not cheerful ones. But this experience gave him an insight into human nature and psychological behaviour.[23]

The most outstanding spiritual experience of this period was his acquaintance with one Raychand Bhai. Raychand Bhai was a jeweler. He was a man of great character and learning. Raychand Bhai was the son-in-law of a brother of Mehta. Mehta was Gandhi's friend and guide in England. Raychand Bhai used to engage Gandhi in serious religious conversation. He was a helper and a guide. Raychand Bhai wanted to see God face to face. Gandhi's goal also was the same in this regard. Raychand Bhai gave Gandhi spiritual books, books on Indian philosophy and religion. In Chapter one of part two of Gandhi's autobiography,[24] Gandhi has certified that three moderns impressed and captivated him. They were Raychand Bhai, Tolstoy and Ruskin. Gandhi's live contact with Raychand Bhai was more important. Gandhi continued his contact with Raychand Bhai in the ensuing years. In fact Gandhi became a bit sophisticated in the two year period from his return from England as a barrister. His mission to South Africa came after two years, for conducting a case for the Gujarati Muslim businessman Dada Abdullah.[25] Gandhi left for South Africa in April 1893, and reached there towards the close of May 1893. In this early part of his career, Gandhi did not show any promise of his future greatness. He showed no brilliance as a lawyer. He failed miserably. What strikes one in his prosaic life was his love for truth.

South African Phase (1893 - 1914)

Gandhi sailed for South Africa in April 1893, leaving behind his wife and two children. As a leader, Gandhi's activity may be divided into two periods. From 1893 to 1914 his field was South Africa; from 1914 to 1947, India. In 1891 Gandhi went to South Africa to argue one of the cases of Dada Abdullah & Co. In 1891 about 1, 50, 000 Indian emigrants settled in South Africa. The Indians were hated by the whites and the Government also was not in favour of the Indians and they were asking them to leave the place. The Indians in South Africa were miserable; they had no rights because they were Indians. Official ignorance, race- prejudice and pride spoiled everything.[26] The impact of the continent of Africa on young Gandhi was unique, fateful and wonderful. Gandhi reached the Dark Continent at the early age of twenty four. South Africa is a rich land. Europeans had long back settled in South Africa. The minority Europeans subjugated the native inhabitants who were the majority. The natives and the migrants from other countries were treated as second class citizens by the white ruling class. Gandhi had substantive, philosophic, procedural and practical experiences in South Africa. These changed the course of his life and transformed him into a Mahatma. At first Gandhi was taken to a court at Durban. He refused to remove his turban when he was ordered to by the European magistrate. He left the court and wrote a letter of protest in the local press. He considered this experience as a challenge to his self-respect as an Indian rather than as a challenge to the traditional customs. This incident marked the beginning of his crusade against racial discrimination.[27]

Some of his substantive experiences were very pronouncing. They were the Maritzburg incident, the coach event, the Balasundaram episode, the Boer War, and the Zulu rebellion. The fame of Gandhi in South Africa was not only based on legal and political work but also on social and humanitarian service to the sick and injured during the Boer War, which broke out in 1889. He volunteered to serve with the British; he formed an Indian Ambulance Corps to nurse the wounded in the war.[28] In 1901, when the Boer War was over, Gandhi decided to return to India. He was having a flourishing practice at that time.

But he felt that he could do greater service to his motherland. It was not an easy job to persuade his friends to let him go. They finally agreed, on condition that he would return to South Africa if they needed him. The philosophic experiences of Gandhi in South Africa were the Christian and Muslim contacts, which enabled him to do comparative study of religions, and the vow of Brahmacharya. The philosophic experiences culminated in the discovery of Satyagraha or Truth Force, a combination of Satya and Ahimsa. The authoring of *Hind Swaraj or Indian Home Rule*, a booklet, was the result of his philosophic blossoming. It contains Gandhi's philosophy of life and his gift for the fight. Gandhi's experiences in the procedural field were brand new and rigorous. They were: the passing of Asiatic Act; the disfranchising of Indians; the verdict of the Cape Supreme Court that all Indian marriages were illegal; the payment of poll tax by Indians; and, the non-violent, non-co-operative agitation against General Smuts, the mighty ruler of South Africa. The practical experiences of Gandhi were historic and personally enriching and apt to change the future course of South Africa, India and the world at large. In conformity with the ideology Gandhi derived from the book *Unto This Last* by Ruskin.[29]

Mahatma Gandhi initiated practical experiments and experiences. Ruskin's classic extolled the dignity of manual labour. It also drew the line of demarcation between social good and individual liberty. To put the ideals of Ruskin into practice Gandhi started the Phoenix settlement. It was in an area of one hundred acres. In this settlement, Gandhi laid the foundation for a community life of different types of families without any class or caste distinction and discrimination. During his militant non-violent fight against General Smuts's administration, Gandhi and his followers sought asylum in the Phoenix settlement and earned a living by hard manual labour. Soon after this, Gandhi founded a Farm named after Tolstoy, the then living Russian philosopher and writer. It was known as Tolstoy farm. This farm was on one of thousand acres. A German friend of Gandhi, Kallanbach, was the owner of this land. Gandhi duplicated the Phoenix settlement on in Tolstoy Farm on a wider scale. The Phoenix settlement and Tolstoy

Farm, in South Africa, were pioneer institutions before the Sabarmati Ashram in Gujarat and the Sevagram Ashram in Maharashtra founded by Gandhi many years later. After founding Tolstoy Farm, Gandhi wrote to Tolstoy about his experiment and agitation and received replies from Tolstoy. Tolstoy also read Gandhi's first biography written by Joseph Doke, a pastor. It was entitled *An Indian Patriot in South Africa*. Tolstoy wrote four letters to Gandhi. In one letter Tolstoy was able to foresee and predict Gandhi's wonderful contribution towards world politics and sociology in time to come. The substantive experiences of Gandhi are very important.

The Maritzburg incident is one of the foremost. This happened within a week of his arrival in South Africa. The Maritzburg incident shows his love for Truth and justice. In the court, Gandhi was not respected by the Europeans. They were not happy with the dress and colour of the Indians. The Indians lived in Maritzburg also divided in the name of religion. Gandhi stood for the justice and fought for equal rights and respect from the Europeans to Indians. He never changed the dress or the style as the Europeans. In this incident Gandhi earned the love, affection and respect of a Muslim man, Sheth Dada Adbulla. The next important substantive experience was the event in a coach. Gandhi had to travel by a stage-coach to Johannesburg and was offered a seat outside the coach on the coach box. The white passengers did not allow an Indian to be in their midst. After some time, the conductor directed Gandhi to sit on a dirty piece of sack on the step below. But Gandhi refused to do so. The conductor pulled him down and rained blows on Gandhi. Other passengers felt sympathy and came to his rescue. Then Gandhi was allowed to sit where he was. This incident also inspired him to do something to put an end to the sufferings of the Indians in South Africa and in India.[30] Another substantive experience was the Balasundaram episode. It was a novel and touching event which laid the foundation of Gandhi's public interest litigation service. It is described in part II, Chapter 20, of Gandhi's Autobiography.[31] One day, a Tamil man in tattered clothes, head gear in hand, two front teeth broken and dislocated and his mouth bleeding, stood before Gandhi trembling and weeping.

His name was Balasundaram. His origin was in Tamil Nadu in South India. He was working as an indentured labourer under a European of Durban. Balasundaram had been severely beaten by his white master. Gandhi nursed him. He obtained an injury certificate from a doctor. He took Balasundaram to a magistrate. A private complaint was launched. The magistrate issued summons against the employer. Gandhi did not want to punish the employer. He met him. The employer was convinced of his violent act. Gandhi made the employer agree to release Balasundaram from his bondage and transfer the indenture to someone else. Gandhi searched and found a new employer. The magistrate found the employer guilty and recorded that the employer had undertaken to transfer the indenture. Balasundaram's case was echoed in far-off Madras in Southern India. This case gave a new confidence to Gandhi and his fellow-beings. This was a significant substantive experience.

The most outstanding substantive experience of Gandhi in South Africa was his participation in the Boer War. It is necessary to put in a nutshell the facts of the war. This was between Great Britain and the Boer Republics of South Africa. The Boers were descendants of Dutch colonials of South Africa. The war took place between 1899 and 1902. Indians were considered to be incapable of taking risks. Gandhi wanted to do service for various reasons. He thought of organizing and setting up an Indian Ambulance Corps. Gandhi met the Natal bishop and explained his intention. Gandhi also organized volunteers. Nearly one thousand one hundred Indians, free as well as indentured, were selected. There were thirty seven members to lead the group. Gandhi and the leaders underwent a nursing course and obtained certificates of fitness. They tendered the offer of service. The offer was accepted. There was a European Ambulance Corps also. The Indian Ambulance Corps did wonderful work for two months. The members of the Corps started work at 5 a.m. They worked till late night. The work was very exhausting. The wounded had to be carried everyday up to twenty five miles, from the scene of action to a hospital. Gandhi had the distinction of carrying the famous General Woodgate from the battle field, when he was severely wounded. This

ambulance Corps made Indians more organized. It widened the circle
of Gandhi's acquaintances. It also gave a good impression about
Indians. The relation formed during Boer war between Gandhi and
the whites was the sweetest. Prabhu Singh of India was singled out
for his bravery. Lord Curzon was the Viceroy of India at that time.
He sent a Kashmir robe to South Africa to be presented to Prabhu
Singh. This work in the Ambulance Corps reinforced Gandhi's belief
in non-violence. The Boer War experience instilled a determination
in Gandhi to fight for India's freedom in a non-violent and truthful
way. The Boer War had caused a metamorphosis in Gandhi's thinking
and mental makeup.[32]

During the time of the Zulu rebellion Gandhi offered his help
to the government. He raised an Indian Ambulance Corps, which
nursed the sick and dying Zulus whom the white doctors and nurses
would not touch. Gandhi's Indian Ambulance Corps was, in effect, a
godsend and a boon. By using stretchers, the wounded were carried for
a distance of thirty to forty families a day. The wounded Zulus would
have been left uncared for, if Gandhi's Ambulance Corps had not
attended to them.[33] The experience from the Boer War and the Zulu
rebellion was extra-ordinary. The substantive experience of the Zulu
rebellion brought about a catharsis in Gandhi's life. The Zulus were
black. The Zulus were the tallest and the most handsome among the
blacks. They were the old inhabitants of Natal when the Englishmen
arrived in South Africa. The Zulu rebellion was a 'misnomer'. The
British wanted to subjugate and eliminate the Zulu tribe. Gandhi
realized the horrors of violence and war from his participation in
the relief work among Zulus more than he did during the Boer War.
The Zulu chief advised non-payment of a new tax to the British. It
was also alleged that the Zulus attacked a tax collector. So the clash
ensued. The British nationals, as in the Boer War, resorted to war.
Gandhi formed an Indian Ambulance Corps. A section of Zulus had
been taken prisoners as suspects. The flogging had caused severe sores
and pestering. The wounded were left unattended. It dawned upon
Gandhi that he could not live after both the flesh and the spirit. In
short, he concluded that the observance of celibacy or Brahmacharya

was a condition for true service to one's brother. This type of thought had seized his imagination since 1900. It was sealed with a vow of celibacy in 1906. That vow was kept intact for the next forty-two years till his assassination. The experiences of the Boer War and the Zulu rebellion culminated in the Brahmacharya vow. The Brahmacharya vow, as a matter of course, resulted in the discovery of Satyagraha, a new type of potential political way sans violence in the interests of the unarmed have-nots and the oppressed.[34]

The Natal Government proposed to introduce a bill to disfranchise Indians in South Africa. Gandhi called this was "the first nail into our coffin".[35] Gandhi was instrumental in forming the Natal Indian Congress. It was not only for political but for moral and social uplifting of its members. Gandhi prepared a petition to the Secretary of State for Colonies in London requesting him to veto such a bill if passed by the local Legislative Assembly. He used letter writing as an effective medium for redressing grievances and building up unity and peace amongst the Indians in South Africa. Even *The London Times* supported the cause of the Indian settlers in South Africa. The Colonial Office, influenced by the agitation organized by him, vetoed the bill.[36] This was a great achievement and the faith of Indian settlers in him immensely increased. He left South Africa in mid-1896 for his country for domestic reasons. Gandhi headed a deputation of Natal Indians to Joseph Chamberlain, the colonial Secretary of the British cabinet. The usual patient hearing and evasive answer of the authority made him stay in South Africa for some more years. He opened his office at Johannesburg and enrolled as an advocate of the Supreme Court.[37]

To learn about the real situation of the Indians living in other countries and the attitudes and practice of developed countries to the developing countries, Gandhi published the grievances of the Indians in South Africa in the 'Green Pamphlet',[38] which circulated widely. He addressed a large public meeting in Bombay.[39] He was also to speak in Calcutta but, before he could do so, an urgent telegram from the Indian community in Natal forced him to return. He sailed for Durban with his wife and children in November 1896. The green pamphlet had enraged the Europeans. Gandhi with his wife and children reached the Durban fort. They were not permitted to land from the ship. Then he was taken to his friend's Rustomiji's house. Some European recognized him. They shouted. Europeans came and attacked him without any mercy. The mob did not allow the family to stay in his friend's house. He was taken to the police station. Mrs. Alexander, wife of the local police superintendent, and the police men saved Gandhi from the hand of the mob. When Joseph Chamberlain, the British Secretary of State for the Colonies, came to know about this incident, he cabled an order to Natal to prosecute all those who were responsible for the attempted lynching. Gandhi's greatness rests in acquitting the assailants.[40]

Gandhi realized the necessity of self-help service. During the second time in South Africa Gandhi's mode of living underwent a gradual change. He began to reduce his wants and his expenses. He studied the art of laundering and became his own washer man. He also learnt to cut his own hair. He not only cleaned his own chamber pots but often of his guests as well. Not satisfied with self-help, Gandhi volunteered for public work and free service for two hours as a compounder in a charitable hospital. He had read books on nursing and midwifery and in fact served as mid wife when his fourth and last son was born.[41] At this time, Gandhi came under the influence of the book *The Kingdom of God is within You* written by Leo Tolstoy. Tolstoy pleaded for the refusal of military service and payment of taxes, rejected the concept of state and for the establishment of a non-violent society which would be economically and politically decentralized. Continuing his religious quest, Gandhi tried to grasp the essence of Hinduism, Christianity and Islam. He read a number of books and a religious fermentation took place within him.[42]

When Gandhi had hardly set up his practice in Bombay, he received a telegram from the Indian Community in Natal. He left his family in India and sailed again and landed at Durban in December 1902.[43] For him "Ahimsa became the basis of the search for truth" and he realized that all are "children of one and the same Creator and as such the divine power within us are infinite".[44] To violate the unjust and Discriminatory Immigration Act, Gandhi led a march of about 5000 indentured labourers from Natal to Transvaal. Women were brought into the struggle in 1912 when the Cape Supreme Court declared all marriages illegal which were not performed according to the Christian rites and registered with the Registrar of Marriages.[45]

Gokhale's visit to South Africa and his discussion with Ministers did not improve the situation. As General Smuts refused to withdraw the Black Act, Gandhi started the struggle again. It was only in July 1914 that the agitation was ended when the Indian Relief Bill was passed in the parliament granting the lost rights.[46] The twenty years' stay in South Africa facilitated several other experiments which transformed his way of life and belief. He made a deep study of the Gita and the Bible and accepted the Gita as his spiritual guide. It was from the Gita that he derived the ideas of non-possession, 'service without self' and action without attachment. Tolstoy's *The Kingdom of God is within you*[47] made a profound impression upon him and he entered into a correspondence with him.

Mahatma Gandhi took a vow of celibacy which he considered to be essential for spiritual development. *Ruskin's Unto This Last*[48] inspired him to make an experiment in simple and community living. He incorporated these ideas in the *Hind Swaraj* which was intended to be a blueprint for India after Independence. He wrote at one stretch his celebrated *Hind Swaraj* or *Indian Home Rule* while he was returning from London to South Africa by ship. The central theme of *Hind Swaraj* was an attempt to answer the youthful Indian patriots. It was written in the form of a dialogue. He questioned the blind acceptance of western civilization going to the basic question of what was true civilization. This book presents Gandhism in a nutshell and it is often claimed as the 'Manifesto of the Gandhian Revolution' and also the 'Sermon on the Sea'. He serialized it in the *Indian Opinion*.[49]

Gandhi returned to India, not as a lawyer, but as a bold experienced organizer in the cause of social justice and equality. The experiences of political struggle for the welfare of human beings in South Africa

widened his mental horizon and field of activity promising India a
ray of hope for the needy in the society irrespective of caste, colour
and creed.

Gandhi's Achievements

Gandhi was a political leader by necessity.[50] After reaching India, he
attended the Calcutta session of the Indian National Congress in 1901,
after which he stayed with Gokhale for a month. His sincerity, zeal
and methods fascinated Gokhale and he prepared the ground for his
entrance into the Indian public arena. Gandhi, with his family, returned
to India on 9th January 1915 at the age of forty five with a burning
desire to serve his people. While Gandhi was still in South Africa,
struggling for his countrymen with his new weapon of Satyagraha,
people in India had begun to call him 'Mahatma,' an appellation which
stuck to him firmly and became a part of his name. Gandhi.

Gandhi-His Gift of the Fight,[51] Gandhi's participation in the Boer
War and the Zulu rebellion which are explained in the foregoing
paragraphs supplied him with an inexhaustible fund of experience.
He met his political guru, Gokhale, and he told Gandhi that he would
spend the first year in India studying the country, with his ears open
but his mouth shut.[52] He founded an ashram in May 1915 on the bank
of the river Sabarmathi outside Ahemadabad. He called it Satyagraha
Ashram, but it came to be known from the place as Sabarmathi
Ashram.[53] Even after the expiry of the year he decided to keep aloof
from Annie Beasant's Home Rule Movement. During the years 1916-
1918, Gandhi did not take active part in politics.[54]

Gandhi substituted it with the word Satyagraha which meant 'Soul
Force' or 'Steadfastness to Truth'. It consisted of Satya, Ahimsa and
Tapasya. Thus, the most potential weapon of the depressed and the
oppressed came into existence, to be known as Satyagraha. The first
act of the new South African Parliament was the passing of the Asiatic
Registration Act. The Transvaal Parliament gave Indians time up to 31st
July 1907 to register. Gandhi and his followers opposed registration. At
that time the number of Indians in Transvaal was thirteen thousand.

Out of these, five hundred Indians got registered and proved to be blacklegs. The Government arrested one Ramasundaram for not registering and taking a certificate. In December 1906, Gandhi and his colleagues received a summons from the Transvaal Court. The next hearing date was 10-01-1908. On that date, Gandhi pleaded guilty. By that time the Court had sentenced a number of Indians to three months' rigorous imprisonment. Gandhi, being the leader, asked for more severe punishment than that given to his co-workers. Gandhi and other Indians were sent to Johannesburg jail. The total number of Indians who were sent to jail at the time was one hundred and fifty. General Smuts and others felt internally guilty and were sorry for the development. Gandhi was sent to jail from the very court where he had practised as an advocate.

Cartwright, editor of a daily, came forward as a mediator. He met General Smuts. He also met Gandhi in jail. A compromise was proposed. General Smuts, ruler of South Africa, also was a barrister like Gandhi. He prepared a draft for the compromise and sent it to Gandhi through Cartwright. Gandhi was taken from Johannesberg jail to Pretoria. He had a long talk with General Smuts. The Superintendent of Police and Cartwright helped Gandhi in the settlement of the dispute. The substance of General Smuts's compromise draft was that, in case the Indians registered voluntarily, the Asiatic Registration Act would be repealed. Gandhi consented to the compromise in order to mitigate the suffering of hundreds of Indians inside the jail. After the talk, General Smuts released Gandhi then and there. Gandhi was given his train fare by General Smuts to go to Johannesberg from Pretoria. This was an excellent instance of the power of the Satyagraha principle. Gandhi could change the heart of General Smuts. This remarkable incident of the first release of Gandhi and other Indians from jail occurred on 30th January 1908. This date is a crucial one.

Gandhi continued with Satyagraha and used it to fight against any injustice which came to his notice. As a result he organized three local Satyagrahas. The first call for help came from Champaran in Bihar in 1917 at the request of Rajkumar Shukla on behalf of the oppressed peasants. Gandhi went to Champaran in Bihar to inquire into the grievances of the peasants of that district. It was an ancient place of great fame but which remained most backward at that time due to the colonialists exploitation. The peasants were compelled by the landlords to cultivate indigo on 15% of their lands and part with the whole crop for rent. He skillfully tackled the problem in a non-violent way.[55] The Government appointed a Committee in which Gandhi was also a member. On the recommendations of the committee, a Bill was passed in favour of the tenant-farmers. The success of his first experiment in Satyagraha in India increased his reputation as a hero in Indian politics.

He had hardly finished his work in Champaran when he got an urgent appeal from the textile workers of Ahmedabad. Their dispute with the mill-owners was taking a serious turn. He reached Ahmedabad and satisfied himself that the workers' demands were legitimate. He advised the workers to go on strike, only if they took a pledge to remain non-violent. The strike went on for 21 days. During the strike, he initiated his maiden fast for three days and his intervention had the desired effect.[56] Gandhi was called by the Kaira (Kheda) District of Gujarat. In early 1918 the crops of Kaira District were washed away by rain. The farmers were left with nothing and could not pay the land revenue. They demanded certain tax concessions. But the government turned a deaf ear to their request. Gandhi advised Satyagraha but he wanted at least one of the workers of the Gujarat Sabha to accompany him and devote all his time to the campaign until it was completed.[57]

Gandhi's first challenge in the form of Satyagraha to the British Government in India came when the Government passed the Rowlatt Act in March, 1919. India had cooperated with Britain during the First World War in November 1918 instead of granting Dominion status, civil liberties were curtailed. He condemned the Rowlatt Act and called upon all people to pledge themselves to 'refuse to obey' such unjust, subversive laws, as a prelude to the launching of a national Satyagraha campaign in the same way as he had done in South Africa. He considered it as the foremost duty to enhance the awareness of the people about the Rowlatt Act.[58] When Gandhi was in Madras, he issued a call to the nation to observe 6 of April 1919 as 'Satyagraha Day' with prayer and fasting and to attend public meetings and special lectures. The whole of India observed a complete hartal on 6th April 1919. Gandhi had stirred the nation over the Rowlatt Act. The movement became more widespread. While Satyagraha day passed off peacefully, a ghostly tragedy was developing in Punjab. The citizens decided to hold a meeting at Jallianwala Bagh in Amristar on April 13 against the arrest of Congress leaders like Satyapal and Kitchlew. General Dyer ordered fire upon a peaceful crowd of citizens, and hundreds of people were killed and more than a thousand people were seriously wounded.[59] The Amristar tragedy had its effect on all the provinces of India.[60]

Gandhi thought that his visit might have saved the Punjab tragedy and he was disturbed as much by the Indian violence in the province as by the atrocities of the Raj. He called the launching of his campaign 'A Himalayan blunder'[61] without disciplining the masses and Satyagraha was suspended. At the same time he observed a three days fast to atone for his mistake. The movement failed to affect any change of heart among the British authorities. But the Rowlatt Satyagraha did not fail entirely. It pushed Gandhi to the forefront of national leadership.

In the meanwhile, the First World War ended with the signing of a treaty on 11 November 1919, but the Turkish Empire was divided inspite of Britain's promise. Gandhi was invited to a Muslim conference where the fate of Turkey was seriously debated and discussed. He searched for a plan of action and found it in non-cooperation with the British Government. Under Gandhi's leadership, the Congress, at the special session in Calcutta in 1920, decided to boycott the elections to be held.[62] This movement formed epoch making in the history of the freedom struggle in India and in the life of Gandhi too. Hindu-Muslim cordiality with national spirit was advanced by him. The Non-violent Non-cooperation Movement got its impetus when he toured the whole country and met people. He started the campaign on 1st August 1920 by returning to the Viceroy the medals and decorations he had received from the government for his war-service and humanitarian work. He was followed by many who gave up their titles and honours. Lawyers, including C.R. Das, Motilal Nehru, Sardar Patel and Rajaji left their practices, students their colleges and schools. Many city dwellers went into the villages to spread the message of non-violent non-cooperation and to prepare the masses to defy the law. Bonfires of foreign cloth took place at various places.[63] People took to the hum of the spinning wheel; women too joined the movement and marched in the streets with men. Gandhi electrified the people by his speeches and writings in his weeklies, *Young India and Navajivan.*

Gandhi toured the whole country and met people. He spoke with patriotic fervour and his ethical values had their effect on both the educated elite and the illiterate masses alike. In November 1921, the Ali Brothers were awarded two years rigorous imprisonment and Gandhi proclaimed that he would lead a mass civil disobedience campaign in the Bardoli Taluk of Surat District in Gujarat. The Prince of Wales visited India on November 17, 1921. India observed a complete hartal on that day.[64] However, the tempo of the movement was hampered in February 1922 due to the outbreak of violence in Chauri Chaura in Gorakhpur District. Due to this incident, on 12th February, Gandhi suspended the Civil Disobedience Movement and decided to concentrate on his constructive programme. Taking advantage of the anti-climax, the British Government arrested him. In September 1922, he decided to wear a loin cloth in order to identify himself with the millions of poor in India. Gandhi was arrested and sent to jail for six years in Yeravda on 10th March 1922.[65]

Gandhi's suspension of the movement was opposed by many Congress leaders. Even though this movement roused the masses and carried the message of Swaraj to the sleepy villages, the news of his arrest and imprisonment magnified his image and reputation. He was released from jail in February 1924 on medical grounds.[66] In 1925, he started writing *The Story of My Experiments with Truth* through *Young India.* The spell of eleven vows came from Yeravda jail. Since 1925, he continued to devote more attention to the Hindu-Muslim problem. Till

1928, he extensively toured and propagated the constructive programme such as communal unity, removal of untouchability, prohibition, khadi, village industries and basic education.[67] The Indian National Congress wanted self-government and considered war for independence. Gandhi naturally refused to support a war but declared that if India was not free under Dominion status by the end of 1929 he would demand independence. Consequently, in 1930, he informed the Viceroy that Civil Disobedience would begin on 11th March. He said "My ambition is no less than to convert the British people through non-violence, and thus make them see the wrong they have done to India. I do not seek to harm your people".[68]

Gandhi decided to disobey the salt laws which forbade Indians from making their own salt. This British monopoly especially struck at the poor. The "Dharma Yudha" was inaugurated with a long march. On 12th , March 1930, he left Sabarmati Ashram at the head of its 78 male and female inmates and set out on foot for Dandi on the west coast. At the time of his departure he took a vow not to return to the Ashram without achieving freedom. His historic march continued for 24 days covering 241 miles on foot. Early in the morning of 6th April,[69] Gandhi went to the beach and broke the salt law by picking up a lump of salt from the shore. It was a signal for the beginning of the Civil Disobedience Movement. To the programme of non-co-operation whose whole emphasis was on boycott, non-payment of unjust taxes and civil disobedience of unjust laws were added. The incident reflected in the whole of India. The government was soon alarmed and resorted to oppressive measures. Gandhi was arrested on 5th May 1930 and Sarojini Naidu assumed the leadership and asked people not to resist the blows of the police. With the passage of time, Gandhi was called to a meeting with Viceroy Irwin in 1931, and they came to an agreement on 5th March. Civil Disobedience was called off. All political prisoners were released unconditionally. The Congress agreed to take part in the Second Round Table Conference.[70]

Gandhi travelled to England and stayed there for eighty four days. By the speeches, press notes and interviews he told the world about the suppression of the Indians by the British, the aim of their struggle and the means they were adopting. He met George Bernard Shaw, Charlie Chaplin and Maria Montessori and others. He was appreciated by many, of course not without criticism. Gandhi gave a vivid picture of the problems and the possible solutions. But the ugly heads of communalism and casteism raised their heads when Jinnah demanded a separate state and Ambedkar demanded a separate electorate. Gandhi was against such communal discrimination which would divide India still further. The Second Round Table Conference ended in failure. He returned to India on 28th December, empty handed.[71] He presented the demands of the Congress. When the British Government refused to accept the demands of the Congress, the Civil Disobedience Movement resumed. Gandhi was arrested in Bombay on 4th January 1932 and sent to Yeravda jail once again on 17th August 1932. The Prime Minister of England Ramsay Mac Donald announced the communal award giving a separate electorate to the depressed classes. Gandhi considered national unity in danger and decided to a "fast unto death" in Yeravda prison from 20th September 1932.[72]

Gandhi wrote a letter to Tagore, "This is early morning. I enter the fiery gates at noon. If you can bless the effort, I want it. You have been a true friend because you have been a candid friend". Tagore sent a telegram to Gandhi, "Our sorrowing hearts will follow your sublime penance with reverence and love" Gandhi's last stroke of Satyagraha worked well and attempts for quiet solutions were made.[73] Tagore's words echoed the sentiment of the whole nation. The heart of every Hindu community was roused as never before. Each held himself responsible for the curse of untouchability. The Hindu Leaders Conference met in Bombay and, in consultation with the leaders of the 'Untouchables,' whom Gandhi called Harijans (Children of God), signed a pact popularly known as the Poona Pact which was accepted by Gandhi. This pact is said to have broken the backbone of untouchability in India.[74]

On 11th February 1932, the first issue of *Harijan* was published. Gandhi was pained to see that the intelligentsia in the Congress was tired of his methods and views; the crucial issue was that the word *non-violence* was not taken into the resolution of the Congress. The Bombay session of the Indian National Congress in October 1934 registered his retirement from the organization and also authorized the formation of the All India Village Industries Association under his guidance. After this, Gandhi's centre of work was the improvement of the rural economy. He devoted his energies for the next six years to the upliftment of the Harijans and for village uplift. This issue was resolved and even Hindu temples were opened to untouchables for the first time. Gandhi had almost settled in Sevagram. Later on, it became the headquarters for his activities. He said, "India lives in her villages, not in her cities, when I succeed in ridding the villagers of their poverty, I have won Swaraj".[75] In the meanwhile the Council Entry Movement was gaining strength. A conference was held at Delhi by the Congress leaders who favoured council-entry under the chairmanship of Ansari. Gandhi did not want to stand in their way and issued a statement on 7th April 1934 suspending Civil Disobedience Movement. Accordingly the government gave up repressive measures and released all political prisoners and also lifted the ban on the Congress.

The Congress was back to contest elections in 1937 after the enactment of the Government of India Act of 1935.[76] Congress Ministries were formed in six provinces, including Madras. The socio-economic programme of Gandhi, especially prohibition and education, were entrusted to the Ministers for implementation.[77] From 1937 onwards, the anti-communal clashes increased between Hindus and Muslims. Discontentment was frequently discussed in all Congress sessions. He was deeply pained by the riots between these communities. He considered it a threat against national integration and solidarity and therefore tried his best to bring about communal harmony.

The outbreak of the Second World War in 1939 and the inclusion of India in the war without her permission resulted in the resignation of the Congress Ministries. Gandhi was genuinely anxious not to embarrass the British during the war. By 1940, an anti-war campaign was launched.[78] Vinoba Bhave, who led an Individual Satyagraha movement, was imprisoned soon.[79] Despite his arrest, the campaign gained momentum. Gandhi once again left the Congress Working Committee as he wanted to pursue his strategy of non-violence for independence and development. He did not want India to become independent under the shadow of war. In 1942, the British cabinet sent the Cripps Mission to India with a new constitutional proposal. Gandhi adopted an uncompromising attitude towards the proposals of the Cripps Mission because those proposals did not satisfy the demands of the Congress.[80] With a clear conscience, Gandhi planned the Quit India campaign for the complete withdrawal of the British from India. The Quit India resolution was passed by the AICC in August 1942. He addressed to the Congress Committee in which he eloquently and emotionally profounded the slogan of "Do or Die". On 9th August 1942, he was arrested and the Congress Committee was declared an unlawful organization. His arrest incited mobs to violence and sabotage. Later, he undertook a 21- day fast at Agha Khan Palace to end the deadlock between the Viceroy and the Indian leaders.[81]

In September 1945, Gandhi went to Bombay with Pyarelal to meet Jinnah in order to find a solution for united India. Jinnah was adamant for a separate nation for Muslims. He would sacrifice anything for Pakistan. Nehru's intervention in this regard was also without success. The Muslim League decided to celebrate 16th August 1946 as "Direct Action Day".[82] It witnessed a powerful outbreak of communal riot in Calcutta never known before in its history. He was deeply shocked. In Noakhali District in East Bengal about 200 Hindu families were massacred mercilessly by the Muslims. In his last years, Gandhi became more of a socialist. He said, "Violence is bred by inequality, non-violence by equality". He went on a pilgrimage to Noakhali to help the poor. He was a lone pilgrim determined to plant the message of love and courage in a wilderness of hatred and terror.[83]

At the age of seventy-seven, he went bare-footed from village to village, mostly on foot, preaching the same message of brotherhood, purity of heart and forgiveness. On 22nd March, Lord Mountbatten came to India and immediately invited Gandhi to come to Delhi. He strongly opposed the decision of the Congress to accept Mountbatten's proposal to partition the country into India and Pakistan. Amidst the situation, partition was accepted by Jawaharlal Nehru and Vallabai Patel and the majority of the Congress Working Committee. Though India became independent on 15th August 1947, Gandhi was not happy over the communal riots and tension mounting in various parts of the country. He spent the day in fasting and prayer.[84] He said with a heavy heart, "My thirty years of work for Independence have come to an inglorious end". He could not rest even after the attainment of freedom.

Gandhi's major Satyagraha campaigns (1917 to 1942) were many. But all the movements under Gandhi's leadership had one thing in common. That was the absence of violence with emphasis on Satyagraha. He also advocated Non-Cooperation methods which was one of the forms of Satyagraha. It needed courage, self-sacrifice as well as moral strength. Its primary aim was self-purification. His fasts and marches were the most effective method of pricking the conscience of the opponent. According to Gandhi, non-violence meant non-killing, had a higher meaning of forgiveness. But forgiveness is the virtue of the strong only; it presupposes the ability to strike. Gandhi created a number of organizations such as the All India Spinners' Association, the All India Village Industries Association, the Hindustani Talimi Sangh, the Harijan Sevak Sangh, the Go Sevak Sangh etc. His ashram served as a training centre for satyagrahis and constructive workers.

Gandhi was a prolific writer. His writings, like his life, are devoid of artificialities. His style is simple, precise and clear. He evolved his own style of writing in both English and Gujarati. Some of his editorials and articles had tremendous political influence and his journals became very popular. Through his writings in the magazines, *Young India and Harijan*, Gandhi was able to work for Hindu-Muslim unity. He elucidated its value and importance through his various articles in *Young India*. He categorically remarked that only harmonious relationship between the various classes and castes could lead to national integration, solidarity and prosperity. He became one with the nation and hence his life could be unmistakably identified with Indian history.

The real significance of the Indian Freedom Movement in Gandhi's eyes was that it was waged non-violently. He advocated non-violence not because it offered an easy way out, but because he considered violence crude and, in the long run, an ineffective weapon. In 1940, for example, *Harijan* was issued in a total of twelve editions in nine languages and in addition, his most important articles were reprinted the next day in all the newspapers of India. The writings of Gandhi have been well preserved in one hundred volumes. *The Collected Works of Mahatma Gandhi* brought out by the Government of India is monumental achievement.[85] He wrote a few books such as *An Autobiography, Satyagraha in South Africa, Discourses on the Gita, Hind Swaraj, Key to Health, From Yeravda Mandir, Ashram Observances in Action, Constructive Programme- Its Meaning and Place* etc. The services of Navajivan Publishing House, Ahmedabad, which was established by Gandhi himself should be mentioned. The world has recorded his activities, speeches and writings remarkably well. A documentary film on Gandhi has also been produced.

Nathuram Godse assassinated Gandhi on 30th January 1948 while he was proceeding to the evening prayer in Birla House, New Delhi. He fell down on the ground uttering the words "Hey Ram". Thus the apostle of non-violence became a victim of violence. The murder was on purpose. Godse had misunderstood Gandhi. He thought that Gandhi was the father of Pakistan. Not only Godse but hundreds of thousands of people inside and outside India thought that Gandhi was responsible for the dissection of India. The sources referred to above prove beyond doubt that partition was effected behind Gandhi's back deliberately and Gandhi was innocent. But the way in which partition was accomplished gave room for misunderstanding about Gandhi in the minds of posterity.[86] At the time of Mahatma Gandhi's assassination Nehru said, "...the[87] light that shines in this country was not an ordinary light. The light that has illumined this country for these many years will illumine this country for many more years".[88]

Mahatma Gandhi was very simple and humble in nature. Once Nehru said, "He did not descend from the above; he seemed to be emerged from the millions of India, speaking their language and certainly in drawing attention to them..."[89] Mahatma Gandhi believed in self-sacrifice and in the concept of non-cooperation, satyagraha and ahimsa. The most distinctive contribution he made to political thought was the concept of Satyagraha. It was the most powerful weapon for fighting against imperialism. It also meant adhering to truth in all circumstances. A true Satyagrahi should love God, Ahimsa, Love, and Peace and suffer willingly. Satyagraha was not a weapon of the weak but a weapon of the strong and excluded the use of violence in any shape or form. Gandhi kept the suffering community in his mind and served for their equality irrespective of caste, colour and creed. To obtain this freedom of life he practised non- violence for which he followed strictly the concept of satyagraha all through the freedom struggle.

Endnotes

[1] *CWMG*, Vol.39, p.7.

[2] *Ibid*, pp.33-44.

[3] *SWMG*, Vol.1, p.4.

[4] C.F.Andrews, *Mahatma Gandhi, His Own Story*, p. 24.

[5] M.K. Gandhi, *The Story of my Experiments With Truth*, p. 23.

[6] *SWMG*, Vol.1,p.10.

[7] *CWMG*, Vol.39,p.10.

[8] Laws of Manu, a Hindu Law giver. They have the authority over Hindu religion.

[9] *CWMG*, Vol.39, pp.10-11.

[10] *SWMG*, Vol.1, p.8.

[11] *CWMG*, Vol.39, p11.

[12] *Ibid*, p. 30.

[13] *Ibid*, p. 31.

[14] *Harijan*, 5.9.1936.

[15] *CWMG*, Vol.39, p.17.

[16] Louis Fisher, *The Life of Mahatma Gandhi*, p. 51.

[17] E.Stanly Jones, *Mahatma Gandhi*, p. 25.

[18] M.K. Gandhi, *Op.cit*, p. 54.

[19] *SWMG*, Vol.1, p.48.

[20] *CWMG*, Vol.1, pp.19-41and pp.42-49.

[21] *SWMG*, Vol.1, p.48.

[22] *CWMG*, Vol.1, pp.19-41 and pp.41-49.

[23] *SWMG*, Vol.1, pp. 58-59.

[24] M.K. Gandhi, *Op.cit*, p.75.

[25] *CWMG*, Vol.39, p.60.

[26] R.M. Gray &M.C.Parekh, p.17.

[27] *CWMG*, Vol.39,p.62.

[28] *CWMG*, Vol.39, p.164.

[29] M.K. Gandhi, *The Story of My Experiments with Truth*, p.249.

[30] *CWMG*, Vol.39, p.69.

[31] M.K. Gandhi, *The Story of My Experiments with Truth*, p.127.

[32] *Ibid*, p.340.

[33] *CWMG*, Vol.1, p.350.

[34] *Ibid*, p. 334.

[35] *Ibid*, P. 115.

[36] B.R. Nanda, p.21.

[37] *SWMG*, Vol.1, p. 326.

[38] *CWMG*, Vol.2, p.55.

[39] A.L. Basham and Arun Bhatta Charjee, *The Father of the Nation*, p. 34.

[40] *CWMG*, Vol.2, p. 56.

[41] *SWMG*, Vol.1, p.237.

[42] *CWMG*, Vol.39, p.114.

[43] *SWMG*, Vol.1, p. 121.

[44] *CWMG*, Vol.1, pp. 220-221.

[45] J.B. Kripalani, *Gandhi: His Life and Thought*, p. 38.

[46] *Ibid*, p.45.

[47] *SWMG*, Vol.1, p. 154.

[48] *Ibid*, p.100.

[49] *CWMG*, Vol,10, pp. 66-68.

[50] Romain Rolland, *Mahatma Gandhi*, p. 27.

[51] J.P. And Marjorie Sykes, *Gandhi- His Gift of the fight*, p.45.

[52] *CWMG*, Vol.39, p.304.

[53] Homer, A. Jack (ed) *The Gandhi Reader*, p. 136.

[54] Dhananjay Keer, *Mahatma Gamdhi: Political Saint and Unarmed prophet*, p.273.

[55] Judith.M. Brown, *Gandhi's Rise to Power in Indian Politics*, (1915-1922), p.106.

[56] Homer, A. Jack, *Op.cit*, pp.154-157.

[57] Judith.M. Brown, *Ibid*, p.107.

[58] R. Kumar, (ed.,) *Essays on Gandhian politics: The Rowlatt Satyagraha*, pp. 82-83

[59] V.P. Singh, *History of Freedom Movement in India*, p. 126.

[60] *FNR*, II Half of April, 1919, TNA, Madras.

[61] D.G.Tendulkar, *Mahatma*, Vol. I, p.136.

[62] *CWMG*, Vol.19,p.359.

[63] *Ibid*, p.46.

[64] *FNR*, II Half of November, 1921, TNA, Madras.

[65] C. Rajagopalachari, *Jail Diary*, 31st March 1922, p.139.

[66] C. Rajagopalachari, *To Devadas Gandhi*, 12th May, 1924.

[67] Ahluwalia B.K. and Shasi Ahluwalia, *Rajaji and Gandhi*, pp.61-62.

[68] *Ibid*, p.63.

[69] A.M. Zaidi and S.G. Shasi, (ed.,) *Encyclopaedia of the Indian National Congress*, Vol .X, pp.35-37.

[70] Pattabhi Sitaramaiyya, *History of Indian National Congress*, p. 465.

[71] Louis Fisher, *Op.cit*, pp. 317-320.

[72] J.P. Krilpalani, *Op.cit*, p.149.

[73] Ahluwalia B.K. and Shasi Ahluwalia, *Op.cit*, pp.70-71.

[74] *Ibid*.

[75] *Ibid*.

[76] *CWMG*,Vol. 44.p.396.

[77] B.R. Nanda, *Mahatma Gandhi*, p. 202.

[78] *CWMG*, Vol. 73, p.2.

[79] *CWMG*, Vol.70, p.315.

[80] B.R. Nanda, *Op.cit*, p.63.

[81] Pyarelal, *Mahatma Gandhi: The Last Phase*, Vol.1, p.65.

[82] *Ibid*, p. 247.

[83] *Ibid*, p. 282.

[84] Pyarelal, *Mahatma Gandhi: The Last Phase*, Vol.II, p.705.

[85] B.K. Ahluwalia. and Shasi Ahluwalia, *Op.cit*, pp.162-164.

[86] Pyarelal, *Mahatma Gandhi: The Last Phase*, Vol.II, p.705.

[87] Jawaharlal Nehru, *Discovery of India*, New Delhi, p. 358.

[88] J.D. Sethi, *Gandhi Today*, p. 47.

[89] Jawaharlal Nehru, *Op.cit*, p.358.

Chapter 3

Social Ideology
of Luther and Gandhi

Social Ideology of Luther

Capitalism emerged due to the aristocratic order. The peasant condition in Germany was deteriorating. In this situation Martin Luther began to work for the people, oppressed and neglected by both the established Church and society. The concern for neighbour occupies a considerable place in the writings of him. He both preached and practised it in his own life. The idea of 'neighbour' got a new explanation and a new dimension in him. Although he did not deal with this matter systematically, he developed it with great zeal. The neighbour, according to him, is everybody, especially he who needs our love ad service.[1] He, therefore, declares that one must accept the needy as his neighbour and extend his love and help to him regardless of his status. For the neighbour can be a servant, a master, a man or a woman. He may be the one who wears purple, or the one who wears rags, or the one who eats meat or the one who eats fish.[2]

The outward appearance need not be the criterion to admit a person to be our neighbour. Even Apostle Paul did not mention any qualification to be one's neighbour. But he simply said 'love your neighbour' (Rom. 13: 9) without any qualification. He did not say you should love the rich, the powerful, the learned, the wise, the upright, the righteous, the handsome or the pleasant.[3] In the same manner, when Jesus commanded us to love our neighbour (Mt. 19:19), he excluded nobody whether he be our friend or enemy, good or evil. So, he concluded that even though they may be a bad person or the one who did evil to us, they do not on any account lose the qualification to be our neighbours. With these assertions, he admonished us to accept the needy ones as our neighbour. In other words, we must accept such persons without any distinction as we accept our own brothers and extend our loving service to them. He also warned us not to apply worldly standards to make a person our neighbour. For the world gives weight to the status and not to the person as such.[4] He went still further and said that we should continue the love for our neighbour even though we may find nothing in our neighbour that deserves our love.[5] With these words he once again emphasized that our concern for our neighbour should not be neglected on the basis of the existing distinctions.[6]

When Luther talked about the love of neighbour he went to the extent of saying even that God requires nothing from us than the love towards our neighbour.[7] We are not called to serve God but our neighbour. God does not need our work and he did not even command us to do anything for him other than to praise and thank him.[8] As to our brothers, sisters and neighbours, God commanded nothing higher than that we love them. [9] Nonetheless, Christians are not coerced by God to service but an act of love towards our neighbour giving expression to our faith in God. Consequently he warned those who withdrew from their neighbours instead of serving them. He criticized monasticism because it was not socially productive and the monks, instead of helping others, lived at the expense of others. He did not see any relevance or meaning in one's fasting or praying unless and until he first loves God and his neighbour.[10] Against those who withdrew themselves from serving their neighbour, he said serving one's neighbour is serving God themselves. He added that Christ and the Apostles never isolated themselves or hid themselves for ever in monasteries; instead they served others.[11]

Luther also contrasted the interpretation of the medieval Church with that given in the statement 'you shall love your neighbour as yourself'. The Roman Church said that self-love was a prerequisite for the love of one's neighbour. But he refuted this interpretation and maintained that the love of self should be replaced by the love of neighbour. In other words, he considered the love of neighbour superior to the love of one's self. Thus he turned the medieval understanding upside down and projected a new explanation. To emphasize his point, he said: Love 'as yourself' it says, no less than you love yourself. But how much you love yourself no one could tell you better than yourself, since you are aware of this very thing which can only be guessed at for you by someone else. For this reason no one could tell you better than yourself what should be done, said, and desired for your neighbour.[12]

On another occasion he said that we should neither judge nor speak evil of our neighbours or do any physical harm to them. No one wishes to endure disobedience, wrath, a wife's impurity, robbery, lying, deceit, slander, but every one wishes to find in his neighbour kindliness, thankfulness, helpfulness, truth and fidelity. All this the Ten Commandments require. Therefore, we should speak the best about them[13] and treat them as God has treated us.[14] We should love them as we love ourselves even without any commandment or rule.[15] He further made it clear that service to neighbour never required a position or standing but one can serve one's neighbour in the capacity of a father, husband, magistrate, teacher or a farmer. In another context he said that even a manual labourer can help his neighbour.[16]

Luther thus inspired everyone to be his neighbour's friend and render him help in all possible ways and means. But at the same time he held that serving one's neighbour should not be evaluated in terms of accident or self-interest or opportunism. Instead it should be viewed and accepted as a call of God.[17] He understood the Christian life as a norm to serve the neighbour. To him, Christian life is composed of two parts, namely, faith in God and love towards the neighbour.[18] And a Christian stands in a faith relationship towards God and in a love relationship towards his neighbour. His love descends towards his neighbour just as his faith movers upward.[19] He illustrated this relationship with an analogy of water pipe of a fountain in which the water flows into us and then it flows out again to our neighbour. [20]

Luther also saw the link between one's faith and neighbourly love. This faith serves God and his works serve the neighbour. In reality it is one's faith in God that produces the spontaneous love for one's neighbour. A Christian, therefore, cannot be idle or without works of love towards his neighbour as he lives not for himself but only for his neighbour. When he sees his neighbour who is in need or in danger of life he should not pass by him like the priest and the Levite and let him lie there and perish. Instead he should voluntarily involve himself to remove the pains of his neighbour. To defend this idea he said that a man does not live for himself but he lives only for others.[21] Nonetheless, he made it clear that the response of the person towards his neighbour ought not to come out of either compulsion or artificiality but from an inner necessity and he explained this with the analogy of trees which bear fruits freely and spontaneously out of natural necessity. To explain this he wrote that good works must follow faith, just as a good tree not only must produce good fruits, but do so freely.[22]

Luther pleaded that one must show sympathy towards his neighbour and he must be even ready to accept the sins of his neighbours as his own. He should even intercede for the forgiveness of sins.[23] Just as God covers our sins with his love, so also we must cover our neighbour's sin.[24] Similarly one should take one's neighbour's weakness, trouble and foolishness as one's very own and should love him despite his frailty.[25] With all these assertions he advised a Christian to identify his or her neighbour in every situation in order to elevate his neighbour's condition to a level better than that of his own.[26] In his conclusion to the Ten Commandments, he talked about the protection given to one's neighbour. He said that one should do no harm, no injury or violence nor in any way molests him whether in respect to his body, his wife, his property, honour or rights even though one may have the opportunity and reason to do it. But he should constantly forgive his neighbour even if he does harm, violence, injustice and bears malice. If he fails, he categorically declares that God will not forgive him.[27] He even went a step further and said that one should examine one's body and mind so that one may be, on the one hand, harmless and, on the other, useful to one's neighbour. If I subdue my body, so that it does not become lascivious, I can also let my neighbour's wife and children alone. Thus if I suppress hatred and envy, I become all the more willing to be kind and friendly to my neighbour.[28]

Luther also spoke of one's responsibility towards one's neighbour. Being a brother, sister or friend, he has the responsibility to make his neighbour aware of the evil he is doing so that he might correct himself and be released from it.[29] On another occasion, he once again drew attention to the dual responsibility of the Christian. First, as a Christian, where his own personal welfare is involved, he should seek nothing else than to serve his neighbor even if his neighbour is his enemy. He must be prepared to suffer injustice without protecting himself and to resist evil, without calling upon the authorities and their judicial power for help.[30] Second, as a secular person fulfilling his office of protecting those entrusted to his care and acting in matters that affect the welfare of his neighbour, he must under all conditions fulfil this duty to protect them, to oppose evil, block it, punish it and use force in resisting it.[31] Thus he showed the dual responsibilities of the Christian in the two realms of existence. In the medieval time good works were sought as a means to righteousness. But he opposed this view very strongly and boldly said that one need not do good works for one's righteousness or salvation since God has already taken care of man's salvation. By faith we acquire everything that God has done for us and, therefore, we need not do anything else in terms of our salvation.[32] Instead he advised Christians to do loving service for the well-being of their neighbours who were really in need of such service.[33]

Commitment towards the neighbour

Luther himself was a committed and practical person and his concern was oriented very much towards the neighbour. He did not only preach and write but also practised it in his own life. For example, when the plague began to decimate the populace of Wittenberg in the year 1527, his concern for his people moved him to remain in Wittenberg itself despite his prince's advice to leave the city in order to safeguard him from the threat of plague. This obviously shows how much love and concern he had for his neighbours.[34] Caring for the neighbour got the priority in all his dealings.[35] He also admonished that everybody must be a little Jesus to his neighbour.[36] In his famous treatise, "The Freedom of a Christian", he spelled out the responsibility of a person in two seemingly paradoxical propositions as follows: First, a Christian is a perfectly free lord of all, subject to none. Second, a Christian is a perfectly dutiful servant of all, subject to all. In the second proposition, he saw the possibility of a Christian being a Christ to his neighbour and giving himself in the service of his neighbour just as Christ had given himself for him.[37] To expound this he said: "I will therefore give myself as a Christ to my neighbour, just as Christ offered himself to me; I will do nothing in this life except what I see is necessary, profitable and salutary to my neighbour".[38]

Thus the epitome of Luther's ethic was that a Christian must be a Christ to his neighbour. A Christian, according to him, lives in Christ through faith and in his neighbour through love. He also suggested that a Christian must offer free service as Christ himself offered to others. He said that one must serve his neighbour most willingly, most freely and most joyfully and that too in humility.[39] He should also do it without anticipating either thankfulness or reward. One cannot serve when he puts his neighbour under obligation.[40] He thus emphasized the genuine commitment to one's neighbour as Christ committed himself to the world. To stress his point he said: "Although the Christian is thus free from all works, he ought in this liberty to empty himself, take upon himself the form of a servant, be made in the likeness of men, be found in human form, and to serve, help, and in every way deal with this neighbour as he sees that God through Christ has dealt and still deals with him. This he should do freely, having regard for nothing but divine approval".[41]

According to Luther good works are worthwhile only when they really serve one's neighbour.[42] Good works are neither for one's own benefit but as enjoined for the benefit of the neighbour. In other words, they are not self service but are done in the service of the neighbour.[43] He insisted that one must freely spend himself and all that he has even if he feels that he wasted everything on the one who is thankless to him.[44] To defend this he quoted Mt. 5: 45, where the heavenly Father distributes all things richly and freely to both the good and the evil. He commanded that faith is to be active in the service of the neighbor because faith needs a secular life and it lives only in the works done to the neighbour. The works are the concrete realization of faith.[45]

The Christian name or baptism or even one's faith are meaningless if he does not help his neighbour and draw him to the faith through his good works.[46] In another context he characterized the life of a Christian as worship and the good works done to the neighbour as worship. He further said that not only he who does evil breaks the commandment but also he who unnecessarily omits a service to his neighbour.[47] In his view, the Christian does not need the government for himself but his neighbour needs it and benefits from it. Therefore, he has to honour and uphold the government for the sake of his neighbour. To acquire peace for his neighbour he has to support the government for the sake of his neighbour, because peace cannot prevail without a government. If the Christian abstains from supporting the government it cannot be strong enough to afford peace or protection. Hence the Christian must accept and uphold the secular government and the office of the sword.[48] To substantiate this Luther said: "Therefore I do not want to be compelled to be subject to secular princes and lords; but I will be subject to them of my own accord, nor because they command me but to render as a service to my neighbour".[49]

Social Ideology of Gandhi

Gandhi was the greatest social scientist ever born. He forged a weapon of truth to fight injustice. It was Satyagraha. His weapon of Satyagraha is an alternative to war. He laid the foundation for peace science. He

changed the status of Indian women overnight. The emancipation of
Indian women, the conferment of equal right to vote on women was
one of the by products of his struggle for freedom. Renuka Ray has
highlighted this reality.[50] He knew the importance of a preliminary
philosophical revolution prior to any final revolution. The sense of a
sociologist enabled him to grant equal rights to women in the matter
of franchise. Socialism is as pure as crystal, according to him. "It,
therefore, requires crystal-like means to achieve it. Impure means
result in an impure end. Hence the prince and the peasant will not be
equalized by cutting off the prince's head... only truthful, non-violent
and pure-hearted socialists will be able to establish a socialist society
in India and the world".[51] Socialism evolved out of his deeply religious
outlook. He may not be accepted as a socialist in the rigid sense. But,
a broader and deeper study of his concept qualifies him to be called
a better socialist than the socialists themselves. The experiments he
gained from the Tolstoy Farm in South Africa and his deep respect
for the yogis inspired him to formulate a unique type of socialism.[52]

Gandhi emphasized certain features of socialism: "He believed in
economic equality and also agreed to the Marxian concept of 'To each
one according to his need'. He was opposed to the private property
as in the case of all socialists".[53]

He believed that every individual has the right to demand satisfaction
of his elementary needs.

- He stood for the full development of man and against any tendency
  of exploitation by the capitalists.

- As the socialists believe, he was also of the opinion that an economic
  order could survive in which production was determined by the
  needs of the individuals and not by personal whim or greed.

Satya and Ahimsa must be incarnate in Socialism. Therefore, only a
truthful, non-violent and pure hearted socialist will be able to establish
a socialist society in India and the world. There is no country in the
world which is purely socialistic. Without the means, the existence of
such a society is impossible.[54] He totally opposed machines when they

master us. He also observed: "I am a socialist enough to say that such factories should be nationalized... It is an alternation in the condition of labour that I want... the labourer must be assured, not only a living wage, but a daily task that is not a mere drudgery. The machine will, under these conditions, be as much a help to the man working it as to the state, or the man who owns it".[55] It could be evident from the above that there is a gradual change in his views on machinery and industrialism. He deviated from his position, i.e., total opposition to machinery and realized the importance of industries in the modern times, not only for the production of comfortable things, but also for the production of basic necessities of human life.

For Gandhi, means and ends are convertible terms.[56] Since they are inseparable and interdependent, they should be equally pure. He compared the means with a seed and the end with a tree. The end grows out of the means and we can control only the means but not the end. The Gita doctrine of Nishkama Karma also teaches us that a good deed produces only a good result. He observed: Means to be means must always be within our reach, and so Ahimsa is our Supreme duty. If we take care of the means, we are bound to reach the end sooner or later.[57]

Gandhi's antipathy to violence and his aversion to the coercive power of the state made him an anti-communist. Inspite of his admiration for the spirit of sacrifice of his communist friends, he could not agree with their method and said, "They frankly believed in violence and all that is in its bosom".[58] As a prophet of non-violence he believed that economic justice could be attained only through non-violent means. He wanted to destroy not capitalists, but only capitalism. He complained that western socialists believed in the necessity of violence for enforcing the socialists doctrine and said: "My Socialism was natural to me and not adopted from any books. It came out of my unshakable belief in non-violence... unfortunately western socialists have, so far as I know, believed in the necessity of violence for enforcing socialist doctrines".[59]

He frankly admitted that he was not well acquainted with Scientific Socialism, but he thought that it was not applicable to our country in its original form. He wanted to solve the same problem which the scientific socialists were trying to solve, but his approach was always and only through unadulterated nonviolence. "If communism comes without any violence, it would not be acceptable to him".[60] He assumed that western socialism and communism are based on the conception that human nature is essentially selfish. Speaking on his conception of Socialism, he said: "Our socialism or communism should be based on nonviolence and on harmonious cooperation of labour and capital, landlord and tenant". [61]

Sarvodaya

Ruskin's work *Unto This Last*, which challenged the classical political economy, had exerted a tremendous influence on Gandhi and he translated it into Gujarati entitled 'Sarvodaya,' which means the welfare of all. Since all men are brothers and no human being should be a stranger to another, Gandhi aimed at the welfare of all. His concept of Socialism is an extension and application of the economic aspect of his Sarvodaya philosophy. In his concept of Socialism all the members of the society are equal. It will provide equal opportunity for the prince and the peasant, the wealthy and the poor, the employer and the employee, the strong and the weak and all are treated on the same level.[62] He claimed that his concept of Sarvodaya is distinguished from and superior to the utilitarian doctrine, which aims at the "greatest good or happiness of the greatest number and the Marxian Socialism, which aims at the welfare of proletariat class only".[63] Hence the real dignified human doctrine, for him, is the greatest good of all.

Non-possession

The central idea of the Gita, according to Gandhi, is the renunciation of the fruits of actions. To Gandhi, "Non-possession is allied to non-stealing". Non-stealing for him means much more than what it commonly meant. It implies, not only not taking another person's belongings without his permission or knowledge, but also not receiving something which one does not actually need.[64] Therefore he said, "A thing not originally stolen must nevertheless be classified as stolen property, if we possess it without needing it. He observed: "God never stores for the morrow. He never creates more than what is strictly needed for the moment. If therefore, we repose faith in his providence, we should rest assured, that he will give us everything that we require."[65] Thus, non-possession implies a total abolition of private property, in all its forms and this view of him seems to be more radical than any other social theory. If all possess equally, there will be no theft. The basic factors of non-possession are,[66]

1. One should get only what is essential to his life. It is a good thing if we get food to eat and clothes to wear.

2. Voluntary renunciation of wants and cultivation of simple habits.

3. Not to accumulate property for future requirements.

4. What he has more than his wants is not his and so he is to be a trustee to use wealth in the service of the poor and the needy.

Equitable distribution of national wealth is the key principle of Socialism. Gandhi believed that so long as the distinction between the rich and the poor continues, the attainment of Socialism will be a far cry and an impossibility. A non-violent system of government is clearly an impossibility so long as the wide gulf between the rich and the hungry millions persists. The contrast between the palaces of New Delhi and the miserable level of the poor labouring classes nearby cannot last one day in free India in which the poor will enjoy the same power as the richest in the land.

Trusteeship

The theory of trusteeship constitutes an integral part of the social order envisaged by Gandhi. He proposed a highly radical approach towards private property. He desired to establish a society without private possession. He tolerated the institution of private property, not on account of its being essential for human progress, but because a truthful and non-violent method to abolish the same is yet to evolve. Hence the idea is to consider private property as 'Trust'.[67] The ideal social order of his dream is one where all the members of the society are able to fulfill their needs, and the rich consider their wealth as held in trust for the benefit of the masses, where the individual freedom is not questioned, where people give more importance to spiritual aspects than material aspects and remain happy with a relatively better standard of living.

Removal of Untouchablity

Gandhi's contribution to the field of social reform was important for the reconstruction of the life of the nation. It can be said that the whole of his constructive programme was devoted to social reform. It was devised to reform our national character. The first and foremost item of this reform was the removal of untouchability. Untouchability is a cruel and inhuman institution. It violates human dignity. It is a social evil for which the society should reasonably be punished.[68] He observed: Hindus will certainly never deserve freed on, not get it if they allow their noble religion to be disregarded by the retention of taint of untouchability.[69] He opposed giving religious sanction to the practice of untouchability. He said that every fight against untouchability was a religious fight for the recognition of human dignity and entrenched citadels of orthodoxy. He therefore suggested that social reformers should take bold steps and allow the untouchables to enter temples and worship there. God cannot be partial to any class or caste. For Gandhi, the caste system was as much an evil as untouchability. He however believed in Varnashrama Dharma. The law of Varna and Ashram is to be traced to our most ancient scriptures.[70] Whereas in our caste system, many unhealthy restrictions were imposed, in Varnashramadharma there was no scope for unnecessary restrictions. Gandhi was against untouchability and therefore he called them as Harijans, means children of God.[71] His fight for the emancipation of the Harijans resulted in Article seventeen of the constitution of India for abolition of untouchability and article forty six of the directive principles of state policy for the promotion of educational and economic interests of the scheduled Caste, scheduled Tribes and the other weaker sections of the community and protect them from social injustice and all forms of exploitation.

Gandhi - Women Supporter

The work of the Gandhi was great in the field of education. He advocated the equality of men and women. His writings on the subjects were influential in raising the status of women in India. With his pen and from every platform throughout his long life of service, he preached against the wrong done to women in the name of law, traditions and even religion. He was in favour of women and he said that women had a low place in our society and were considered inferior to men in intelligence or wisdom. In his opinion, Hindu society always assigned a high position to women and history was witness to that. In his opinion women should be given a much higher status in the society than even men. For him, a woman was the incarnation of Ahimsa and personification of self-sacrifice. He held that both were of equal rank and supplementary to each other and that without one the existence of the other could not be justified.[72]

The census of 1912-1922 shows the scheduled caste women students account for only 0.5%. The socio – economic factors made them a negligible proportion. The social degradation of the society affected very much the willingness of Adi Dravidians families to send their children to schools and colleges. The women became victims to untouchability in the institutions. It kept them from the mainstream of the national life. Another major problem that they faced was the cost of university education. Due to these problems they were prevented from enjoying the fruits of higher education.[73] He said: "Woman is the companion of man gifted with equal mental capacities. She has the right to participate in the activities of man and she has an equal right of freedom and liberty with him". He was against all social and religious barriers to widow remarriage. He was against child marriage, dowry system, purdah system etc. Nobody in modern times has done more for the uplift of women than Gandhi.[74] His contribution to the financially backward class women, particularly low caste women, was noteworthy.

Prohibition

"Drinking is not only a bad habit but also a disease"[75] said Gandhi. For him drinking was evil and the nation which was developing and depending on such revenues was to be cursed. So he introduced prohibition as one of his constructive programmes. He instigated people to picket the liquor shops in non-violent ways. He observed: "For me, the drink question is one of dealing with a growing social evil against which the state is bound to provide while it has got the opportunity... It is a gigantic problem. The prohibition I have adumbrated in the beginning of the reform. We cannot reach the drunk as long as he has the drink shop near his door to tempt him".[76]

Gandhi was of the opinion that drinking liquor in India was more criminal than the petty thefts which starving men and women committed and for which they were prosecuted and punished. He considered drinking the most dangerous of all social evils. These evils cause untold sufferings to the masses. In 1937, when Congress Ministries were formed in many Provinces, he advised every legislator to champion the cause of prohibition on the floor of the Assembly. It should be the foremost duty of all legislators to pledge themselves to the task of successful implementation of prohibition. According to Gandhi, the state could use its power to force the people to be moral by law. What prohibition is concerned with is not only the drink addict but the non-drunkard whom it wishes to protect from the evils of the liquor trade. Compulsion is felt only by the drink addict and the liquor trade. But it is right that the state should step in and compel them to give it up.[77]

For Gandhi, socialism was not limited by class constraints. He believed in classless society but did not think that this involved the destruction of the individuals who constituted the propertied classes. And he was not willing to identify himself with land lords and capitalists and he said 'I am a part and parcel of the whole'. He also claimed for his socialism of sarvodaya and trusteeship the ability to survive on a sustaining and permanent basis which, he held was not, possible in the case of the socialism or communism of the Marxian conception.

The theory of socialism through trusteeship was the alternative that he presented to the scientific socialism and communism evolved by the western thinkers. He was not able to elaborate in it because of his involvement for the political freedom of our country. He recommends for six principles of social order(said in Pyarelal pp.23-94) Equality and equal distribution of wealth irrespective of gender, caste, color, ethnicity and creed were prime motives of his social ideology that may enable the people to live without discrimination and enable them to enjoy the breadth of unity in diversity.

For Luther, a neighbour is the one who is in need of one's help, love and service. To put it differently, the neighbour according to him, was the neglected, the poor and the needy and he never meant it in the general sense. He maintained that loving one's neighbour is the most important and indispensable act and affair which has no substitute or replacement. He was saying on the priesthood of all believers, showing no disparities among the human beings in the name of religions and position in the state. For Gandhi, equality and equal distribution of wealth irrespective of gender, caste, color, ethnic and creed were prime motive of his social ideology that may avail the people to live without discrimination and enable them to enjoy the breadth of unity in diversity.

Endnotes

1 William H. Lazareth, *Luther on the Christian home*, p. 83.

[2] *Luther's Works*, Vol.27, p.31.

[3] *Luther's Works*, Vol. 27, p. 351.

[4] *Luther's Works*, Vol. 30, p. 304.

[5] *Luther's Works*, Vol.27, p. 67.

[6] *Luther's Works*, Vol. 3 0, p. 277.

[7] *Luther's Works*, Vol.27, p. 55.

[8] Lewis W. Spitz, " *Luther's Social Concern for Students*", *The Social History of the Reformation*, p. 259.

[9] J.N. Lenker, *Luther's Large Catechism*, p. 31.

[10] *Luther's Works*, Vol.51, pp.104-105.

[11] *Luther's Works*, Vol.46, p.151.

[12] *Luther's Works*, Vol.17, p. 352.

[13] *Luther's Works*, Vol. 51, pp. 158-159.

[14] *Ibid*, Vol. 51, p. 95.

[15] *Luther's Works*, Vol.27, p.355.

[16] *Luther's Works*, Vol.21, p. 237.

[17] H.G. Koenigsberger, ed. Luther: A Profile, London, Macmillan, 1973, 136.

[18] *Luther's Works*, Vol.30, p. 47.

[19] *Ibid*, Vol. 30, p.198.

[20] *Luther's work*, Vol.31, p. 371.

[21] *Ibid*, Vol.31,p. 364.

[22] *Luther's Work* , Vol.34 p.111.

[23] *Luther's Works*, Vol.31, p. 371.

[24] *Luther's Works*, Vol.30, p. 123.

[25] *Luther's Works*, Vol. 31, p. 302.

[26] *Ibid*, Vol. 31, p. 304.

[27] J.N. Lenker, *Op.cit*, p.75.

[28] *Luther's Works*, Vol.30, p.118.

[29] *Luther's Works*, Vol. 23, p. 23.

[30] *Luther's Works* , Vol.45, pp.101-103.

[31] *Luther's Works*, Vol.21, p. 113.

[32] *Luther's Works*, Vol.31, p. 365.

[33] Walter Altmann, '*Interpreting the Doctrine of the Two Kingdoms: God's Kingship in the Church and in Politics*', pp. 43-44.

[34] Walter Altmann, Op.cit, pp. 51-52.

[35] *Luther's Works*, Vol.44, p.71.

[36] *Luther's Works*, Vol.31, pp. 364-365.

[37] *Luther's Works*, Vol.35, p. 120.

[38] *Luther's Works*, Vol.31, pp. 367- 368.

[39] *Ibid*, Vol.31, p.365.

[40] *Ibid*, Vol.31, pp. 368-369.

[41] *Ibid*, Vol.31, p. 366.

[42] *Luther's Works*, Vol. 31, p. 370 also see Karl Holl, *The Cultural Significance of the Reformation*, p. 33.

[43] Edward D. Schneider, 'Lutheran *theological Foundations for Social Ethics*', p.191.

[44] *Luther's Works*, Vol.31, p.367.

[45] *Luther's Works*, Vol.45, p. 286.

[46] *Luther's Works*, Vol.51, p.116.

[47] J.N. Lenker, Op.cit, p. 47.

[48] *Luther's Works*, Vol.30, p. 74 & Vol.13, p.44.

[49] *Ibid*, Vol.30, p.79.

[50] Dastur Aloo.J. Usha Mehta, *Gandhi's Contribution to Emancipation of Women*, p. 46.

[51] *Harijan*, 13. 07.1947.

[52] *Harijan*, 20.02.1937.

[53] *Harijan*, 01.06.1947.

[54] *Harijan*,13.07.1947.

[55] *Young India*, 13.11.1924.

[56] *Harijan*, 26.12.1924.

[57] N.K. Bose, *Selections from Gandhi*, p. 14.

[58] *Harijan*, 04.08.1946.

[59] *Harijan*, 20. 04.1940.

[60] *Haijan*, 13.02. 1937.

[61] *Ibid.*

[62] *Harijan*,13.07.1947.

[63] *Ibid.*

[64] *Harijan*,13.02.1937.

[65] *Ibid.*

[66] *CWMG*, Vol.50, p.213.

[67] *Harijan*,16.12.1939.

[68] M.K. Gandhi, My *Philosophy of Life*, p. 148.

[69] *Young India*,02.10.1920.

[70] *Harijan*,28.09.1934.

[71] B.C.Das, *Gandhi in Today's India*, p.17.

[72] *Harijan*, 24.02.1940.

[73] B.D. Bhatt & S.R. Sharma, *Women's Education and Social Development*, p. 175.

[74] *Harijan*, 05.01.1947.

[75] Sudanthira Sangu, 27.06.1931, p. 5.

[76] *Harijan*, 05.01.1947.

[77] Bharatan Kumarappa, *Why Prohibition?* p.8.

Chapter 4

Political Ideology
of Luther and Gandhi

In Germany in the sixteenth century and in India in the nineteenth century, the political reigns were mostly in the hands of the educated and wealthy people. In Germany politics was in the hands of the Popes and the rulers. The poor and the needy were not able to get the ordinary benefits that were extended to them from the government. High rates of tax were imposed and allotment of hard work on less payment were practised by the government. In India, the colonial power deprived the welfare of the ordinary people and they were treated as slaves. Indians were not allowed to enjoy power in their administration and the entire politics was in the hands of the white people. In this particular context both reformers stood for a clean political ideology, needed to raise the people from their oppressed status.

Political Ideology of Luther

Appreciation of Secular Government

Politically speaking, Germany was seeking autonomy both from the Emperor and from the Papal taxation. Kings as well as Arch- bishops were compelled to give large amounts of money to meet the Roman administration's expenses. In this context, Martin Luther taught the political involvement of the people in the state. During the time of Luther, there was strong opposition to Christian participation in temporal activities. The Anabaptists argued that Christians should not participate in the institutions of this world such as property, law, oath-taking, exercise of authority, affairs of state, police work and any kind or war.[1] Likewise, the passive Enthusiasts asserted that Christians should radically withdraw from the world. But Luther boldly and openly opposed both the views and declared that Christians should neither leave these worldly affairs nor refuse to accept the offices and responsibilities of the temporal government since they are necessary for life in the world.[2]

Andor Muntag states that the Church's attitude of refusing to accept its responsibility in the sphere of politics resembles the attitude of the priest and the Levite when they turned away from the man on his way to Jericho.[3] Luther defended the legitimacy of the temporal government and all its offices. To him, it was also a divine institution: and God established it to maintain law and order in the world by way of punishing the evil, protecting the good and preserving the peace. To strengthen this view further, Luther quoted Jesus and John the Baptist. Luther stated that when Jesus stood before Pilate, Jesus uttered, 'If my kingship were of this world, then my servants would fight that I might not be handed over to the Jews' (Jn. 18:36). On this verse, Luther commented that Jesus had a positive view of the temporal government and endorsed its legitimacy. For if Jesus thought that the secular government was wrong and displeasing to God, he could have condemned it.[4]

Luther also defended the work of soldiers as right and godly.[5] To him, to be a soldier was in no way harmful or anti-Christian. In doing so, Luther declared that a soldier who goes to war can kill and rob as the military law requires. For these works are neither sinful nor unjust at the time of war. The killing along with all other things that accompany war time behaviour has been instituted by God.[6] Thus, Luther upheld the legitimacy and the authenticity of the temporal government and its offices as it was, to him, a divine institution established by God himself.

God's Kingship of the Secular Government

Luther was a man of the middle ages where a Christo-centric concept of the state was in vogue. Luther, therefore, had a positive view of the temporal government. To him, it was an inestimable blessing of God and an evidence of God's continuing mercy to mankind. For, without the secular government, there would be no peace on earth but only war and destruction. He also affirmed that God had established the secular government as part of his overall plan for the world. God only ordained all authority and all nations received their authority only from God.[7] Hence, no one need to doubt that the temporal government is in the world by God's ordinance and will.[8] Luther also made it clear that all the secular laws are confirmed by the Holy Spirit.[9] In doing so, Luther also advocated that one should be thankful to God for the gift of the secular government because through it God graciously preserves human life.[10] He also narrated the biblical warrant for the divine origin of the temporal government.[11] In another context Luther affirmed the same idea. He stated that the secular government is part of the 'divine order' and the gift of God. For no man can create it by himself or survive without it. To emphasize this point Luther further said that the temporal Government is purely and solely God's gracious gift which no man can establish or maintain by his own wisdom or strength. He was of the opinion that the secular government remains God's gift even though the secular rulers misuse and exploit it for their own vested interests and benefit.[12]

Luther described the secular government as God's servant.[13] For Luther believed that without secular government the life of man on earth would be solitary, poor, nasty, brutish and short. The purpose of the temporal government, according to him, is not merely to punish the wicked but also to prevent the wickedness. As such the temporal government stands between man and chaos and it is only through the temporal government that man can be prevented from violence and rebellion. Luther held that disobedience and rebellion against the secular government are disobedience and rebellion against God himself.[14] So Luther advocated that one should obey the temporal government since it is established by God and used as a means for caring for human life. Luther had a high regard for the secular rulers because he thought that God was in the secular rulers. He called them 'gods' and advocated that they must be treated as 'high' and 'glorious'.[15] They must not be either disobeyed or despised and doing such things is doing them to God himself.[16] Luther also described them as 'fathers' and as 'saviours' of the country. For he believed that the secular rulers should act in the capacity of fathers and should have a fatherly heart towards their subjects.[17]

In another context Luther said that the secular rulers, by the administration of just laws, support all their subjects as a father supports his children.[18] In his small catechism, Luther placed the rulers alongside parents and advocated that we should show respect for the secular government as we honour our parents. When Luther described the temporal government as God's servant, he pictured the rulers as God's ministers, just as the ministers of the Word of God, but in a different way and in a different capacity. Due to his controversy with the Papal court, Luther categorically emphasized that the secular rulers derived their authority directly from God and not from the Pope. He also denied that the Pope could in any way be the source of the temporal authority. Thus, Luther had a high opinion about the secular government and the secular rulers as well.

Luther's opinion, on the Sword

Luther asserted that God honours the sword as it is established by his word and commandment. It is also a divine institution and those who use it properly are not only serving God but are also obedient to his word.[19] Luther also said that if the governing authority is divine, then everything that is essential and connected with the authority is also divine and the bearing of the sword becomes a divine service.[20] Harold J. Grimm says that, for Luther God has given rulers 'the power of the sword,' because of the original sin and man's natural inclination towards evil.[21] God charged the government, which has the means, to look after the general welfare of the subjects. Therefore, the secular authority bears the sword not in vain but it is God's servant for the good of the people and an avenger upon those who do evil.[22] The hand that wields the sword and kills with it is not man's hand but God's. And it is not man but God who hangs, tortures, beheads, kills and fights. All these are God's works.[23] With this understanding, Luther called the sword 'the wrath of God'.[24] He was of the opinion that the sword also existed from the very beginning of the world. When Cain slew his brother Abel, God placed a special prohibition that no one was to slay him (Gn.4:14-15). Similarly, after the Blood, God reconstructed and confirmed this law of the sword when he said 'whoever sheds the blood of man, by man shall his blood be shed' (Gn.9:6).

It was once again confirmed by the Law of Moses in Exodus 21:14, 'if a man wilfully kills another, you shall take him from any altar that he may die'. Besides, Christ also affirmed it when he said to Peter in Mt. 26:52, 'He that takes the sword will perish by the sword'. John the Baptist too taught the same thing when he said to the soldiers 'Do neither violence nor injustice to anyone' (Lk. 3:14). Above all, from the beginning of the world, all the saints have wielded the sword. Abraham rescued Lot (Gen. 14: 8-16). Samuel slew king Agog (I Sam., 15:33). Elijah slew the prophets of Baal (I King 18:40). Likewise Moses, Joshua, Samson, David and all the kings of Israel wielded the sword.[25] In the New Testament, when Philip converted the Ethiopian, he permitted him to remain in the same office, although without the sword he could not possibly be an official under the Queen of Ethiopia.[26] Hence, it is certain and clear that God himself has granted the sword and it existed from the beginning of the world. And in granting the sword, God has a special purpose. He wants to punish the wicked and to protect the upright by means of the sword.[27]

Nonetheless, Luther objected to all notions of violence and resistance because it was nothing but satanic influence. In his address "To the Christian Nobility of the German Nation", he appealed to the secular authorities to bear the sword and to intervene in order to carry out reforms on behalf of the community. However, he rejected revolution and rebellion because both were contrary to natural as well as divine law. For rebellion or revolution cannot take palace without injury and shedding of blood. Hence, he always objected to rebellion and declared that rebellion was punishable with death.[28] When he allowed the secular rulers to use the sword, he advised them to fight chaos and rebellion in order to preserve order in creation so that there would be peace on earth and protection to human life. But at the same time he criticized the secular rulers when they attempted to impose total control in their territories with the power of the sword. He cautioned them that no one should wield or invoke the sword for his own cause. On behalf of others, however, he may and should wield it in order to restrain wickedness and to defend godliness.[29] He did not forget to put forth the idea that the sword or force can be used only after the wrong has been legally condemned.[30] He, thus, disclosed God's sanction for the law of the sword and the ethics behind the sword.

Luther's Attitude to War

Luther's attitude to war is for the most part conventional. His ideas are based very largely on the traditional concept. Cargill Thompson says that Luther's teaching on war was simply an elaboration of the traditional medieval doctrine.[31] Nonetheless, in principle, he was a man of peace and this concept was repeated often in his sermons. He stated that since all wars are disastrous it is better to seek peace by negotiation in accordance with dated 10. 10.1520 and that pastors must always admonish rulers to seek peace by all means before waging war.[32] Thus, Luther naturally regarded war as evil because it was the product of Satan leading to destruction. In his exposition of Psalm 14, Luther, stated that pagan poets praise war but war is a horrible and extremely cruel thing in the sight of God. It destroys both religion and government and high prices and pestilence are only like foxtails when compared with war. It is better to fall into plague than into the hands of soldiers. War is one of the greatest plagues that can afflict humanity; it destroys religion, it destroys states, it destroys families. Any scourge, in fact, is preferable to it. Famine and pestilence become nothing in comparison with it.[33]

To Luther, war was like fishing with a golden net. The risk of loss is always greater than the catch can be. Victory never makes up for what is lost by war. Nonetheless, Luther did not mean that war is always to be condemned or that one must never get involved in it. On the contrary, he defended war and the work of the sword. He said that if people were good and wanted to keep peace, war is not necessary. But when people do not keep peace but fight with each other and exploit the weak, war becomes a necessary thing. In his treatise on whether soldiers, too, can be saved, he said that if one punishes a thief or a murderer or an adulterer, that punishment is inflicted only on a single evil doer. But in a war a whole crowd of evil doers are punished at once.[34] So, war is an instrument for several purposes. It is a work of Christian love to protect humanity.[35]

Luther published in April 1529, his treatise on war against the Turks while whole Germany was expecting the great Mohammedan invasion, was primarily a theological study explaining the Mohammedan religion. Luther revised, at the same time, the litany as a special prayer to God against the enemies of the Church. Likewise, when Suleiman was planning his great invasion into central Europe in 1529, Luther advised Christendom to fight. In addition, he himself took active part in the war by preaching sermons and writing books in order to arouse the nation to arms against the enemy. In doing so, Luther condemned those who took a lax or disloyal attitude. Thus Luther, through his sermons and writings, was instrumental in helping Europe to stop Suleiman and creating the will for a united Christian resistance against the Mohammedans, which finally saved western civilization by destroying the Turkish sea power at Lepanto in 1573.[36]

According to him, the first kind is of the devil because God does not give good fortune to the man who wages that kind of war. The second kind is a human disaster and God helps them. Thus, he defended defensive wars but he objected to aggressive wars because aggressors are the cause of the universal lack of peace. He forbade war against the head of the state because force should not be exercised against the lawful authorities. Fighting against the legitimate government was equivalent to rebelling against the order instituted by God.[37]

Luther emphasized further that no prince, regardless of his rank, may take up arms against those that God has placed over him. In case the emperor or an overlord attacks him, he must not resist him by force of arms. He may protest against such injustice but if his protest goes unheeded the prince must endure all abuses for the Lord's sake.[38] When the emperor unjustly molested the subjects, he should be met with armed resistance. But such active resistance could be offered only by those entrusted with the common interest. When a ruler is attacked by a fellow ruler of equal rank or an outside power; he should protest and go to war. But prior to his attack he must see whether all peaceful means have been tried to avoid the attack. When all these efforts fail he and his subjects may go to war in the defence of their land.[39]

Thus, Luther allowed a war between equals, provided an offer of peace had been refused. But when the prince is clearly in the wrong, any command to take part in war should be unheeded by the subjects because no man should act unjustly. But he had a dread of revolution. He considered it unscriptural and unwise. He did not even encourage active resistance against the Papists.[40] He did not grant the right to rebel even though the rulers broke the laws which they had sworn to uphold. For the subjects have no right either to judge or to punish their rulers. Instead they should obey and endure them because God is the only judge.[41] Rebellion against the political authority would be an encroachment on God's judicial function.[42] God would bring revolution through early forces and punish such rulers.[43] Thus, he dealt with the positive as well as the negative connotations of war and its consequences.

Medieval Christendom helped that a Christian should not participate in politics. He should not be a magistrate, executioner, policeman or a soldier.[44] The Anabaptists too took the same position that a Christian could neither be involved in politics nor bear arms in any circumstances. According to them, a Christian is a subject of the Kingdom of God where Christ alone rules. Hence, he should neither fight nor wield the sword not resist evil.[45] They thought that their government was a spiritual government and they were the subjects of no one save Christ. But, for Luther, political questions were moral questions about how the Christian should behave as a subject or as a ruler. His approach was another way of defining a Christian's relationship to God in the temporal order. He says that only the lawless need the government, as Paul says in I Tim. 1:3. The law is not laid down for the just but for the lawless. They only need the law to instruct and compel them to do well.[46] As the whole world is evil and there is scarcely a single true Christian, and no one serves God but all devour one another, the world is reduced to chaos and for this reason God has ordained the government.[47] But the Christians need no secular government if the whole world is composed of real Christians, that is, true believers. For the Christians need nothing from their worldly rulers and there is no need for any suit, litigation, court, judge or sword. The temporal law finds no work to do among them since they do much more than the laws demand. In short, the secular government is neither necessary nor useful for them because they have in their hearts the Holy Spirit, who both teaches and makes them do injustice to no one, love everyone and suffer injustice and even death willingly and cheerfully at the hand of anyone.[48]

Nevertheless, Luther stated that Christians need the secular government for the sake of their neighbours in order to achieve justice, protection and help, as much as they can achieve for themselves.[49] He, therefore, exhorted the Christians to esteem the secular government as highly as the estate of marriage or any other calling which God has instituted.[50] To maintain this view, he quoted Paul and Peter, who commanded obedience to government (Rom. 13:1-4; I Pt.2: 13-14). He also urged the Christians to accept civic responsibilities.[51] There are legitimate callings or offices in the temporal order which are ordained by God. The Christians can carry out the obligations of such callings, if they are called to such offices. For the government is the most beneficial and necessary to preserve peace, punish sin and restrain the wicked. So the Christians should submit most willingly to government services and they lose nothing by doing those services as they are in no way harmful. On the contrary, they are of great benefit to their neighbours as well as to the whole world.[52] To him, political service is also a service to God and a Christian belongs to two spheres of life-the spiritual and the secular. Two types of offices are combined in him.[53] He is both acting on his own behalf and on behalf of his neighbour. In other words, he acts as a 'private person' and a 'public person'. As a private person he should not resist evil, but as a public person or as a secular person he should oppose every evil.[54]

Luther suggested that a Christian can serve in various capacities. He can be a father of a family, a local magistrate and a town councillor.[55] His active part in the governmental services is the finest thanks-offering and the highest service to humanity.[56] The political office provides the opportunity for the noblest kind of helping activity.[57] One can devote himself to serve the people by way of accepting the offices in the secular government.[58] He further admonished that Christians should be ready to fill such offices. Otherwise those offices may be easily misused by someone who has selfish motives, who, then, no longer serves but tyrannizes and carries out his own arbitrary and vindictive purposes. So, he advised the Christians to be always available whenever and wherever they have the opportunity to serve, no matter, what form such service may take. They should not selfishly seek a particular service which is attractive in the eyes of the world or attractive to them personally. They should only consider how necessary the service is.[59]

In his tract "Secular Authority: To What Extent It Should Be Obeyed", Luther advocated that Christians have the right to serve as soldiers because the office of the soldier is as godly, needful and useful to the world as any other office.[60] Christians can even serve as magistrates, which involves the exercise of force because the use of force is justified in the temporal law. The Christians need not evade such functions on the pretext that they are not responsible for secular affairs. For nothing is secular to the Christian conscience.[61] When the ruler calls on a Christian to serve as a soldier and to take part in a war in the defence of his fellow citizens, he should oblige and do so. If he rejects it as unnecessary, his action would be misunderstood by his fellow-men. Putting differently, a Christian must submit himself to lawful authorities just because of his love for his neighbour and his readiness to protect his neighbor. If he is killed in the war, he dies a good death. He is found obedient to his ruler and to God.

The Christian can refuse the call of his ruler only when his ruler commands him to go to war in an unjust cause or to take part in a rebellion against the overlord. In such cases, the Christian must be prepared to suffer the consequences of his disobedience. If the ruler is wicked, one need not plan to avenge him, because God has plans to punish him. He can raise foreign rulers, as he raised the Goths against the Romans, the Assyrians against the Jews. God does not allow him to be wicked forever, because he is right behind him.[62] Luther never taught that the Christian must obey his ruler unconditionally. A Christian can obey his ruler as long as material things are involved. But, in matters pertaining to conscience and faith, he is free from secular restraint. For worldly law and order do not extend beyond outward bodily things. Putting otherwise, one need not obey when the ruler's command goes contrary to the teachings of the scripture. When the ruler invades the domain of faith contrary to one's convictions, a Christian can refuse to obey in accordance with Acts 5:29, which reads, 'We ought to obey God rather than man'.

When the emperor or an overlord violates the law and puts god-fearing innocent citizens and preachers to death, the citizens are released from their duty to obey, because such rulers are no different from murderers on the highway.[63] Luther knew that the rulers will not tolerate such disobedience but will seize one's goods and punish. In such circumstances he advised people to make great sacrifices so that God's commands could remain.[64] He, thus, exhorted the Christians to take an active part in the offices of the secular government since it stands as an opportunity to serve God and humanity.

Two Kingdoms Doctrine

Luther's doctrine of two kingdoms or two governments is one of the most valuable and enduring treasures of his theology. It is wholly determined by the scripture rather than an invention of his own wilful speculative thinking or what the medieval political authorities wanted him to say. In other words, it is closely related to the biblical dual perspective. Hans Schwarz rightly affirms that Luther's faithfulness to the scripture and his personal awareness of the political activities of his time paved the way for the emergence of this doctrine.[65] He constructed this doctrine on the exegesis of the Sermon on the Mount (Mt.5-7) and Rom. 13, with its parallel I Pt.2:13ff.

Nevertheless, Luther never formulated it systematically. It underwent a process of change and development. The medieval ideology confronted by Christendom as well as by society led him to formulate this doctrine. For example, the Roman Church had defined itself as the spiritual power in its own hierarchy. Similarly monasticism considered it less holy to work in the sphere of the temporal realm than to do work that was specially organized by the Church. In sharp antithesis to these views, he placed his doctrine and said that it was improper to apply the term 'spiritual power' to anything except the Spirit of God himself. In like manner, he replied to monasticism that people must also take part in temporal affairs and demonstrate their faith and love through constructive service and witness. As such, he established the political foundation upon which he made his proposal for the reform of the community.[66]

Luther hammered out his doctrine of two kingdoms in opposition to two counter theories, that is, medieval Catholicism and Anabaptism. He proclaimed the independence of the secular government from clerical control, which claimed supremacy over secular power. Likewise, he stressed the divine origin of secular power and defended participation in the secular realm. He advocated this against the Anabaptists, who argued for religious separatism.[67] Luther used different metaphors such as 'God's right hand' and 'God's left hand' and the 'masks of God' to describe the two modes of God's role.[68]

Two Kingdoms - An Overview

Luther strongly believed that God had instituted two kingdoms, namely the spiritual and the secular, and it is possible to find a great many passages in his writings in which he asserted it quite explicitly. The spiritual kingdom belongs to all believers and the secular kingdom belong to all others, that is, the people of other faith. Thus, he saw humanity dived into two groups, Christians and people of other faith. In his treatise "World Authority", he divided the people into two groups that are, those who are of the kingdom of God and those who are of the kingdom of the world. All those who believe in Christ belong to the Kingdom of God and they need neither sword nor law. But people who do not believe in Christ belong to the kingdom of the world and they need the sword and the law. He maintained the relationship of these kingdoms as found between the law and the gospel. He described the two kingdoms as a two-fold strategy or two-fold way of God's rule in the world.[69]

God administers the secular government with his left hand and where God himself reigns is called his right hand, but the same God stands behind both kingdoms. According to his goodness and love, he offers twofold blessings to humanity through these two governments, namely law and order, and eternal salvation. The two governments not only constitute the instruments through which God governs but also represent the weapons which God employs in his struggle against the kingdom of the devil. God directs both the governments against the power of the devil. They act in two different ways but with one goal.[70]

With this doctrine, Luther described God's struggle against the kingdom of the devil. The doctrine of two kingdoms is also universal. God established both the kingdoms for all people.[71] John Tonkin supplements further that Luther's doctrine of two kingdoms could be applied to all, regardless of their system of atheistic convictions.[72] Trutz Rendtorff says that one can conclude from the doctrine of the two kingdoms that even non-believers like Marxists and atheists alike are able to provide a government that is good and that serves the community well. For the words of Luther show us clearly that neither faith nor the ethical conduct of a government's office-holder is a prerequisite for the formation of a government, but what is solely important is whether they work for the well-being and peace of the society.[73]

Spiritual Kingdom

God governs mankind with the spiritual order in which he governs people through his word and carries out his work of redemption. It is essentially an inward and invisible government. It is heard but not seen. Unlike the secular government it extends upward towards the invisible Kingdom of God. It directs people radically to God so that they might be saved and do right. Putting differently, it is a government of the soul since it is concerned only with people's eternal salvation. God operates secretly in people's hearts to draw them away from sin and to make them righteous. Luther called this kingdom a 'government of hearting' (*ein Horreich*) because it is only through the instrument of the Word and not by force that people can enter into the Kingdom of God.[74] Spiritual government helps people to achieve true righteousness and therewith eternal life. Christ brings the gospel to men who are in bondage to sin and therewith freedom from all the demonic powers. Thus, the constitutive element of the spiritual government of Christ's Lordship is freedom.[75] And force is not used in this kingdom because everything takes place voluntarily through the compelling power of the Spirit which is interested in the word of gospel.[76] Luther called this power the 'spiritual sword' of God's word.[77] Luther included parents in the spiritual government since they too proclaim the gospel to their children.[78] The primary goal of this kingdom is to liberate people from all sorts of bondages which come forth by the power of the evil.

Secular Government

The temporal government is God's left hand which he instituted for the punishment of sin and the maintenance of external peace in the world and through which God provides the needs of people's earthly existence. It serves physical, earthly, temporal life and thereby preserves the world. It is, therefore, also a divine order established by God and ruled by the law and the sword, stretching its power visibly over the entire world. God has made it subject to reason and law because it is not directly related to the salvation of souls. However, God wants it to be a symbol of true blessedness and a mark of the heavenly kingdom. It builds a bridge to spiritual government since it takes care of the earthly welfare of the people. The very real presence of Satan makes the secular government necessary for repressing sin and for restraining the evil tendencies of people. In the human realm, it represses evil and contests the kingdom of Satan with the law and the sword so that body, property and family may remain secure. God governs people by means of temporal laws and the power of the sword which he has entrusted to secular rulers to exercise on his behalf. It is therefore, purely external government, and its primary function is the enforcement of law and order in the world. For, without it, human life would be in chaos.[79]

To the wicked and the unbeliever it may appear a veritable hell due to its use of the sword. Nonetheless, these requirements should not mislead one to identify it with the kingdom of the Devil. Although it exists because of sin it does not have its source in sin. Instead it is a divine institution and God's own work and creation. Indeed, it was established by God in opposition to the devil.[80] In Augustine's opinion, it is a product of the fall, corrupted by sin. God created and ordained it as his means for acting upon men. But Luther recognized the elements of temporal government even before the fall. In him, it was present from the beginning of the world. God committed it to Adam when he said, 'Be faithful and multiply and fill the earth and subdue it' (Gn.1:28).[81]

M.D.J. Cargill Thompson goes still further and says that Luther used the term *temporal government* in a broader sense to refer to the whole external order of society and all the institutions such as family, property, trade and other temporal occupation. From this point of view, the temporal government, he advocated, cannot be regarded simply as a product of the fall as it is part of God's original creation.[82]

It too, like the spiritual government, remains an expression of divine goodness that bears equally upon the total life of the people. Hence, it is neither evil itself nor subordinate to the spiritual government as it has been established by God himself and has all the blessing of the earthly life.[83] Luther felt the necessity of the temporal government because it does much to restrain evil and uses its power and force to safeguard humanity. It contributes to the preservation of this earthly life.[84] Nonetheless, Luther never allowed it to interfere in the realm of conscience which belongs purely to the realm of spiritual government.

The Unity of the Two Governments

Luther found a dialectical relationship between the two governments. To him both are based on one foundation and God is the Lord of both. Both have a common goal, binding themselves reciprocally. The state regulates the Church as a social institution in matter of property and the Church proclaims God's will to the State to work for social, political and economic transformation.[85] Moreover, secular authorities function within a temporal order under the direct rule of God. And the notion of an autonomous secular state functioning independent of divine control would have been incomprehensible to Luther.[86] Even though the two governments are distinct in character and function and differ in so many ways, they need not be viewed simply as the antitheses of each other. For example, in the spiritual government, all are equal before God because of their relationship to God. In the secular government God instituted differences among people and made for dependence upon others.[87] In the spiritual government everything is voluntary whereas the secular government rules with force and compels people to obey[88] while the spiritual government consists of forgiveness, the secular government exercises retribution and punishment.[89]

Nevertheless, both the governments are complementary and they are God's two ways of governing. They are essentially interdependent and need each other. They need not be seen in a static juxtaposition between two spheres, one political and the other spiritual. Instead they can be viewed as a single reality because they are not in opposition to each other but, side by side, both contend against the devil, one guided by the gospel and the other by the law. Against the devil, God uses both the governments as his weapons[90] What Luther wished to express was not two mutually exclusive areas of life but the twofold activity of God in the world. They both stand as the right and left hands of God to combat Satan. They are both involved directly in the conflict to suppress the power of evil. They are separated or divided because the two different aspects of God's activity occur in them. In Luther's view the two must ever remain separate and distinct as far as possible since the devil acts on both sides to brew and cook the two together. John M. Headley says that the separation is not between two different forms of order or between two different conditions within each order but rather between creature and creator.[91]

In Luther's opinion, each is independent in itself. Nonetheless, one cannot exist without the other.[92] Putting differently, the two exist for each other because one is insufficient without the other. For this reason one must carefully distinguish between these two governments. Both must be permitted to remain; the one to produce righteousness, the other to bring about external peace and prevent evil deeds; neither one is sufficient in the world without the other. No one can become righteous in the sight of God by means of the temporal government, without Christ's spiritual government.[93] Thus, he saw the link between the two. Luther's doctrines of stations and hierarchies are also not coextensive but complementary. For example, the institution of marriage creates new members for Christendom. The political government on the other hand preserves peace. Christendom does not have the resources to establish this peace as it has only the gospel through which one cannot rule the world. For the gospel does not force people as the sword does.[94] On this point he said: 'I have often taught that the world ought not and cannot be ruled according to the gospel and Christian love, but by strict laws and force, because the world is evil. It accepts neither gospel not love, but lives and acts according to own will unless compelled by force".[95]

Likewise, the secular government needs the spiritual government as much as the spiritual government needs the secular government. For example, no society properly maintains law and order if it lacks the knowledge of God which can be provided only by the spiritual government. Moreover, the authorities of the secular government are inspired by the proclamation of the Word of God and preserve peace and order.[96] It also instigates the common people to respect the secular government and its various stations. In other terms, the spiritual government makes the heart righteous and helps one to behave well inwardly while the secular government produces outward obedience.[97]

Although Luther advocated that both governments need each other, he also stated that the two should not be mixed. For, the two remain two different entities just as heaven is separated from earth despite the fact that both serve the same purpose.[98] But, at the same time, he was of the opinion that the secular government is subordinate to spiritual government as it serves only this earthly life and passes away together within this life while spiritual government stands in the service of eternal life which is God's ultimate purpose.[99] Luther further insisted that though the secular government indirectly serves the good by way of providing access to the preaching of the gospel and peace for Christendom, it is never anything more than a means to achieve it.

Findings of the state
Luther's doctrine of two forms of God's rule explicitly explains the disastrous nature of human history, that is, wars, rebellion and tyrannies. It also reveals the impressive truth that God is struggling to overcome the power of evil and thereby to preserve justice, peace and fraternity. In other words, the doctrine ascertains that his world is not just a place of sin and evil but belongs to God and it's under the control of God. Andor Muntag rightly says that we are not in a foreign country but in God's Kingdom. He explains this idea thus:

We have learned from Luther when we serve in the world we are not in a foreign country but in God's kingdom. The whole world, despite its basically sinful nature, belongs to God. God the creator and preserver can also work through political organizations, even if the political leaders do not fear him. Thus the entire political organization functions as a 'larvadei'.[100]

The doctrine also reveals that God is taking care of the total humanity. His two governments care for the total life of a person-one for internal and another for external betterment. Both play vital and significant roles to bring God's creation home where it belongs. Luther's doctrine serves as a basic agent or guideline for social change. For example, Christians, by preaching the gospel, take part in the struggle against the power of evil and exploitation in all the areas of human life, as part of their contribution to redress the power of Satan. The gospel message inspires as well as conscientizes the oppressed and discourages the oppressor so that they may repent and change their exploitative attitudes. With this doctrine Luther had a concrete vision for the best possible world. Eric W. Gritsch says that Luther's two kingdoms ethic helped the secular authorities to invent new forms of international alliance. [101] It mobilized public opinion and created new policies for the first time in history, which was a sign for the prosperity of the world. Luther's doctrine discloses not only the link between God and the world but also embodies the fact that God is continually active in his creation. He is involved in the world in order to uphold and direct it because he wants both the governments to be symbols of true liberation of humankind. He administers the spiritual kingdom by means of his word through which men are to become good and righteous so that with this righteousness they may attain eternal life. He committed the gospel to the preachers so that they may envisage this righteousness through their preaching. God's other government, which is worldly government, works through the sword so that those who do not want to be good and righteous may be forced to become good and righteous.

Therefore, one need not look on the temporal government as profane or one should not say God is not much interested in it, but is interested only in the spiritual kingdom. For Luther's doctrine makes it clear that God is responsible for both the governments and he is at work in each one of them. In other terms, Luther's doctrine is his attempt to describe the manner by which God exercises his lordship over the world and human as well.[102] This doctrine provides fundamental guidance for people. It reminds them to carry out their responsibilities as secular persons. To Luther, to be a Christian is to have internalized the will of God in order to express that will externally. In other words, Luther wanted the Christian life to penetrate secular affairs and renew the worldly kingdom.[103] The Christian, being a member of two worlds, has obligations to fulfil in both worlds and this obligation includes the exercise of a political responsibility. Luther's biblical realism forced him to compel Christians to assume their social responsibilities. Since civil occupations too serve God's creating and preserving purpose, Luther insisted that the Christian should participate in social affairs for the sake of the society which God created. Luther' doctrine of two kingdoms affirms God's constant activity. God did not cease his activity with creation. Rather it is a continuing process which is still going on with his two kingdoms. God is continually active in his creation by way of upholding and sustaining it. Ulrich Duchrow says that Christians should actively participate in the struggle to improve economic, social and political institutions even at the risk of enduring persecution and the cross.[104] According to Luther, the first and the best place of Christians to put into practice the gifts which have been bestowed upon them were the human institutions of the Church, the home and the economic and political life. Edward D.Schneider too asserts that Luther's doctrine underscores the social responsibility in which Christians should act as a willing tool of God's saving and preserving purpose.[105]

Luther's doctrine affirms that both the kingdoms are charged with important responsibilities to attain the spiritual as well as material benefits which could enable every individual to reach his or her full potential and rights and thereby the establishment of the Kingdom of God on Earth.[106] Walter Altmann observes three tasks in Luther's interpretation of Psalm 82. to guarantee the free preaching of the gospel precisely. Critical and prophetic preaching is to defend justice and to fight for the rights of the weak and the abandoned and to guarantee the order, peace and protection of the poor.[107] This idea also underscores that God has not left the world to its own devices but keeps it under his control and rules it by his own means, that is, the two kingdoms. Gordon Rupp says that Luther's doctrine of two kingdoms makes it clear that the spiritual office is by no means confined to purely 'spiritual matters' but it must be applied to the condition of a specific place and time. In other words, the spiritual matter must be conditioned by its own context and related to its own situation.[108] This is why Luther advocated that Christians on earth should always be seen not merely as 'spiritual persons' who exist only in relation to Christ, but also as 'temporal persons' who live in the world with bodily needs and social responsibilities as do other people.[109] As a result, Luther condemned the Enthusiasts who wanted to spiritualize the world.[110]

With this doctrine Luther proclaimed the liberating message that the secular government need not to be under the control of the Church, which was the idea prevalent in his day. But, at the same time, it was not the only aim of Luther to defend the state from the interference of the Church or to protect the Church from the control of the state but to call both to participate in the struggle for justice and human rights. Walter Altman too states that Luther's two kingdoms doctrine is not an attempt to make a clear separation between state and Church but an attempt to return the state to its proper competence in administering secular affairs.[111]

Mahatma Gandhi's Political Ideology

Gandhi's political ideology is so comprehensive that it has left no aspect of human life untouched. Gandhi was a true democrat and lover of individual and national freedom. In his philosophy there are very clear indications of his love for individual and national freedom. He very fervently believed and unhesitatingly declared that the state was not an end in itself but only a means to an end and that the fullest development of man's faculties was the end of the state.[112] He said, "I do not divide life into water-tight compartments. The life of a nation like that of individuals is an indivisible whole and also for me there is no politics without religion, not the religion of the superstitious and the blind, religion that hates and fights, but the universal religion of toleration".[113] Politics without morality is a thing to be avoided.

Gandhi's Views on State

Gandhi's concept of a state was not evolved out of political theorizing but out of his personal encounter with the living reality. His opposition to the state is an outcome of his personal encounter with the racialists in South Africa and the British imperialism in India. He was greatly repelled by the coercive character of the state and looked upon the state as "an organ of violence in a concentrated and organized form". Since Gandhi believed in the inherent goodness of man, he thought that men were capable of developing their moral capacities to such an extent that exploitation could be reduced to the minimum. He held that human by their nature is consciously divine, national and sociable and, therefore, has an inborn capacity to govern themselves. He stood for self-help and self-regulation, in which the state is totally uncalled for. Inner freedom, for Gandhi, springs from self-control and self-purification. He repudiated the state because the compulsive nature of the state takes away the moral value of all individual action. It is out of this basic approach that Gandhi developed his anarchistic views. Hence he held, "I look upon an increase in the power of the state with greatest fear, because, although, while apparently doing good by minimizing exploitation it does the greatest harm to mankind by destroying individuality which lies at the root of all progress."[114]

Political power, for Gandhi, "is not an end in itself but one of the means of enabling people to better their conditions in every department of life." Gandhi conceived the state as a 'soulless machine'. The state represents violence in a concentrated and organized form. He held that "The individual has a soul, but as the state is a soulless machine, it can never be weaned from violence to which it owes its very existence".[115] His concern for the excessive concentration of power in the state made him concede merely a minimal role to the state. At the same time he made a clear-cut distinction between a democratic and an authoritarian state. In his earlier years, he considered a self-regulated stateless society as his ideal, but, with the passage of time, the imperfections of human compelled him to search for a practicable ideal. Hence he preferred a predominantly non-violent democratic government which governs the least.[116] He accepted the classical statement of Thoreau, that Government is the best which governs the least. Thus, inspite of his great opposition to the state, Gandhi as a realist, accepted a perfect democratic government as the next best alternative, in which the individual is the architect of his or her own government.

Democracy

Gandhi was influenced by the 19th century democratic movement of the West and regarded democracy as an ideal solution to harmonize the interests of the individual and the state. He also championed the cause of democracy as it can better protect the 'weak' and 'respect the individuality of man' which lies at the root of all progress.[117] He defined democracy as the art and science of mobilizing the entire physical, economic and spiritual resources of all the various sections of the people in the service of the common good of all.[118] Centralization of power in any branch of social life, for Gandhi, was an evil. Since centralization of political power is conducive to violence, he pleaded for a decentralized democratic form of government. He opposed to the imposition of power from above and felt that the power should evolve upwards starting from the village level. Therefore, he visualized an ideal non-violent state based on a federation of self-governing autonomous village republics with equality pervading every sphere of life. Gandhi observed, 'True democracy cannot be worked by twenty men sitting at the centre. It has to be worked from below by the people of every village'.[119]

With the help of decentralization Gandhi wanted to establish the political organization of the country on a non-violent basis through village communities. He wanted to make every village a unit, free and active for the total good. He said, "My idea of village is that it is a complete republic independent of its neighbours for its vital wants, and yet independent for many other things in which dependence is a necessity".[120] If village cottage industry flourishes, it will not only make villages self-reliant but also preserve and maintain the environmental balance stably. Thus every village will be a Republic or a Panchayat having full powers. It follows, therefore, that every village has to be self-sustained and capable of managing its affairs even to the extent of defending itself against the whole world.

Individual Freedom

The essence of democracy, according to Gandhi, lies in individual freedom. He had no regard for the quantitative principle of democracy, but emphasized the quality of opinion on merits. Referring to majority rule, he observed, "Opinion of an individual should have greater weight than the opinion of many, if that opinion is sound on merits. That is my view of real democracy".[121] For Gandhi, individual liberty is the basis of all social progress. No society can possibly be built on a denial of individual freedom. If individual liberty goes, then surely all is lost. Individual freedom can make man voluntarily surrender himself completely to the service of society. If freedom is wrested from him, man becomes an automation and society is ruined.[122]

At the same time Gandhi believed that both individual and society are inseparable and interdependent. He could not ignore the fact that humans are essentially a social being who has risen to their present status by learning to adjust their individualism to the requirements of social progress. He observed that, "Unrestricted individualism is the law of the beast of the jungle... willing submission to social restraint for the sake of the well-being of the whole society enriches both the individual and the society of which he is a member".[123] Gandhi was not interested in changing the power from one set of rulers to another set. The freedom he sought for the nation was not merely the absence of alien bondage; the power must belong to the people. He held that politically free nations were nominally free in the sense that real power did not belong to the people. This keen sense of reality led him to enunciate his ideal of Swaraj as: "My notion of democracy is that under it the weakest should have the same opportunity as the strongest".[124]

Political freedom, for Gandhi, does not represent the fulfillment of a nation's dream. It only provides scope and opportunity for the renewal of a nation's life. He was aware of the fact that political freedom devoid of its economic content was a mere philosophical abstraction. He wrote: 'A starving man thinks first of satisfying his hunger before anything else. He will sell his liberty and all for the sake of getting a morsel of food. Such is the position of millions of the people in India. For them, liberty, God and all such words are merely letters put together without the slightest meaning. They jar upon them. If we want to give these people a sense of freedom we shall have to provide them with work... which would give them at least the barest living'.[125] The Swaraj of his dream was a condition under which the nation was free to make its own choice both of good and evil. It also meant ability to regard every inhabitant as our own brother or sister. In his own words, "A nation which allows it to be influenced by the fear of death cannot attain Swaraj, and cannot retain it if somehow attained".[126]

Swaraj

His philosophy of Swaraj was not merely a political concept but an all-round awakening. According to him is the Government of many.[127] Since swaraj means self-government, people must learn to rule themselves.[128] It was also an arrangement under which all communities, classes and races living in a country lived with perfect harmony. He felt that there was no substitute for Swaraj or independence. For him the parliamentary democracy system is more concerned with power than the welfare of the people. There can also be unreality about the choice by voters, the influence on them being of the newspapers, of powerful orators, of those who have appeared to them at a particular moment as the best.[129]

Luther's proposal was that political powers should be returned solely to the secular authorities which God intended to exercise them. Luther invited the Christian nobility to carry out reforms. He called upon them to see in their baptism the basis for their calling to exercise their authority to guard against political chaos and to administer political matters justly. Mahatma Gandhi was not against elections and representation but the point he wanted to make was that there was a need for a disciplined and politically intelligent electorate. To Gandhi decentralization may be the greatest guarantee for democracy and not the parliamentary system.

Endnotes

[1] Paul Althaus, The Ethics of Martin Luther, p.63.

[2] Luther's Works, Vol. 21, p.113.

[3] Andor Muntag. "Theory and practice of the Doctrine of the Doctrine of the Two kingdoms in the Lutheran Church in Hungary", p.76.

[4] Luther's Works, Vol.46, pp. 97-99.

[5] Ibid, Vol.46, p. 94.

[6] Ibid, Vol.46, p. 95.

[7] Luther's Works, Vol.13, p.44.

[8] Luther's Works, Vol.45, p.85.

[9] Luther's Works, Vol.14, p.14.

[10] Luther's Works, Vol.14, p.52.

[11] Luther's Works, Vol.45, pp. 85-87.

[12] Luther's Works, Vol.46, p. 56.

[13] Luther's Works, Vol.45, pp.99-102.

[14] Luther's Works, Vol.21, p.23.

[15] Luther's Works, Vol.13, p.44.

[16] Ibid, Vol.13, p. 44.

[17] Ibid, Vol.13, p. 53.

[18] Ibid, Vol.13, p.58.

[19] Luther's Works, Vol.46, p. 98.

[20] Luther's Works, Vol.45, p.103.

[21] Harold J. Grimm, "Luther's Conception of Territorial and National Loyalty", p. 88.

[22] Luther's Works, Vol.45, p.99.

[23] Luther's Works, Vol.46, p. 96.

[24] Ibid, Vol.46, p.99.

[25] Luther's Works, Vol.45, p.96.

[26] Ibid, Vol.45, p. 98.

[27] Luther's Works, Vol.45, p.86.

[28] Luther's Works, Vol.46, p. 101.

[29] Luther's Works, Vol.45, p.103.

[30] Ibid, Vol.45, p. 114.

[31] W.D.J. Cargill Thompson. The Political Thought of Martin Luther, p. 112.

[32] Eric W. Grietch, Martin Luther 0' God's Curt jester, p. 123.

[33] Hugh Tomson Kerr, (ed.,) A compend of Luther's Theology, p. 197.

[34] Luther's Works, Vol.46, pp. 98-99.

[35] Luther's Works, Vol.30, p. 76.

[36] Armas k. E. holmio, "Luther and War", p. 273.

[37] Luther's Works, Vol.46, p.91.

[38] Luther's Works, Vol.45, p.124.

[39] Ibid, Vol.45, p.125.

[40] Lowell C. Gree, "Resistance to Authority and Luther", p.344.

[41] Luther's Works, Vol.13, p.45.

[42] Luther's Works, Vol.46, p. 112.

[43] Luther's Works, Vol.13, p. 68.

[44] Gord on Rupp. "Luther and government", Luther A Profile H.G. Koenigs-berger, (ed.,), p. 135.

[45] Luther's Works, Vol.46, p.90.

[46] Luther's Works, Vol.45, pp.89-90.

[47] Luther's Works, Vol.45, p. 91.

[48] Luther's Works, Vol.45, p. 89.

[49] Ibid, Vol.45, p. 101.

[50] Ibid, Vol.45, p.100.

[51] Ibid, Vol.45, p. 95.

[52] Ibid, Vol.45, p.94.

[53] Ibid, Vol.45, p.122.

[54] Luther's Works, Vol. 21, p.113.

[55] Luther's Works, Vol.45, p.122.

[56] Luther's Works, Vol.46, p. 241.

[57] Luther's Works, Vol.13, pp. 51-53.

[58] Luther's Works, Vol.45, p.122.

[59] Ibid, Vol.45, pp.103-104.

[60] Luther's Works, Vol 47, p.97.

[61] Eivind Berggrav. "State and Church – The Lutheran View", p. 360.

[62] Luther's Works, Vol.46, pp. 109-110.

[63] Eivind Berggrav, Op.cit, p. 369.

[64] Luther's Works, Vol.44, p.100 and Luther's Works, Vol.45, p.112.

[65] Hans Schwarz, "Luther's Doctrine of the Two Kingdoms – Help or Hindrance for Social Change", p. 62.

[66] Craig L., Nessan, "Liberation Theology's Critique of Luther's Two kingdoms Doctrine", p.258.

[67] Timothy George, Theology of Reformers, p.99.

[68] Luther's Works, Vol.46, p.96.

[69] W.D.J. Cargill Thompson, Op.cit, p.48.

[70] Jurgen Moltmann, On Human Dignity: Political Theology and Ethics, p. 68.

[71] W.D.J. Cargill Thompson, Op.cit, p.175.

[72] John Tonkin, The Church and the Secular Order in Reformation Thought, p. 57.

[73] Trutz Rendorff. " The Doctrine of Two Kingdoms or the Art of Drawing Distinctions Research concerning the Theological Interpretation of political Affairs", p. 51.

[74] W.D.J. Cargill Thompson, Op.cit, p. 170.

[75] Luther's Works, Vol.34, p.199.

[76] Luther's Works, Vol.34, p.55.

[77] Luther's Works, Vol.45, p.101.

[78] Luther's Works, Vol.21, p.109.

[79] Luther's Works, Vol.45, p. 101& Vol.21, p.109.

[80] Ibid, Vol.45, p.91.

[81] Ibid, Vol.45, p.111.

[82] W.D.J. Cargill Thomposn, Op.cit, p. 179.

[83] John. M. Headley, Luther's View of Church History, p. 6.

[84] Luther's Works, Vol.21, p.29.

[85] Walter Altman, "Interpreting the Doctrine of the Two Kingdoms God's Kingship in the Church and in Politics", p. 47.

[86] Craig L. Nessan, Op.cit, p. 260.

[87] Luther's Works, Vol.31, p.949, Vol. 21, p.214 & Vol.26, p.97.

[88] Luther's Works, Vol.45, p.92.

[89] Luther's Works, Vol.47, pp.79-80

[90] William A. Johnson, "Luther's Doctrine of Two Kingdoms", p. 242.

[91] John M. Headley, Op.cit, p. 4.

[92] Luther's Works, Vol.13, pp.193-194.

[93] Luther's Works, Vol.45, p.92.

[94] W.D.J. Cargill Thompson, Op.cit, p. 50.

[95] Luther's Works, Vol.45, p. 91.

[96] Luther's Works, Vol.46, p. 227-228.

[97] Luther's Works, Vol.45, p. 92 & Vol.46, p. 242.

[98] Ibid, Vol.45, p.92.

[99] Luther's Works, Vol.24, p.229.

[100] Andor muntag, Op.cit, p. 76.

[101] Eric W. Gritsch and Robert W. Jenson. Lutheranism, Philadelphia, p.186.

[102] William A. Johnson, Op.cit, p. 240.

[103] Ibid, p. 247.

[104] Ulrich Duchbrow, Two Kingdoms – The use and Misuse of a Lutheran Theological Concept, p. 9.

[105] Edward D Schnieder, "Lutheran Theological Foundations for Social Ethics", Geneva, p. 20.

[106] Anza Lemo, "The Doctrine of the Two Kingdoms – Its Socio Economic Implications in our Societies", p. 41.

[107] Walter Altmann, Op.cit, p. 54.

[108] Gordon Rupp, Op.cit, p. 140.

[109] W.D.J. Cargill Thomposn, Op.cit, p. 780.

[110] Hans Schwarz. Op,cit., 63.

[111] Walter Altmann, Op.cit, p. 47.

[112] Harijan, 20.02.1937.

[113] Young India, 27.11.1924.

[114] Young India, 02.07.1931.

[115] Hind Swaraj, pp. 80-81.

[116] Young India, 02.07.1931.

[117] Harijan, 27.05.1939.

[118] Ibid, p. 143.

[119] Harijan, 18.01.1948.

[120] Harijan, 28.07.1946.

[121] D.G. Tendulkar,Mahatma, Vol.6,p.283.

[122] Harijan, 01.02.1942.

[123] Harijan, 27.05.1939.

[124] D.G. Tendulkar, Mahatma, Vol.5, p.343.

[125] Young India, 18.03,26.

[126] Young India, 01.05.1930.

[127] Young India, 28th July, 1921, p.238.

[128] B.C. Das, Gandhi in Today's India, p.3.

[129] Young India, 10.09.1931.

Chapter 5

Economic Ideology
of Luther and Gandhi

ECONOMIC IDEOLOGY OF LUTHER

Martin Luther's economic theory was based on Aristotelian and scholastic economic principles. He accepted the Aristotelian economy that labour is the source of all wealth and the scholastic view that money cannot produce money. However, he went a step further in analyzing the nature of business practices and capitalist profit. He brought to light the evil practices found in the trade and commerce of his time and without hesitation he exposed the greedy and avaricious attitude of the economic institutions. He also declared that if labour is the source of all wealth then wealth without labour must be from somebody else's labour which is not only unjust but also evil as well. In addition, he stated that it was impossible for money to make money but that only work could increase wealth.[1] Thus he played a significant role in the sphere of economy and made relevant contributions in order to transform the areas connected with the economy.

Trade

Fundamentally Martin Luther affirmed the necessity of trade because production of goods was not enough.[2] But at the same time he did not fail to share the medieval distrust of trade. He commented that trade was a necessary evil.[3] By its very nature trade leads to temptation and the persons involved in it become greedy and avaricious. The disparity in wealth, according to him, was nothing more than the result of the greed and avarice of the merchants. He advocated that trade ought to be done according to the principles of justice and fairness. In other words, the proper conduct of trade constantly occupied him. Nonetheless, he vigorously opposed free trade because he heard that capital would thereby gain control of the crafts which would in turn crush the poorer classes who ought to be the beneficiaries of trade. They would be smashed due to the unlimited competition created by the outside people.[4] Luther objected to importing foreign goods, especially luxury items. To him, it was an extravagant and superfluous spending. The extension of trade to distant countries drained so much money out of the country. As a result, even the nobility and the rich were impoverished. Again, it served only a limited number of people who were rich in terms of refinements and luxury in their style of life. He therefore advised that trade ought to be limited to those things that are really necessary and not produced in one's own country. In so doing, he opposed the import of spices and silk from Asia that was being introduced into Germany.[5]

Owing to these drawbacks, Martin Luther insisted on agriculture rather than trade and commerce. He considered agriculture godly, better and more important than trade and commerce. Since so much land was uncultivated, he exhorted people to increase agriculture and seek the livelihood from it rather than with the tricky, selfish and unjust traders.[6] He was also extremely critical of world trade. He objected to the practices of trading companies and their monopolies. To him, such kind of commerce was nothing more than simple robbery and he used this word repeatedly in both his speeches and writings. He used this harsh word because the merchants sold their goods at a higher price than was commanded in the common market or than was customary in the trade. They raised the price of their wares for no other reason than that they knew that there was no more of the commodity in the country so that supply would shortly be exhausted, and people must have it. In reaction, he criticized the proprietors of these companies as they converted the people into beggars while they became more powerful and richer than kings.[7]

Furthermore, these companies were the instruments of the power pressure through which they broke and shattered the small merchants and producers. They sold some products below cost in order to gain a monopoly but recouped the difference by overcharging on other products. He was also critical of the rise of capitalism. To him, the whole economy based on money was unjust and corrupt because it was possible for one to accumulate great possessions worthy of a king. He questioned how it could be right that a man in a short time could grow so rich that he could buy out kings and emperors.[8] He particularly aimed his comments on Fugger's because they became richer and richer by way of usury. Against these he said that we must put a bit in the mouth of Fugger's and similar companies.[9] He also exposed the abuses, lies and tricks found in trade and reacted harshly.[10] He boldly declared that the majority of the merchants were poor with God but rich with the devil.[11] When the merchants complained about the highway robbers, who in fact were a problem at the time, he criticized the merchants who robbed all the time and complained about the thieves who robbed occasionally.

In such situations, Luther advised the temporal authorities to stop such atrocious deeds and to take from them everything they acquired and suggested to banish them from the country. Thus, he simultaneously brought to the light the abuses practised by the merchants and conscientized the masses about the exploitation and corrupt practices of the greedy merchants. With regard to setting prices, he said the best and safest way would be to have the temporal authorities appoint wise and honest men to compute costs of all sorts of wares and accordingly set prices. When the price was not fixed either by law or custom, the individual must fix it himself according to his conscience without overcharging his neighbour. For selling was an act performed towards one's neighbour and, therefore, it should rather by governed by law and conscience. Moreover, it must be directed more towards doing no injury to one's neighbour than towards gaining profit for oneself.[12] He also asserted that the purpose of selling should satisfy the real need of the masses.[13] Otherwise it would be a practice of shame, unjust and illegal.[14] He was not in favor of higher price as it was a burden of the masses.

Accumulation of Goods

Martin Luther upheld the accumulation of goods only when it was not for self-interest or monopoly but for the right cause. In other words, he backed the idea of accumulation when it was done for the good and betterment of the community as a whole. For example, accumulating becomes necessary when there are natural disasters so that the people can get their share out of it. For instance, Joseph gathered grain not to sell as dearly as he pleased nor did he do it out of greed or self-interest but for the benefit of the country and people. He did it with good intentions so that people might not perish when famine arose. But when the merchants accumulated the goods for their selfish motives, he denounced it and declared that any accumulation regardless of the land or people was a grave sin.[15] In another context he said that the accumulated or piled up possession need not be considered possession; it ceases to be 'goods' at all. They are evil and damnable possessions because they have not been distributed or shared with the needy but simply heaped up out of selfish and avaricious motive.[16] Thus he condemned the property that one owns in excess apart from his own needs. To him, it was owned unjustifiably. Such property was stolen property because he refused to share it with the needy and the poor. In other words, the excess possession ought to be used to alleviate other people's needs. Otherwise the property is deemed illegal.[17] In conclusion, one can easily see that his ethics on trade and commerce was not in favour of the rich merchants but on the contrary it was solely for protective and safe measures for the poorer classes.

The Practice of Usury

No other economic question occupied Martin Luther so much as usury. He first criticized the practice of usury in a series of sermons preached in the years 1516 and 1517. In 1519 when Eck renewed his activities in the interest of Fugger's, he again preached on this subject and published his first tract "Short Sermon on Usury". This he enlarged in the same year and later published under the title "Long Sermon on Usury". In 1520 in his famous tract "Address to the German Nobility", he spoke out against usury. All these ideas were combined in his tract of 1524 under the title On "Trade and Usury". It was published in the context of economic transition, characterized by increased reliance on money. His intention in writing this tract was to call attention to the unjust behavior of the usurers. As early as April 1539, Luther turned to the town councillors, to Mayor Lukas Cranach and to the local prince asking them to take energetic steps to prevent starvation, price increase, speculation and usury. However, there was no great improvement. He, therefore, wrote another treatise in 1540 called "An Exhortation to the Pastors to Preach against Usury", which was an attack on those who practised usury. In all these writings, he compared the previous years with the present and concluded that the present was worse than the past.

Luther said that, in the previous years, the merchants were noblemen and therefore people were happy. But at present the nobles and princes became traders and oppressed the people just for the sake of money. Twenty years ago, said Luther, one said that to take ten goulden on a hundred was usury but now the moneyed fellows extracted exorbitant interest. They demanded twenty or thirty percent and some of them charged forty or sixty percent as interest for a year. It was obvious that the devil was in the game and usury was a sign and proof that the world had been sold to the devil. Even though people pleaded with the emperor and the princes to lessen their burdens which they suffered due to the practice of usury, they did nothing because they themselves were immersed in the scheme. At this critical juncture, he began to plead for the masses and objected to the idea of living on the interest from the wealth earned by a previous generation. To him it meant becoming a parasite on society.[18] He thus spoke in favour of the masses and showed his resolve in order to annihilate their passions and pains. Since Christ had shed his blood and sacrificed his life for everyone, one might not even contemplate defrauding his poor neighbour by way of usury.[19] For, when one deceives the poor by way of usury, he also deceives God.[20] When the usurers crushed the poor masses without minding their sufferings and pains, Luther boldly called them murderers. For they not only failed to help the poor but also snatched the crumbs from the starving mouth, the bread which God has given for their sustenance.

Luther condemned the practice of usury as a form of clever theft and as the 'worm' eating within the apple. To him, whoever practices usury breaks the seventh commandment. He listed usury along with gluttony, adultery, manslaughter and murder and called it a sin both against God and neighbour.[21] John T. Nooonan also supplements that usury has to be treated without hesitation as a sin against justice.[22] For these reasons, he said that when one sees a usurer, he should go to him in secret and admonish him to give up his sin.[23] If he will not listen, he should take two others with him and admonish him once more in a brotherly way to give up his sin. If he scorns that, he should tell the pastor before the whole congregation and accuse him before the pastor in the presence of the people. The pastor should exclude him and put him under the ban until he comes to himself.[24]

E.G. Schwiebert says that usury to Luther did not mean merely an exorbitant rate of interest on money that had been loaned but rather the taking unjust advantage of a specific situation.[25] One who loans the money can take reasonable interest, but he should not secure annual interest but only on the gain that was reaped by the one that had assumed the loan. If the gain is high, on that were well off and if the gain is low, both should suffer. Thus the creditors should show a real interest in the debtor.[26] Otherwise, he said, the usurers would die unusual and sudden deaths or come to other terrible ends as tyrants and robbers deserve. For God is the judge of the poor and the needy.[27] With regard to the rate of interest, he allowed the earning of interest only to those who were not able to work such as aged people, widows and orphans. They must be allowed on the basis of love and natural equity and the rate of interest should not exceed six percent.[28]

When a loan is offered to the poor and the needy it is sinful to charge interest. But, on the other hand, when a loan is given to a businessman who expected to use the money as an investment, he permitted the charging of five or six percent interest which seemed to him reasonable. Again it must be dependent on the success of the enterprise. Since Christ taught to lend expecting nothing in return (Lk. 6.35), the Christians, as disciples of Christ, should observe this rule and beware of interest as a real sin. For charging interest was contrary to nature as well as Christian teaching. He added that experience also shows that riches gained in this manner are cursed by the Lord.[29] He called those who charged interest on loans un-Christian. Whoever demands more in return than he has given was a usurer. The one who possesses more than what is required to meet their own needs and the needs of their family ought to lend without charging interest. In favour of this discipline, Luther cited the sermon of the Mount, Deuteronomy and the Church Fathers as well.[30]

Since the usurer misuses their fellow-man's plight in order to earn money, they commits a crime against the community. They use their economic power to subdue their neighbour. Such persons, said Luther, do not believe in God but Mammon. They are idol worshipers and place themselves outside the believing community. They therefore ought to be excluded from the sacraments and must not be buried as Christians if they do not repent before they die.[31] Even in the case of a penitent, he said that he or she must become a Zacchaeus and return what they stole in excessive interest to those out of whom they squeezed it. Otherwise theirs is not truly repentant. According to civil law, he or she cannot keep such money with good conscience. He also warned those who had fellowship with such persons. Whoever eats and drinks with them, said Luther, makes themselves a participant in their sins.[32]

Martin Luther further emphasized that it was the duty of the preachers to deal with the problem of usury and to expose the injustice connected with it in their preaching despite the fact that the problem belongs to the lawyers' area of competence. Those who fail in the struggle against usurers, said Luther, become in practice Antinomians. When the scholars and priests gave loans with interest with a view to seeking to improve the churches, and divine worship, he condemned them vehemently. He declared that the churches have neither authority nor freedom to break God's commandments on brother, neighbour and practising usury. With the practice of usury the divine worship did not improve but was corrupted. To serve God is to keep his commandments and not to steal, or rob the poor by way of usury in order to build churches or altars, which God has not commanded.[33] Even if the whole world had the custom of usury, the churches and the clergy should do the opposite. A person who does otherwise is doing so not to improve the churches or ecclesiastical property but for their own greed.[34] Therefore it is the duty of the Pope, bishops, emperor, princes and everybody else to watch over the matter of usury and to rescue people from its gaping jaws. They should abolish this practice because it is not directed towards love but towards self-seeking.[35] In addition, he argued that any Church which deals with finances in order to take interest should not be called a Church. For the Church has been established to give a good example to the world and not to practise usury.[36]

In conclusion, from his "Brief Sermon on Usury" (1519), to his "Admonition to the Clergy to Preach against Usury" (1540), Luther consistently preached and wrote against the expanding money credit economy as a great sin. Usury, argued Luther, affects everyone. It occurs in all cities and is found in the market and the kitchen. The usurers are eating our food and drinking our drink. Just like the big fish eats the little fish, big thieves hang the little thieves.[37] He declared that usury was the greatest misfortune of the German nation. He commented that after the devil there was no greater human enemy on earth than a usurer because the usurer desires to be above everyone. Although tyrants are evil person, they allow the people to live and they are somewhat merciful. But an usurer desires that the entire world should be ruined in order that there be hunger, thirst, misery and need so that they can have everything and so that everyone must depend upon them and be their slaves as if they were God.[38]

Luther's denunciation of economic abuses reveals that he had a strong concern and commitment to justice. Owing to this, he saw a permanent conflict between people's need and profit making. In other words, his views on economics radically centered on the basic needs of the people. His criticism on the economic principles of his day had a double effect. On the one hand, it brought to light and to the public notice the exploitation of the merchants. On the other hand, it conscientized the masses and created radical awareness among them which ultimately pushed them to reform the field of economics. In other words, the economic criticism of him was at the right time and its was context-oriented. He connected his theology with historical reality.[39]

Luther on Poverty

During the medieval period the Church theologized as well as institutionalized the idea of poverty. The poor were thought of as favoured people in the sight of God. The care of the poor was related to the good work of salvation. The idea of 'holy poor' was created and, according to this, those who bore poverty patiently without complaining to God were exhorted to receive the reward of the heavenly city. By the same token the rich were also exhorted to redeem themselves from their sins by generous alms-giving. By giving alms to the poor, the rich could atone for their sins and receive salvation. In other words, the poor were thought of as their scissors for the rich whose material benefits they could repay with spiritual benefits as spiritual persons richer in faith. Thus, the theological idealization and legitimizing of poverty served the poor and the rich alike. In addition, the monks who had taken a vow of poverty were seen as being spiritually more perfect than the laity who still had private possessions. Similarly, those who were outside the monastery, yet poor, were also seen as being in a blessed state. The laity who gave alms to the poor were seen as the ones who did the most important good works. To continue this good work even after their death, they formed charities and endowed foundations.[40]

In other words, poverty was no longer seen primarily as an injury to the human spirit but as a virtue to attain salvation. It was understood in religious terms rather than as a social concept. However, the care for the poor declined due to the emergence of capitalism and secularization of society and the Church. The religious orders which had played an important role in relieving poverty experienced great difficulty in adjusting to new circumstances. The declining income of the religious foundations and endowments and the natural disasters such as wars, famine and pestilences added to the difficulties of poor relief programmes.[41] In short, the late medieval period lacked both the theoretical and practical resources to deal with poverty. Carter Lindberg estimates that around thirty percent of the population may have been paupers and vagrants during the middle Ages.[42]

Having recognized the serious nature of poverty in his time, Luther offered theological as well as practical suggestions and solutions to achieve complete elimination of poverty.[43] His theology of poverty became a protest against the medieval ideology of poverty.[44] Since he understood righteousness before God by grace alone, he rejected the traditional idea that the poor are the means of good works through alms giving. He also denied the plight of the poor as a peculiar form of blessedness and alms giving as merit for salvation.[45] In short, he de-ideologized the medieval approach to poverty and vehemently stated that there was no salvific value in bringing poor or in giving alms.

On the contrary, Luther stressed that salvation was the source rather than the goal of the life. He also emphasized that giving should stem from honour of God and love of neighbour and as a concern for the common welfare. He further stated that poor relief should not only be the individual duty of consideration and helpfulness towards the needy neighbour but it must also be the duty of the community to take care of those unable to work, the weak and the poor.[46] He thus determined the place at which help to the poor should begin in a manner different from the current practices of his day. Karl- Holl declares that Luther considered not only the lowest strata of the already completely pauperized but also those of the middle class whom poverty was threatening or who were just struggling out of it.[47]

Luther also rejected the position of Eck and Aquinas that poor relief was not necessary unless the needy were in extreme wants. Luther said that to withhold help until extreme wants, was an evasion of the commandment and a deception of the Holy Spirit.[48] Instead, he suggested following the example of St. Ambrose and Paulinus who at one time melted down the chalices and everything that their churches had, and gave to the poor.[49] He added that this was the reason that the possessions of the Church were formerly called *bona ecclesiae*, that is, common property for all, especially for the poor and the needy.[50] His concern for the poor pushed him further to speak even against the monks. He said that the property of the monastery, when it was deserted, should be used for the needy and the poor. Having seen the false poverty of the monks and the real poverty of the people, he strongly objected to raising large sums of money from the common folk in order to keep the monks in their status. He asserted that the monks should be put to work if they want to eat. For him, they were the major financial drain on resources that should go to the poor.[51] In addition, Luther hated their claim that their poverty put them in an exalted state before God.

Luther also criticized the medieval 'Brotherhoods' which were originally intended for works of charity but had degenerated into self-seeking means of salvation through the proliferation of masses and the accumulation of good works. He protested against this attitude and insisted upon service to the needy and poor. He said: "If men desire to maintain a brotherhood, they should gather provisions and feed and serve a tableful or two of poor people for the sake of God, or they should gather money into a common treasury, each craft for itself. Then in cases of hardship, needy and fellow workmen might be helped to get started, and be lent money, or a young couple of the same craft might be filled out repeatedly form this common treasury".[52]

Thus, Luther advocated that 'Brotherhoods' should serve as the free servants of the community. In another context, he criticized the self-centeredness of the Brotherhoods. In contrast to this ego – centricity, he emphasized community rooted understanding for the betterment of humanity, especially for the poor and the needy.[53] He also asserted that it was much more essential and urgent to help the needy and the poor than to give to the churches made of stones. He wrote: "To speak boldly, it is sheer trickery, dangerous and deceptive to the simple-minded, when bills, letters, seals, banners and the like are displayed for the sake of dead stone churches and the same thing is not done a hundred times more for the sake of needy, living Christians. Beware, therefore, O man! God will not ask you at your death and at the Last Day how much you have left in your will, whether you have given so and so much to the churches. But he will say to you, 'I was hungry and you gave me no food; I was naked, and you did not clothe me'".[54]

Luther himself crossed this threshold already in his ninety five theses when he wrote that he who gives to the poor or lends to the needy does a better deed than he who buys indulgences. He added that he who sees the needy and passes him by, giving his money for indulgences, does not buy Papal indulgences but God's wrath.[55] A few years later, he said that any contribution to the poor would shine more brightly than the contribution to the institutional life of the Church. He thought that individual acts of charity were always insufficient. So he sought for a system which can be accompanied by structural change. He envisioned the common chest as a structural means of dealing with poverty. He also felt that it would make it possible to ensure that assistance would go to the truly needy.[56] So he institutionalized poor relief and the first effort took place in Wittenberg. The city council had issued an order for the creation of a place in Wittenberg. In the year 1522 the city council issued an order for the creation of a 'common chest'. The noteworthy element was that the poor should be supported in developing their vocational skills beyond their social station so that they might overcome dependency. Stress was also laid that those who were able to work should have the responsibility to work.[57]

Luther developed this idea of poor relief more fully in the "Ordinance for common Chest of the Town of Leisnig" (1529).[58]

Carter Lindberg says that by way of his assistance to the town of Leisnig in establishing a poor relief order, he developed his early model of congregationalism.[59] He also declares that this was the first effort which translated Luther's theological ethics into social legislation.[60] Karl- Holl also says that it was the decisive theoretical breakthrough and the first seed for the development of the welfare state.[61] Following his suggestion, the Leising Ordinance established the common chest on the basis of the universal priesthood of all believers, which was one of the reformative doctrines of Luther. He hoped that, as a result of the leising example, there would be a great decline in the existing foundations, monastic houses, and those horrible dregs which had fattened on the principle that all the internal as well as external possessions of Christian believers should serve the honour of God and the love of neighbour.

Luther further stressed that all the ecclesiastical assets should be placed in the common chest after fulfilling special obligations to provide for those who wished to remain in the cloisters, giving transitional support to those who wished to leave the monastic life and partial restoration of funds to the needy families of donors. He advised that all the receipts from 'Brotherhoods' that had been collected and were then available together with their written documents and records should be assigned to the common chest. Voluntary gifts made during days of good health and by will at the time of death should be given to the common chest. He also advised the parishioners to make liberal contribution to the common chest to meet insufficiency in the future. He stated: "That every noble, townsman and peasant living in the parish shall according to his ability and means remit in taxes for himself, his wife and the children a certain sum of money to the chest each year".[62]

When the extent of poverty was more than the handling of the common chest, Luther stated that everyone should have to pay for the support of poor. He also requested the clergy to contribute towards the common chest. He also suggested that the congregation should take over all Church properties within the parish and establish an organization to administer schools and to assist the poor and the needy.[63] He advocated that the same procedure in the case of bishoprics, foundations and chapters can be followed and the possessions should be divided between the impoverished and the common chest.[64] He thought that if these suggestions were carried out there would be a well-filled common chest for every need which could diminish and eventually end three crying evils. The first of these was beginning which does so much harm to land and people. The second was the terrible misuse of the ban, which served no other purpose than to torture people in the interest of the possessions of priests and monks. If they had no possessions, there would be no need of this ban. The third was the cursed usury contact, which had asserted its validity even in the matter of ecclesiastical properties.[65]

The common chest was responsible for a variety of services. The maintenance and construction of common buildings such as the church, school, and hospital and store room to store grains were met from the common chest. The people of the whole parish could have resource to these stores for bodily substance in times of scarcity.[66] Needy workmen were allowed to receive loans and the daughters of the poor and the neglected orphans were provided with appropriate dowries so that they were given in marriage. Sons of the poor were educated so that there would be learned people to preach the gospel and lead the worldly government.[67] Those who were impoverished by force of circumstances and left without assistance by their relatives and those who were unable to work because of illness or old age and were as poor as to suffer real need could receive help as the occasion demanded. This should be done so that their lives and health may be preserved from further deterioration, enfeeblement and foreshortening through lack of shelter, clothing, nourishment and care. For no impoverished person need ever publicly cry out, lament or beg for such items of daily necessity.[68]

Similarly the poor and neglected orphans should be provided with training and physical necessities out of the common chest until such time as they can work and earn their bread. If there be found among such orphans, or the children of impoverished parents, young boys with an aptitude for schooling and a capacity for arts and letters, they should be supported out of the common chest.[69] He was against begging which was the consequence of poverty. He viewed begging as a theological and social problem. His position on begging, therefore, was a consequence of his theology of justification by grace alone which denies any salvific benefit to alms-giving. During Luther's time, begging became respectable through the activities of the several mendicant orders. The beggars who flocked to the streets, inns and market places were using crude devices to call attention to their begging. Among these were many professional beggars who disliked work and found begging both congenial and profitable. Hence, when he made his attack on begging, it was directed at the heart of the medieval theological and ecclesiastical system.[70] He vehemently objected to begging because he thought that unrestrained begging would bleed Germany to death.

Although efforts were made to control begging, the medieval Church did not do anything to eliminate begging completely. In other words, the medieval ordinances failed to do away with begging by an ordered poor relief programme.[71] He advocated the abolition of all begging in contrast to the pre-Reformation efforts to control begging. He emphasized that the civil authorities should abolish all begging since God has ordained them to punish the wicked and protect the good.[72] He encouraged political authorities to enforce laws against begging. He also urged the princes not to build hospitals for the poor but to make their whole land into a kind of hospital in terms of aid to the truly needy so that there would be a no beggar in the land.[73] He suggested that every city should take care of its own poor and an organized system of poor relief should be set up to replace the current haphazard system.[74]

Luther was also against 'professional begging' as it was painful and harmful to the common people. He said that if each of the five or six mendicant orders[75] visit the same place more than six or seven times every year along with the usual beggars, the common people would be in a critical financial condition as the tribute was above that the secular authorities demand by way of taxes and assessments.[76] He, therefore, argued that no monk of whatever order he may be, should beg or have others beg for him.[77] He also emphasized that the monks should work if they want to eat. He perceived laziness as a form of evil as it is living off the labour of another.[78]

In sum, Luther made a critical contribution to the understanding of poverty which facilitated structural social change and the development of modern social welfare. His availability to various councils such as Leisnig reveals that he was ever ready to serve the poor in order to annihilate poverty thoroughly. His immediate response to those requests also reveals his extreme concern for service to the poor and the needy. For instance, he pleaded through his friend Palatine for the poor with the El ector, whom he called the patron of the poor. He interceded for a widow who wished to cancel her bequest of her house to the commons because she needed to help her sister. Luther pursued this case for two years. Likewise, he involved himself in numerous appeals on behalf of widows, the poor, invalids and prisoners.

Luther was also active on behalf of poor pastors and monks, nuns who had left the cloisters. He was very much concerned to prevent begging at its very source. He declared: "For so to help a man that he does not need to become a beggar is just as much of a good work and a virtue and an alms as to give to a man and to help a man who has already become a beggar".[79] Thus, by way of introducing poor relief programmers, he helped people to be liberated from the wrong ecclesiastical notion of this time, avoided the constant dependency of the poor and the needy, elevated the social stance of the neglected and raised the oppressed masses of his time to attain their fundamental and basic rights. Carter Lindberg rightly observes that, with the suggestions for poor relief, Luther spoke highly of the poor, particularly on the fundamental human rights of equality, freedom and brotherly love.[80] The economic ideology of Luther was highly useful to the people of Germany and the masses were very much convinced by his teaching, preaching and writing. His writings were widely circulated and people also stood with him in support of the Reformation.

ECONOMIC IDEOLOGY OF GANDHI

Gandhi is a universally recognized economist. His ideas on economics are based on morality and an economy of permanence. There is a branch of Economics known as Gandhian Economics. Gunnar Myrdal and Schumacher are world famous economists. In the celebrated works *Asian Drama and Small Is Beautiful* respectively, there are references to the economic ideas of Gandhi. Dr. J. C. Kumarappa was the outstanding exponent of Gandhian economics. It is pertinent to underline that Gandhi's Economics is being recognized by western countries. If all economic ideas of Gandhi were reduced into one word, it is the idea of trusteeship. According to Gandhian Economics a rich man is only the trustee of the riches in his possession. The Marxists want to confiscate the properties of the rich but Gandhi wanted to take over the rich men also along with their wealth. His idea was to permit the rich man to continue his avocation and work for the welfare of the society as a trustee. This economic idea has revolutionary implications. But they have not been put to test, due to his untimely death and the rulers' indifference.[81] He said "My theory of trusteeship is no makeshift, certainly no camouflage. I am confident it will survive all other theories"[82]

Gandhi had his own approach to the economic problems facing our times. Gandhian economy was an economy of conservation, as opposed to the economy of exploitation. His economic ideas were shaped by his own practical experience and intensive reading of John Ruskin, Leo Tolstoy, the Gita etc. He viewed economics and economic problems in a different way. His economic ideas were rooted in spiritual and moral grounds. He insisted that the objective of human conduct should be moral and spiritual development. He had no faith in an economics which is devoid of morality. That economics is untrue which disregards moral values.[83] He championed the cause of the poor and the semi-starved millions of India and wanted to provide them a decent and high standard of living. He used to judge any economic system or institution on the basis of the common good or human welfare. He viewed property relations from a moral point of view and said: "I suggest that we are thieves in a way. If I take anything that I do not need for my own immediate use and keep it, I thieve it from somebody else ..."[84] Thus he opposed capitalism purely on the moral grounds. He realized the fact that changes in the existing economic system is a necessary step for improving the living conditions of the poor. He wanted to put an end to the rule of the capital. He not only opposed the British imperialists for imposing poverty upon the Indian masses, but also condemned the exploitation of the poor by the Indian capitalists.

True economics stands for social justice and promotes the good of all. According to Gandhi, true economics never militates against the highest ethical standards and an economics that inculcates Mammon worship and enables the strong to amass wealth at the expense of the weak 'is a false and dismal science'.[85] True economics never conflicts with the moral standards, as all true ethics must be also good economics. He said, "I do not draw a sharp line or any distinction between economics and ethics. Economics that hurts the moral well-being of an individual or a nation is immoral, and therefore, sinful".[86]

Gandhi considered true economics as indispensable for a decent life. He was influenced by the famous saying of Christ that, "Man cannot live by bread alone." But it is also a fact that he cannot live without it either. Matter may be less important than the spirit; but in human beings the spirit manifests itself and works through the flesh. Also, freedom is the very essence of our being. It is a primary condition for the progress of the individual, the group and the nation.[87] He has given a spiritual interpretation of human history. He observed that the essential difference between man and the brute is that "The former can respond to the call of the spirit in him, can rise superior to the possessions that he owns in common with the brute".[88] The spiritual and moral progress made by man during all these centuries must also be borne in mind in determining the future course of human destiny. He observed, "I do not believe in the existence of class struggle".

Though Gandhi pleaded for limitation of wants, he recognized that human life needs some amount of material goods for a decent life. He accepted the necessity of a certain degree of physical harmony and comfort and said, "No one has even suggested that grinding pauperism can lead to anything else than moral degradation".[89] But he opposed an unlimited number of wants and satisfying them. At the same time, he denounced the enforced grinding poverty of the masses since it morally degrades them. Thus Gandhi regarded that possession of wealth and material things beyond certain limits would make man unhappy and enslaved instead of facilitating a good life. One should, therefore, limit his wants to the basic necessities of life. If the wants grow in number, some of them cannot be satisfied. Pain will be the consequence, reducing the size of welfare. When the purchasing power is limited, it is good to have only a few wants and to get them satisfied fully so that pleasure and welfare become positive and maximum. He also wanted to reduce the number of wants to the minimum so that they are satisfied and satisfaction is got in every sense and consequently welfare is maximized. He stood for a simple and, more or less, self-sufficient living in rural surroundings. He had an ideal of simple living and high thinking. He stood for voluntary reduction of wants. According to him, "Craze for multiplicity of goods is destructive of contentment, peace and tranquility".[90] He advocated the establishment of ideal villages in India where the people could pursue the ideal of 'Simple living and high thinking'. He also advocated, "I do not believe that multiplication of wants and machinery contrived to supply them is taking the world a single step nearer to its goal".[91] He argued that all wealth is socially produced and therefore, must be equally divided among the members of the society. The basic necessities of life should be freely available to all like God. Their monopolization by any country or a group of persons was unjust and the neglect of this simple principle is the cause of the destitution that we witness today throughout the world. He argued: "Nature produces enough for our wants from day to day, and if everybody took enough for himself and nothing more, there would be no pauperism in this world, there would be no man dying of starvation in this world".[92] He wanted that everybody should be provided with sufficient work to enable him to make two ends meet. This ideal, according to him, "God created man to work for his food and said that those who ate without work were thieves". Again, "If everybody lives by the sweat of his brow, the earth would become a paradise. If everyone laboured physically for his bread, poets, doctors, lawyers and others would consider it their duty to use those talents gratis for the service of humanity. Their output will be all the better and richer for their selfless devotion to duty".[93]

Bread labour shall be the foremost duty of every member of society. He derived the concept of 'bread labour' from Tolstoy and Ruskin's *'Unto this Last'*. He also claimed that the same principle has been set forth in the third chapter of the Bhagavad Gita[94] where, it has also been said that those who eat without putting in any labour eat stolen food. He argued "How can a man, who does not do body labour, have the right to eat?" He quoted the famous Biblical saying, "In the sweat of thy brow shalt thou eat thy bread". To Gandhi, intellectual labour could not be a substitute for bodily labour.[95] He wanted that everyone should do some sort of manual labour to earn his bread. He believed that bread labour would bring about a steady and silent revolution in the society. In his own words: "If all laboured for their bread and no more, then there would be enough food and enough leisure for all. Then there would be no cry of over-population, no disease and no such misery as we see around. Such labour will be the highest form of sacrifice... There will then be no rich and no poor, none high and none low, and no untouchable. If we did so, our wants would be minimized, our food would be simple. We should then eat to live, not live to eat. Intellectual labour is for the soul and is its own satisfaction".[96]

Economic Equality

Gandhi condemned the concentration of wealth in the hands of a few which led to the glaring economic inequalities in the society. He said: "Today there is gross economic inequality. The basis of Socialism is economic equality. There can be no Ramarajya in the present state of iniquitous inequalities in which a few roll in riches and the masses do not get even enough to eat."[97] His ideal of non-violent society presupposes economic equality. He therefore held that "A non-violent system of Government is impossibility so long as the wide gulf between the hungry millions persists". The establishment of a non-violent society implies the abolition of external conflict between the rich and the poor. Economic equality, for him, does not mean that everyone should literally have the same amount of worldly things, but it means that everybody should have enough for his needs. Hence the real meaning of economic equality is 'to each according to his need'.[98] He wanted to reconstruct the entire social order in such a way that each man would be provided with all his natural needs and no more. His ideal of socialism is all should get equal wages.[99]

Gandhi's ideal of economic equality involved complete non-possession or at best retention of only that amount as was necessary to meet the basic needs of existence. He applied the same principle not only to material property but also to the intelligence, skills and other productive attributes of human beings that constituted their inseparable private property. In spite of his belief in economic equality, he did not like to cramp the talents of any individual. He allows every individual to earn as much as he can, but the bulk of his earnings must be used, not for himself, but for the good of the society. If every man looks upon himself as a servant of society, learns for its sake, spends for its benefit, he visualised a peaceful revolution in the society.

Swadeshi

Gandhi believed that Swadeshi should be accepted as a creed. It was always essential to use indigenous goods even if those were comparatively bad. He said, "My definition of swadeshi is well known. It is never vindictive or punitive. It is in no sense narrow. I refuse to buy from anybody anything, however nice or beautiful, if it interferes with my growth or injures those whom nature had made my first care and I buy useful healthy literature from every part of the world. But I will not buy an inch of the finest cotton fabric from England or Japan or in other part of the world because it has injured and increasingly injures the millions of the inhabitants of India."[100] In the economic sphere, his doctrine of swadeshi stands for self-sufficiency of the country. Here swadeshi implies production of all necessary things of life in one's own country. Though Gandhi was an ardent supporter of swadeshi, he was not against importing certain limited necessary things for our growth which India herself cannot produce.[101]

Khadi and Village Industries

The concept of constructive work was put to test and action at the instance of Gandhi. According to him, constructive work was as important to a Satyagrahi as drill and daily exercise is inevitable for a military or police man. In the first list of constructive work there were twenty three items. Hindu-Muslim unity, Removal of untouchability etc. Hindu-Muslim unity, Removal of untouchablity and khadi were given prominence in the agenda of the constructive work. The seven and a half lakhs of villages in composite India were considered to be the units for constructive work. During the recess when there was no Satyagraha struggle in the course of the independence movement constructive work was undertaken by freedom fighters. The constructive work widened the horizon and social outlook and social sensitivity of freedom fighters.[102]

Gandhi wanted to make every village self-supporting for its food and clothing through khadi. He conceived khadi as a universal industry.[103] It ensures the proper utilization of human labour. It would provide work to millions of villages. It would give them hope where but yesterday there was blank despair. To him, spinning must be a compulsory objective of every able-bodied man. He conceived spinning as an emblem of non-violence or a doctrine that had its roots in the purest ahimsa. He considered 'khadi' as the symbol of a unit of economic freedom and equality; decentralization of the production and distribution of the necessities of life. Its message is one of simplicity, service to mankind, being so as not to hurt others, creating a bond between the rich and the poor, capital and labour, the prince and the pauper. In addition to khadi, he mentioned some village industries like hand grinding, tanning, hand pounding, soap-making, oil-pressing etc. Without khadi, these industries cannot have an existence of their own. Village industries were to be improved. For this reason, he regarded 'khadi' as a necessary corollary of the principle of Swadeshi and the first indispensable step towards the discharge of 'Swadeshi Dharma' towards society.[104]

Gandhi wanted India to evolve a system of non-violent occupations instead of industrialism. He believed that large scale production, with its competitive economy, would not be compatible with the concept of a society, equal and free. Hence he favoured a rural economy. The village was to be the basic unit of the economic system. It was to be self-contained and self-sufficient. He explained: "My idea of Village Swaraj is that it is a complete republic, independent of its neighbours for its own vital wants, and yet interdependent for many others in which dependence is a necessity. Thus every village's first concern will be to grow its own food crops and cotton for its cloth".[105] He wanted the village to produce all that is necessary for the consumption of its own people. His idea was the establishment of several independent village units or republics which could manage their own affairs with the least governmental help and outside interference. Thus, every village will be a republic or a panchayat having full powers. It will be an oceanic circle whose centre will be the individual.[106]

Views on Machinery and Industrialism

In his earlier years, Gandhi was totally opposed to all machinery, but, with the passage of time, he gradually changed his views on machinery and said: "Machinery has its place; it has come to stay. But it must not be allowed to displace necessary human labour. Again he said: "I am uncompromisingly against all destructive machinery. But simple tools and instruments and such machinery as saves individual labour and lightens the burden of the millions of cottages, I should welcome".[107] He condemned industrialization because it accentuates materialism and spreads moral corruption. He remarked, "I would prize every invention of science made for the benefit of all".[108] He was not opposed to machinery as such, but his objection was only to the craze for machinery, the craze for labour-saving machinery, which will throw thousands of men on the open streets without work to die of starvation. Machinery, under capitalism, was enabling concentration of wealth in the hands of a few capitalists thereby helping a few to ride on the back of millions. He opposed this trend of machinery.[109]

Economic Decentralization

Gandhi realized that effective decentralization in social and political spheres depended upon decentralization of the economic structure. Decentralization will mean that industries should produce essential commodities in villages and for villages, using local raw materials and simple processes and tools that can be acquired by the villages easily, and run with the aid of human or animal power since they are easily available. To him, economic exploitation was the essence of violence in society and wars in future could be eschewed only by following a bold policy of decentralization through the organization of largely self-sufficient village communities. Self-sufficiency does not mean narrowness. "Man is much self-dependent as inter-dependent; when dependence becomes necessary in order to keep society in good order, it is no longer dependence, but becomes co-operation where each is equal to the other". Decentralization also leads to self-dependence, mutual respect and sound economic internationalism by avoiding international dependence. For capital and labour, he thought that if all the labourers could combine in the true non-violent spirit, capital would inevitably come under their control. He advised the workers to refuse to serve under degrading conditions and for insufficient wages. He told workers: "I would honour you as brave men if you would accept a state of utter starvation rather than that you should labour on such insufficient wages as would render it impossible for you to observe the primary laws of morality".[110] He pleaded for mutual love between capital and labour. He wanted to replace the traditional relations between the employer and the employee as master and servant by that of father and children.

Luther's economic reform was fully based on the word of God. He did not give a place for the rich to enhance their financial position in the world by collecting more interest from the poor people in the society and the Church. His preaching and writings consisted of equal distribution of wealth and payment of labour. Degrading the people on the basis of their economical position was also condemned by him and he declared this type of activities as evil and against the word of God. Gandhi demanded equal status and dignity for capital and labour to avoid conflict between them. He was against the theory of abolition of private property on the basis of trusteeship. He believed in liquidating class interests by conversion and not by coercion. He was of the opinion that total economic equality was neither possible nor desirable to be established. He regarded the individual as the supreme architect of his own government and preferred minimum state or governmental interference in his private and public life. His ideal of Rama Rajya was based on this.

Endnotes

[1] *Luther's Works*, Vol.45, p.233.

[2] *Ibid*, Vol.45, p.246.

[3] W.D.J. Cargill Thompson, *The Political Thought of Martin Luther*,p. 165.

[4] Heinrich Bornkamm, *Reformation and Society in 16ᵗʰ Century Europe*, p. 264.

[5] *Luther's Works*, Vol. 45, p. 246 & *Luther's Works*, Vol. 44, p. 212.

[6] *Luther's Works*, Vol.44, p.2 14.

[7] Walter Altmonn, *Luther and Liberations*, p.109.

[8] *Luther's Works*, Vol. 44, p. 213.

[9] *Ibid*.

[10] *Luther's Works*, Vol. 45, pp. 264-266.

[11] *Ibid*, Vol.45, p. 245.

[12] *Ibid*, Vol.45, pp. 248-249.

[13] Walter Altmann, *Op.cit*, p.105.

[14] *Luther's Works*, Vol.45, p. 247.

[15] *Ibid*, Vol.45, p.263.

[16] *Luther's Works*, Vol.14, p.219.

[17] Martin Brecht, *Marthin Lutehr: Shaping and Defining the Reformation*, p. 146.

[18] E.G. Achwiebert, *Luther and His Times*, p. 453._

[19] *Luther's Works*, Vol.24, p. 250.

[20] *Luther's Works*, Vol.43, p. 20.

[21] *Luther's Works*, Vol.51, p.374.

[22] John T. Noonan, *The Scholastic Analysis of Usury*, p. 20.

[23] *Luther's Works*, Vol. 51, p.97.

[24] *Ibid*, Vol.51, pp.97-98.

[25] E.G. Schwiebert, *Op.cit*, p. 451.

[26] Hans Schwarz, *"Lutehr's Doctrine of Two kingdoms – Help or Hindrance for Social Changes"*, p. 69.

[27] *Luther's Works*, Vol.45, p. 305.

[28] *Luther's Works*, Vol.54, p. 369.

[29] *Luther's Works*, Vol.2, p. 263.

[30] *Luther's Works*, Vol.45, pp. 289-290.

[31] Per Frostin, "God versus *Capitalism: Would Luther have Enjoyed Mars?*" pp. 331-424

[32] *Luther's Works*, Vol.54, p. 398.

[33] *Luther's Works*, Vol.45, p. 306.

[34] *Ibid*, Vol. 45, p. 294.

[35] *Ibid*, Vol. 45, p. 297.

[36] E.G. Schwiebart, *Op.cit*, p. 260.

[37] *Luther's Works*, Vol.21, pp.180 & 221, Vol. 25, p. 172 & Vol. 13, p.60.

[38] Carter Lindberg, *Beyond Charity: Reformation Initiatives for the poor*, p. 112.

[39] Richard P. Hordern, " *Lutheran Economics: In Community with the Poor"*, p.30.

[40] Carter Lindberg, *"Through a Glass Darkly"*, p. 43.

[41] Harold J. Grimm, *"Luther's Contribution to Sixteenth Century Organization for Poor Relief"*, p. 222.

[42] Carter Lindberg, *"There shall be No Beggars Among Christians: Karlstadt, Luther and Origin of Protestant Poor relief"*, p. 317.

[43] Richard Hordern, *"Lutheran Economics: In Community with the Poor"*. p. 34.

[44] *Ibid*, p.30.

[45] *Luther's Works*, Vol.31, p.204.

[46] Karl Holl, *The Cultural Significance of Reformation*, p.77.

[47] *Ibid*, p. 92.

[48] *Luther's Works*, Vol.45, p. 287 & *Luther's Works*, Vol.31, p.203 where Luther first attacked this idea.

[49] *Luther's Works*, Vol.45, p. 289.

[50] *Ibid*, Vol.45, pp.172-173.

[51] *Luther's Works*, Vol.44, p.110.

[52] *Luther's Works*, Vol.35, p. 69 & *Luther's Works*, Vol. 44, p. 193.

[53] *Luther's Works*, Vol. 35, p. 72.

[54] *Luther's Works*, Vol.45, p. 286.

[55] *Luther's Works*, Vol. 41, p.29 & Theses 43 and 45.

[56] *Luther's Works*, Vol.44, p.189.

[57] *Luther's Works*, Vol.44, pp. 189-191.

[58] *Luther's Works*, Vol. 45, pp. 169-194.

[59] Carter Lindberg, Beyond *Charity: Reformation Initiatives for the poor*, p. 99.

[60] *Ibid*, 119.

[61] Karl Holl. *Op.cit*, p. 95.

[62] *Ibid*, p. 192.

[63] *Ibid*, p. 165.

[64] *Ibid*, p. 174.

[65] *Ibid*, p. 176.

[66] *Ibid*, p. 191.

[67] Carter Lindberg, *"Property and poverty in the History of the Chruch". Christian Ethics — Property and poverty*, Bela Harmati (ed.,), p. 43.

[68] *Luther's Works*, Vol. 45, p. 189.

[69] *Ibid*, Vol.45, p. 190.

[70] Carter Lindberg, *Beyond Charity: Reformation Initiatives for the Poor, Op.cit*, p. 106.

[71] *Ibid*, p. 135.

[72] *Luther's Works*, Vol. 44, p. 130.

[73] *Ibid*, Vol. 44, p.130.

[74] *Ibid*, Vol.44, p. 189.

[75] Carter Lindberg, *"There shall be No Beggars among Christians"*, p. 331.

[76] *Luther's Works*, Vol.44, pp. 189-190.

[77] *Luther's Works*, Vol.45, pp. 185-186.

[78] *Luther's Works*, Vol. 31, p. 360 &Luther's Works, Vol.14, pp. 114-115.

[79] *Luther's Works*, Vol.13, p.54.

[80] Carter Lindberg, *"There shall be No Beggars among Christians", Op.cit*, p. 331.

[81] Cherian Gudalur, *Gandhi's Concept of Truth and Justice*, p.180.

[82] M. K. Gandhi, *Economic and Industrial life and Relations*, Vol.1, p. 157.

[83] *Young India*, 26.11.1924.

[84] N.K. Bose, *Selections from Gandhi*, p. 75.

[85] R. K. Prabhu & Rao (ed.,), *Op.cit*, p.264.

[86] *Ibid*, p.263.

[87] J.P. Kripalani, *Gandhi : Life and Thought*, p.367.

[88] R. K. Prabhu & Rao (ed.,), *Op.cit*, p.264.

[89] N.K.Bose, *Op.cit*, p. 76.

[90] V.C. Sinha, (ed), *Khadi Gramodyog*, November, 1982.

[91] *Young India*,17. 03. 1927.

[92] N.K.Bose, *Op.cit*, p. 75.

[93] D.G. Tendulkar, *Mahatma*, Vol. VII, p. 389.

[94] M.K. Gandhi, *My Socialism*, p. 60.

[95] *Harijan*, 29. 06.1935.

[96] *Harijan*, 29. 06.1935.

[97] *Harijan*, 01.06.1947.

[98] *Harijan*, 31. 03.1946.

[99] *Harijan*, 24.10.1948

[100] *Harijan*, 29. 06.1935.

[101] *Young India*, 17.06.1926.

[102] Cherian Gudalur, *Op.cit,* p.183.

[103] *Young India*, 30.09.191920.

[104] *Young India*, 17.09.1925.

[105] *Harijan*, 26.07.1942.

[106] *Harijan*, 28.07.1946.

[107] *Young India*, 17.06.1926.

[108] *Harijan*, 22.06. 1935.

[109] *Young India*, 13.11.1924.

[110] D.G.Tendulkar, *Mahatma*, Vol. II, p.297.

Chapter 6

Religious Ideology
of Luther and Gandhi

RELIGIOUS IDEOLOGY OF LUTHER

In Martin Luther's time the religious condition was becoming worse every day. The Popes and their subordinates were very much interested in money rather than religion. The poor people were not able to pay and buy indulgences. For this they were punished by the priests in various ways. In short, the spiritual atmosphere was very poor and the Church was not at all helpful in relating people to God. In this particular climate the Augustinian hermit Luther started to protest and try to bring about a peaceful life among the people with the help of his 95 theses. He nailed the world famous ninety five theses on the north door of the Castle Church in Wittenberg. It was this concern for the people that provoked the sensitive monk to attack the medieval Church and its practices. The theses were terrible blows to the authorities as well as an invitation for correction. Above all, the theses reveal Luther's concern which he especially showed towards the naïve people. The occasion of the ninety five theses was the sale of indulgences by Johann Tetzel in the neighbourhood of Wittenberg for the building of St. Peter's Church in Rome. Pope Leo X had authorized Archbishop Albrecht of Mainz to sell a plenary indulgence in his provinces in Germany.[1]

The proceeds from this indulgence were designated for the construction of the new Basilica in Rome. The proceeds were also being used to pay off debts which Archbishop Albrecht had incurred to the Pope for his elevation to the archbishopric of Mainz and for the Papal permission to hold simultaneously two additional ecclesiastical offices. Archbishop Albrecht, who was heavily indebted to the Papacy for holding three offices, he borrowed a huge amount from the banking house of the Fugger. In return, the Fugger and he were to get half of the proceeds and the other half was to go to the Papal treasury. Albrecht appointed as sub-commissary Johann Tetzel, a Dominican monk who had sold indulgences for the Papacy since 1504. Tetzel and his indulgence preachers gave false assurances to the people in order to collect money from them. They persuaded the common people that the indulgence would grant complete remission of penalties both in this world and in the next to all who made suitable contribution for the building fund. They also told them that there was no sin that cannot be forgiven, including raping the Mother of God.[2] To put it differently, they preached instant salvation.[3] In so doing, they sold the merits of religion in exchange for money.[4] They further induced the recipients that their souls in purgatory would be released from the pains if they bought the indulgences immediately. They also promised the buyers of indulgences that they could choose their own confessor. In other words, the buyers of indulgences could even refuse to go to their own parish priests. As soon as these ideas caught on, the common people became anxious to procure this advantage for their relatives in purgatory. They believed that the souls would escape from purgatory as soon as they placed a contribution in the chest.[5]

They were also convinced that when they bought indulgence letters their salvation was guaranteed.[6] Thus, the Roman Church commercialized religion and paralyzed the ethics of Christianity. It impoverished both religion and ethics.[7] Its indulgence scheme eliminated the love of God and encouraged a self-love piety based on good works. It sold what was free for all and exhorted the people to perform faithless good works instead of accepting God's free gift of grace. He of course had no direct access to hear all these claims of the indulgence preachers since they were not allowed to enter the region of Electoral Saxony. The Elector did not want to lose the income from the indulgences which could be obtained at the All Saints' Chapter in Wittenberg.[8] Consequently, the vendors of indulgence did not enter the region of Electoral Saxony but they came close enough so that Luther's parishioners knew about this indulgence traffic. Only through his parishioners he learnt of it when they produced the indulgence letters at the time of penitence.[9]

Luther was very much irritated when he heard about the impious and irrational preaching of the indulgence preachers. He found that the indulgence scheme devoured both the body and the soul of the common people.[10] It inculcated a wrong state of mind and complacency rather than contrition. It created a false understanding that remission of sins depended on the ability to pay. The venders of indulgence persuaded the common masses even to sell their clothes in order to buy the indulgence letters.[11] All these things pricked the conscience of him because he not only noticed the bad effects of the indulgence system but also comprehended the bad instructions given by the indulgence preachers. This unusual and unprecedented happening hurt him very much. As a pastor, he was responsible for the welfare of his flock and whenever there was any pitfall, he had to safeguard his sheep. So he decided to eradicate the evil of indulgence himself by way of imparting the evangelical accuracy. For he, believed that when people were informed wrongly, they would be open to wrong ideas.[12]

The ninety five theses therefore, were a written document designed to meet the needs of a critical time. It was a treatise displayed openly in order to find a solution to a practical problem which disturbed not only Luther but also the great majority of the people. In other words, the ninety five theses were the outgrowth of the crisis that took place in his heart. Gordon Rupp substantiates this in the following lines: We must set his Ninety-five Theses: no afterthoughts, no external affair of an ecclesiastical scandal, but something much deeper, a crisis of conscience of one Christian man first and then for the whole world.[13] Indeed the crisis in his heart was expressed in the form of the ninety five theses. Being conscious of responsibility, he protested against the nature and power of the indulgences and his protest took the shape of a challenge in the form of the ninety five theses. His theses were the comprehensive output which he exposed in his sermons prior to the appearance of the ninety-five theses. Scott H. Hendrix says that Luther extended his protest through ninety five theses which he had previously confined to lectern and pulpit.[14]

Luther considered some of the prevailing evil religious, political and social practices and felt that they should be purified or replaced by human values. He approached the problem of indulgence with pastoral concern. In other words, pastoral concern was more abundant that anything else. James Atkinson rightly says that his approach was not theological but essentially practical. He saw the matter from the pastoral point of view, considering the effect of such practices on the soul of the ordinary man.[15] Putting somewhat differently, the ninety five theses were his pastoral protest against the exploitation of the poor souls. He did not send the theses to the people but he sent it to the Archbishop of Mainz and to the Church leaders. They were the ones responsible for the grave abuse of indulgences. He, therefore by sending the thesis to such people, wanted to eradicate the misuse of the indulgence system and to save the innocent masses. In this thesis, he employed the phrase 'Christians are to be taught'.[16] This obviously confirms the pastoral concern of Luther because he wished that everything should be sufficiently informed and discussed among the common people (thesis 56) so that there may not be any misunderstanding or pitfalls. Otherwise people may erroneously think and accept what is false as the truth.

It is true that Luther made a major attack against the dominant theological system of the medieval Church.[17] Nonetheless, his principal concern, as mentioned earlier, was not theological but anthropological. Any theology, whether false or true will ultimately affect the people. Even if we say that his concern was theological, his ultimate goal was to protect the people from false theology and superstitious belief. Robert E. McNally ratifies this idea in the following lines: "The ninety-five theses are objective and controlled in spirit. Their principal concern is pastoral: the correction of an abuse which by all standards was a formidable obstacle to the Church's apostolate and to the development of Christian life."[18]

Luther and Sacred Relics

Frederick the Wise of Saxony, who was Luther's prince, had shown much interest in relics. He collected the relics from various places and displayed them to the public. Roland H. Bainton says: "Luther's prince was a man of simple and sincere piety who had devoted a lifetime to making Wittenberg the Rome of Germany as a depository of sacred relics. He had made a journey to all parts of Europe, and diplomatic negotiations were facilitated by an exchange of relics".[19] Knowing pretty well that his prince had reverence for relics, his concern for this parishioner led him to publicly criticize the abuse of the indulgence system and the reverence of relics. To put it in other words, he boldly opposed his own prince's attitude because it steered the people to follow the path of their prince.[20] Carl Arthur Piepkorn rightly substantiates the above view thus: "But it needs to be remembered that in his attack on indulgences the Augustinian Hermit was involving himself not only with the pope and with the primate of Germany but with the prince on whom he depended for personal protection."[21]

Luther's concern for the poor souls also guided him to thwart the Archbishop of Mainz. He wrote an angry treatise in December 1, 1522 when Archbishop Albrecht announced a campaign to sell indulgences. Luther called the sale of indulgences 'idol' and, therefore, his treatises were named "Against the Idol of Halle". In this treatise he advised the Archbishop to stop the sale of indulgences since it robbed simple poor people of money as well as their souls. If the idol (sale of indulgences) was not halted, he gave an ultimatum that he would attack him publicly as he did the Pope.[22] Besides, he advised the Archbishop to refrain from leading the poor people astray and from robbing them. He also cautioned him to present himself as a bishop and not as a wolf.[23]

Luther, indeed, drafted his theses in opposition to the official instruction of the Archbishop which he gave to his indulgence preachers.[24] Hendrix says that he mailed his theses to the Archbishop in order to show how debatable his view on indulgence was.[25] He, thus, directly challenged the authority of the Archbishop and the claims of the indulgence preachers. Again, it is clear that his interest in the common people forced him to go to such an extreme. He was also against the externalization of the notion of punishment because, according to him, it eventually affected the masses. In the middle ages, pilgrimages, which involved the buying of relics and giving reverence to saints, were linked with the indulgences and people were encouraged to do such things to obtain forgiveness of sins and to achieve salvation. In other words, the medieval Church made the salvation very expensive, which consequently affected the ordinary people like peasants and artisans. And this was the reason for his objection to such practices.

Luther and Pope

Luther's interest in the masses did not allow him to exempt the Pope. He raised antipapal slogans against his avarice love of money and unholy attitude. In theses 5-7 he argued about the limitations of the Pope. In these theses he categorically criticized the practice of the Pope in the matters of the forgiveness of sin, and said, Pope is not having the power to forgive sins or having the vested power to withdraw the penalties imposed on the individuals. Penance was a matter between the individual and God and the Pope had no power to remit it. Similarly, in theses 8-29 he questioned the Pope's capability and bluntly denied his immoderate authority. In theses 81-91 he recalled the grave pastoral responsibilities of the Pope. In doing so he criticized the disposition of the Pope towards his sheep. For example, theses 82 asks: Why does not the Pope empty purgatory because of this superlative love and the pressing need of the soul that are there, rather than for the puny reason of raising money to build a church, build the church with his own money rather than the wealth of the legendary Croesus, build the Church with his own money rather than with the money of poor believers? He would do better to sell St. Peter's church and give the money to the poor folk who are fleeced by the hawkers of indulgence. If the Pope knew the exactions of these vendors, he would rather that St. Peter's should lie in ashes than that it should be built up with the skin, flesh and bones of this sheep.[26] He thus raised an anti-papal voice for the sake of the poor souls.

Luther and Indulgence

The indulgence system was evil in Luther's eyes because it did not let God be the gracious, forgiving Father. Again it was not based upon the love of God but the fear of men. He says: "The indulgence sellers as an effort to frighten us in the same manner as men desire to frighten little children by the use of mass".[27] He also said that the indulgences were religiously invalid. If God, he argued, had really wanted these indulgences, why did he not say so in the Holy Scripture. He also declared that the indulgences were ethically unsound and his theses 40-47 were concerned with the disastrous ethical results.[28] In another context he described the indulgence traffic thus in his Leipzig debate with John Eck in 1519, he confidently declared that the indulgences were not a pious fraud, but an infernal, diabolical and anti-Christian fraud, larceny and robbery whereby everybody's money is sucked and enticed away to the place of this unspeakable harm.[29]

Although Luther disapproved of the indulgence system on various grounds,[30] the primary reason was humanitarianism. He denounced the system as it was only a net with which money was taken out of the pockets of the simple-minded[31] and was not concerned with the people but with money.[32] The clerical peddlers took financial advantage of the poverty – stricken peasants and artisans. Feeding on their fear of purgatory, these 'ordained parasites' forced men to purchase indulgences when they were not even able to provide for their own families' needs. He lamented: 'But there are many who have neither bread nor proper clothing and yet, led astray by the din and noise of the preachers of indulgences, rob them and bring about their own poverty in order to increase the wealth of the indulgence sellers".[33] He denounced the system through his theses and, therefore, the ninety-five theses were, to a great extent, his objection against the shameless exploitations.

Ian D. Kingston Siggins aptly says that indulgence traffic and its financial consequences were the primary causes for the emergence of the revolt against Rome.[34] Another reason for his disapproval was that it created a class society of making some people rich and the majority poor.[35] Thomas M Lindsay too confirms this. He says: "A capitalist class gradually arose in Germany. Large profits, altogether apart from trade, could be made by managing, collecting and forwarding the money coming from the universal system of indulgences".[36]

It was true that the indulgence system elevated the financial condition of the authorities in whose domain the indulgences were conferred. For example, the indulgence revenue which Pope Leo X had arranged with Archbishop Albrecht brought 52,286 ducats out of which Albrecht received 26143 and the other half went to the Pope.[37] He was not happy with this system because it created an asperity between the rich and the poor. The rich readily got large indulgences but the poor none, because they had no money to pay for it.[38] He was also very much distressed when the money collected from the people was spent in dishonest ways. He was deeply pained when the shepherds devoured their flock in the name of God. The following quote shows how Luther yelled at the unholy attitude of the authorities: Following studiously after their faithful shepherd, his lambs strayed about in the land with indulgences; wherever there is a parish festival or an annual fair these beggars gather like flies in summer and all preach the same song, 'Give to the new building, that God and the holy lord St. Nicholas may reward you, 'Afterward they go to their beer or wine, also 'for God's sake' and the commissioners are made rich from the indulgences also 'for God's sake'.[39]

All these appalling deeds provoked Luther and he became the voice of the voiceless and argued on their behalf. He debated vehemently that the money and the property which the indulgence sellers fraudulently stole from the people ought to be given back to the people.[40] It is worth mentioning here that Luther was the first pastor who made such an appeal and argued in such a forceful way for the betterment of the masses. In the place of indulgences, Luther preferred the works of men performed with charity and gave the first priority to such deeds.[41] In his theses 41-52 he admonished people to do works of mercy rather than buy indulgences. For the good works, in his opinion, satisfy God as well as one's neighbour whereas the indulgences were useful to neither the buyer nor his neighbour. In thesis 32 Luther put the counterpoint against the indulgence sellers and advised them to love and serve one another by ignoring the indulgences.[42] In thesis 42 Luther insisted that giving alms to the poor and the needy is a better deed than the acquisition of indulgences.[43]

To conclude, Luther's concern for the common people is spread throughout his theses. He wanted to awaken the conscience of the many through his theses and to protect them from all sorts of exploitation. The eagerness of Luther pushed him to criticize and condemn all the persons who were responsible for the oppression of the naïve people irrespective of their status or office. It was obvious that people of all walks of life and especially those belonging to the lower strata of the medieval society welcomed the protest of Luther because he sounded the call to wage war upon the un-questioned abuses existing in the Church. Hans J. Hillerbread says: Abuses under which Germany had for long groaned, a responsive chord vibrated in the hearts of nearly all thoughtful, earnest Germans who were looking for some relief from papal exactions. His ninety five theses were immediately published in the tongue of the common man and swiftly scattered over Germany. Men of all classes welcomed them and praised the Witten Burg. The content of the thesis became the voice and reflect so boldly what was in the heart of every true German.[44] People were of course very much conscientized by his theses and they began to raise their voice against all sorts of illegal acts and exploitation. They began to oppose the evil elements that destroyed their theses. The theses, profoundly changed not only the inner life of the people but also the political and cultural structure of the West.[45]

Luther and the Word of God

Luther was very much involved in advancing the people's status by implementing a new pattern of work that may please and edify them to move further in all levels of life. To bring about religious reformation he worked hard to print the Holy Bible in the vernacular language of the common people. The word of God was not permitted or allowed to the ordinary people and it was considered to be the personal property of the priests and the Pope. Therefore he went in for Bible translation. The translation of the Bible into German is his noblest achievement and the greatest single work. It is both a literary and religious achievement.[46] It is a classic not only of German but of world literature.[47] His eminence is universally recognized because it is the earliest and most successful arrival since the Vulgate and superior both in accuracy and in literary quality. Heinz Bluhm states that the German Bible is the greatest and the most enduring achievement of all the great achievements of Luther.[48] Erasmus observes its uniqueness in the following lines thus: 'Our Lord also illuminated the German language through Doctor Martin so that as long as the world has stood, no human has written or spoken the German language as well as he".[49]

Nietzsche too praised the monumental piece of work.[50] Roland H. Bainton declares that it is an incomparable treasure to the Germans.[51] Indeed Luther's translation of the Bible into German has been regarded by many as the greatest of the contributions to the German people and to Christendom. It is appropriate to mention here that his published portion of his translation of the Old Testament was prior to his publication of the German Bible. And those portions had already been embodied in the editions of the first complete Protestant Bible which appeared in 1529 in Zurich and Worms.[52] His translation of the Bible was by no means the first to appear in German. There had been German translations of the scripture even before him. For example, the fourteen High and Low German Bibles and the German Psalters prevailed. Nonetheless, none of them had the majesty of the diction, the sweep of vocabulary, the native earthiness and the religious profundity of him.[53] And the bridging of the gap between intellectuals and the far wider public did not obtain full development until the age of Luther.[54] But his Bible was very much appreciated and regarded by all due to it plain, simple, unscholastic and unpedantic style and because of this reason it reached all sections of the people in the society. He himself said: "The German Bible (this is not praise for me but the work praises itself) is so good and precious that it is better than all other versions, Greek and Latin and one can find more in it than in all commentaries, for we are removing impediments and difficulties also that other people may read in it without hindrance".[55]

Luther did not like to use the existing translations. They were not based on the original tongue but on the Vulgate. In other words, they were translations of a translation.[56] He, therefore as a professor of sacred letters, followed the original rather than the Vulgate. Translating is not an art that everyone can practise. It requires a right, pious, faithful, diligent, God-fearing, experienced and practical heart.[57] He himself accepted that it was a laborious job. He once said: "We are sweating over the work of putting the Prophets into German. God, how much of it there is, and how hard it is to make this Hebrew writer talk German."[58]

Despite this Luther resolved to take up the job. Heinrich Bornkamm rightly says that it was the love for his German people that pressed the pen into his hand for the great work of translation.[59] He corroborated it when he said. 'I am born for my Germans, whom I want to serve.[60] And about a month later, he involved himself in the great task of translation.[61] With this translation he met the need of the hour. J.A. Faulkner rightly says that Luther did not write his books as a scholar or investigator but to meet some popular emergency.[62] Indeed he aspired to furnish a body of literature to his people in the form of educational and instructive tools. When Marin Bucer of Strasburg urged the Wittenberg theologians to get out into the world and preach, he replied with the pregnant words: 'We do that without books.'[63] In another context, he rejected the claims of common men to devise theologies or to direct religious movements. The scripture, to him, contained the redemptive force. Hence he resolved to bring forth the idiomatic German bible and to put down the heresies. John C. Cooper sees Luther's Bible as an attempt to make the Bible speak to human in their own language.[64] People could understand the gospel truth only when it is supplied in the language of the people. Carter Lindberg too sees the German Bible as a first step toward universal education.[65]

The third reason the idea of his justification. The Bible was the sole weapon of his conflict against a thousand-year-old Papal system. Luther, therefore, wanted to justify his reformatory deeds by producing the scripture in their language. It goes without saying that his Bible afforded the Reformation the possibility of extensive operation since the language of the vernacular penetrated very much into the society and touched almost every home. Ian D. Kingston Siggins aptly says that the German Bible played an all-important role not only in the establishment of Protestant piety but also in the very evolution of modern German.[66] Heinrich Bornkamm says that he opened the portals of the future for the High German dialect by the very act of his translation.[67] Indeed his contribution helped to evolve the modern German language.[68] This in turn created unity among the German people.[69] Luther's genius is interpreted as the 'awakening sun' that shone over the development of modern High German.[70] With his care and his influence he strengthened the young shoot of the common language to such an extent that it gradually grew to a tree overshadowing the whole of Germany.[71] His opening of the Bible to the public is considered as one of the most important phases of national importance.

Luther was a translator but at the same time he was a theologian. As a theologian he was keen as far as doctrinal matters were concerned. With regard to his translation, he was committed not only to the letters but also to the sense of the text.[72] Being convinced by the concept that the just shall live by faith alone and not by works of the law in the light of the Pauline Corpus, he wanted to project this very idea and thus impress his people. His goal, therefore, was not merely translating the words but to evolve a translation with theological significance. During his time the word of God was hidden to the laity and was spoken to them in the mass only by the priests.[73] But he opened the Bible to the common people which was a revolutionary deed. He broke the exclusive control of the elite over the word of God and by doing so, he removed the deprivation of enjoying the word of God by the common people.[74] But at the same time his vernacular Bible helped the preachers to expound the scripture thoroughly and to refute false doctrines.[75] Many of the preachers could not read the original tongues and the Bible since their education was poor. Knowing all these factors, he felt the immediate need of a German Bible and thus there emerged the German Bible.

It is quite natural that if a translation is to reach the people, it must be in the language of the people. Since Luther most definitely made the translation for the common people, he gave utmost care to put it in the language they used in their day-to-day life. To succeed in venture, he observed the existing spoken, written and printed language of his people. Besides he collected German pictures, rhymes and songs to pick up the familiar terms used most frequently by his people. Above all, he listened to the people and learned from them what was to be learned.[76] To him there was no doubt where the living language was to be found. He went to the homes and market places to find out the language of the people. He employed the phraseology of the household and the market place and that was the yardstick by which he measured the language of the Bible.[77] A. G. Dickens says that Luther deliberately used the linguistic forms intelligible to the Germanic people from Austria to the borders of the Low Countries.[78] With regard to the language of the Bible, Luther himself once said: "We must inquire about this of the mother in the home, the children of the street, and the common man in the market place. We must be guided by their language, the way they speak, and do our translating accordingly. That way they will understand it and recognize that we are speaking German to them."[79]

As a most prolific writer, Luther knew how to coin the telling phrase, and the core of the subject which could easily move the common man.[80] Heinrich Bronkamm says whatever stock of raw material Luther received from his adoptive dialect, he gave back after qualifying it for the greatest role in the history of the German language.[81] He translated the Bible into German which consisted of a variety of dialects. However, he did not use the scholar's medium of Latin but the German idiom of his time. He took incredible pains to coin suitable idioms. To accomplish this task, he travelled to different places and gained the familiarity of various dialects. He made repeated trips to the slaughter house and enquired of the butcher the terms used for the sacrificial victims in the book of Leviticus. In order to name the precious stones among the gems of the New Jerusalem, he examined the court jewels of the Elector of Saxony.[82]

For the coins of the Bible he consulted the numismatic collections in Wittenberg. In conclusion, it was the language of the masses that Luther listened to, it was their mouths he watched in order to determine the nature of truly idiomatic German. He consequently made the Bible available to the common people in their own language. He usually made a literal translation of the original text and put forth the freshest and the most suitable synonyms for each word. However, he understood that the task of translation is not that of reproducing in one language words exactly equivalent to the words of another language but of reproducing to his neighbours[83] in vigorous vernacular idiom the meaning of what was originally expressed in a foreign tongue. Along with his translation, he gave the Biblical perspective.[84]

Luther offered a free rendering whenever and wherever it is necessary in order to catch the spirit of the terms of the original tongue and to make the people understand it in the fullest sense. In doing so, he always preferred indigenous words which had local connotation and familiarity. For example, Luther offered 'Liebe Maria' to the literal translation of the Vulgate 'Hail, Mary full of Grace'. For the Germans, according to him, could not conceive the meaning if it was translated literally. He explained that one can easily understand the meaning of the term "a purse full of gold' or 'a keg full of beer'. But no one can understand the term 'a girl full of grace'.[85] He presented a free rendering wherever it was possible just to help the people grasp the actual spirit of the passage. Likewise, he offered the word 'only' (sola) in Romans 3:28. He added this word although it is not found in the original tongue. He included the term just to convey the real sense of the text. Luther said that the word 'only' ought to be inserted there in order to make the translation more clear and vigorous.[86] He identifies the geography of Palestine with the German scene just to give an indigenous description. For example, when he read about the streams he acknowledged it with the medieval location. He transplanted Judea to Saxony and the road from Jericho to Jerusalem to the German Thuringus Forest. Hans J. Hill brand says: "Luther transformed Galilee into Saxony and Jerusalem into Wittenberg. The Personages of the Gospel, their speech, their customs and their environment became those of the sixteenth century. When Jesus spoke to his disciples, he spoke as the man in Wittenberg or Nurnberg would speak".[87]

Above all, Luther's Bible was richly illustrated and there were five hundred woodcuts in various editions.[88] The woodcuts were not the choicest expressions of art, but they did Germanize the Bible. In other words, then illustrations were inserted in order to make the text more intelligible to the masses. For example, in the first edition of the New Testament in September, 1522, the scarlet woman sitting on the seven hills wears the Papal tiara, as also does the great dragon. The beast out of the abyss had a monk's cowl. In the New Testament of 1530 he introduced an annotation explaining that the frogs issuing from the mouth of the dragon were his opponents, Faber, Eck and Emser.[89]

Luther also gave his time and work to the instruction of the young and the uneducated. He wanted to explain to them the Ten Commandments, the Creed, the Lord's Prayer and the Sacraments. Luther, therefore, published literature of edification like the Catechism, apart from his Bible translation. There was no literature of this kind in Germany.[90] The people, especially those who lived in the villages, seemed to have no knowledge whatever of Christian doctrine and many of the pastors were ignorant. He stated that this little book was planned for the instruction of children and the uneducated.[91] Though there was training of pastors and teachers to instruct the people, Luther thought that it was not sufficient to meet the needs of the masses. Similarly he was not at all satisfied with the literature produced by Erasmus and the Bohemian Brethren as they were so scant and crude. Eck, therefore, resolved to produce literature of edification which could meet the needs of the people and the outcome was the Catechism.

J.M. Reu says that next to the translation of the Bible, the small Catechism claims attention to show Luther's influence on the German language. It was the first and the only German reader for many and was therefore committed to memory by all people.[92] He produced two Catechisms in the year 1529 and he himself explained it as the true Bible of the laity. The Large Catechism was for adults with a long section on marriage, scarcely suitable for the young and the Small Catechism was for children. In the Large Catechism the exposition was comparatively full and the tone was polemical while the Small Catechism was devoid of all polemics but contained an inimitable affirmation of faith. He prepared the Catechism not in lofty and subtle words but in brief and simple words so that it could impress the young ones and penetrate deeply into the hearts and be fixed in their memories.[93] Norma Everist states that the Catechisms contributed to an international revival of Christian religious life at all levels of society from the peasant's farm in Germany to the education classes at top levels of English society.[94]

Luther published those Catechisms with quaint woodcuts of episodes from the Bible suitable to each section. For instance, the creedal statement 'believe in God the Father Almighty' was illustrated with a view of creation and the statement in the Lord's Prayer 'Hallowed be thy name' was illustrated by a preaching scene. Similarly he wrote the explanations to the commandments where he said that the ministry of the word was for the youth and the poor multitude.[95] In the medieval period, village congregation members were peasants, and town congregational members were artisans. The worship was conducted in Latin, which was not intelligible to the ordinary folk.[96] He, therefore, revised the liturgy in the vernacular despite strong protests, because the renewal of social life entailed the reform of worship.[97]

The whole service was in German except for the Greek refrain 'Kyrie Eleison'. One of the principal parts of the German order of worship was a plain and good instruction to the youth.[98] The sermon occupied the central and larger place. In other words, the divine service was more of the scriptural than of the instructional. The words sung had a greater effect than the words spoken. Knowing this fact, Luther composed a great number of hymns based on the scripture as an additional tool and inspirational instrument. His hymns served as a powerful instrument for disseminating the teachings of the Reformation. Kysle C.l Sessions says that he wrote hymns ultimately for pastoral purposes, to instruct and train his flock correctly in the evangelical doctrines.[99]

To sum up, Luther's concern for the common people pressed him to create this literature. With this literature he strove to eliminate the existing heretical elements and the abuses imposed by the Roman Church. Luther's writings awakened the masses and they began to resist all sorts of unjust acts. Walter Altman rightly says that his own writings often proved the best springboard, provoking better and more appropriate discussion and leading to creative and challenging insights. His literature also invented a common as well as a modern German language which ultimately aided the nation's unity. Eric W. Gritsch too substantiates this view. He said that Luther's Bible was, above all, the instrument of religious renewal in Germany, changing simple baptized Germans into biblically trained common priests united by a common language.[100]

RELIGIOUS IDEOLOGY OF GANDHI

Mahatma Gandhi had respect for all religions. Gandhi's religion was a national and ethical one. He would not accept any belief which did not appeal to his reason or any injunction which did not commend itself to his conscience. This rational approach towards religion did not prevent Gandhi from paying almost reverence to the scriptures of Hinduism. But he tended to explain and interpret every text to suit his rationality. He looked upon the Ramayana and the Mahabharatha as mere allegories and Rama was just a name for God with him. Gandhi's religion was Hinduism, which, for him, was a religion of humanity, including the best of all religions known to him. For him Hinduism was based on the firm foundation of truth and non-violence. To define his religion fully, he regards truth as God. Like every Hindu, he believed that all religions are branches of one tree and the same tree- the tree of truth.[101]

Gandhi emphasized the equality of religions.[102] Therefore he said "as all religions were rooted in faith in the same God, all were of equal value, while each was specially adapted to its own people.[103] He read the Gita, the Bible, the Koran and the Zend Avestha. Gandhi was profoundly influenced by the world's great religions like Hinduism, Jainism, Buddhism, Islam and Christianity. His thought and action were moulded by this great religion. He was brought up in a religious atmosphere. He belonged to a Vaishnavite Hindu family influenced to some extent by Jainism. His mother was a devout woman. His father often invited the learned of different faiths to discuss religious problems. They would have talks with his father on subjects both religious and mundane. Besides he had Musalman and Parsi friends, who would talk to him about their own faiths and he would listen to them always with respect and often with interest. These many things combined to inculcate in him toleration for all faiths."[104]

Gandhi calls himself a Sanatani Hindu because he believes in the Vedas, Varnashrma Dharma, protection of cows and idol-worship. He considers the Bible as a part of his scriptures. He himself declared that he is not a blessed Hindu. He was always to be a humble and impartial student of religion with great leaning towards Christianity. The New Testament particularly the Sermon on the Mount endeared Jesus to him. For Gandhi the Gita is his Bible and Eternal Mother. Gandhi accepted Christ as a great teacher of humanity. He rejected the belief that Christ was the only begotten son of God. The idea of conversion also was not much appreciated by him. He says, "Hinduism tells everyone to worship God according to his own faith or Dharma, and so it lives at peace with all the religions". Therefore he was much moved by self-discipline and the passion for the poor. To attain the passion he maintained Satya very strictly in his life.[105]

Regarding his attitude towards religion, Gandhi said: "You must watch my life; how I live, eat, sit, talk, and behave in general. The sum total of all these in me is my religion."[106] Essentially, he was a religious and spiritual soul. His passion for religion was immense; so he said: "I could not live a single second without religion"[107] He said, "If I did not feel the presence of God within me, I see so much of misery and disappointment every day that I would be a raving maniac and my destination would be the Hooghli"[108] His aim was to spiritualize politics, economics and society. He believed in the absolute oneness of God and therefore also of humanity. He remarked, "If one gains spiritually, the whole world gains with him, if one man fails, the whole world falls to that extent."[109] His philosophical perception was that "religion is beyond all speech."[110] For him, God [truth] is one and so humanity also is one.[111] For Gandhi, true religion and true morality are inseparably bound with each other. Religion is to morality whatever is to the seed that is sown in the soil.[112] There is no religion higher than truth and righteousness.[113] For him, the basic principles of this morality were truth and non-violence. He found the essence of religion in morality or ethics. For him, "God is truth and love; ethics and morality"[114] God can never be realized by one who is not pure at heart. Identification with God or man is impossible without self-purification or morality. Moral life is necessary for reaching spiritual purification.[115]

Gandhi's religion may be characterized as ethical spiritualism. To him, any religion without a moral foundation ceased to be a religion. He recognized that prayer was the very core of man's life, since it was the most significant part of religion. Prayer was an effective means to bring to the surface the divine element in every human being. Service to human is the worship of God. Gandhi observed: "Man's ultimate aim is the realization of God and all his activities, political, social and religious have to be guided by the ultimate aim of the vision of God. The immediate service of all human beings becomes a necessary part of the endeavour simply because the only way to find God is to see him in his creation and be one with it".[116] Next, the Gita occupies a pre-eminent place. His first acquaintance with the Gita was through Thoreau and Emerson when he was in England. He studied many important commentaries on the Gita and also it was translated from Sanskrit to Gujarati. Hence the 'Gita' became Gandhi's 'infallible guide of conduct' and 'dictionary of daily reference.' Among the

Hindu scriptures, the Iso Upanishad and the Gita have a distinct and definite influence on Gandhi.[117] "...if all the Upanishads and all the other scriptures happened all of a sudden to be reduced to ashes, and if only the first verse in the Iso Upanishad were left intact in the memory of Hindus, Hinduism would live forever."[118]

Gandhi adopted the principles of the Gita and formulated the qualifications essential for a Satyagrahi such as truth, non-violence, non-attachment, renunciation, austerity, celibacy, self-sacrifice, self-control, gentleness, cheerfulness, purity of means and so on. Concepts such as non-possession and equality in the Gita shaped his thought in the formulation of his 'theory of trusteeship'. The ideal of service of the Gita without self and of 'action without attachment' broadened his vision and equipped him with extra ordinary stamina and faith for his public life.[119]

The concept of ahimsa (non-violence) is the bedrock of Jainism and Buddhism. Jainism is the religion of ahimsa par excellence. Buddhism also believes in ahimsa and karuna to all living beings. Gandhi was first introduced to the principles of Islam through the study of the essay "The Hero as Prophet" in Carlyle's "*Hero worship*".[120] He was impressed very much by the voluntary poverty and the humility of the Prophet. His deep interest in and devotion to Christianity made him realize its importance. 'The Sermon on the Mount' especially created an indelible impression on his mind. He said, "I have not been able to see any difference between the Sermon on the Mount and the Bhagavad Gita."[121] He was deeply religious. Without religion life for him was not worth living. He used the term religion in a wider sense. *Religion*, Gandhi believed, "is always subject to a process of evolution and re-interpretation. Progress towards truth, towards God, is possible only because of such evolution."

Gandhi considered all castes and communities equal. He was secular in the sense that he was against coercion to seek conformity to certain creeds. Gandhi's view in a nutshell is, "after long experience, I have come to the conclusion that: [1] All religions are true, [2] all religions have some error in them, [3] all religions almost are dear to me as my own Hinduism.[122] Another remarkable contribution of Gandhi to religious pluralism is the acceptance of a common humanity. Gandhi always appealed to the religion of humanity underlying all religions.[123] He always disbelieved in the illusion of forming one single religion. He believed in the harmony of religions. Once he said, "If the Hindus believe that India should be peopled only by Hindus, they are living in dreamland."[124]

Gandhi believed in ecumenism and unity of religions before ecumenism was born. He suggested, how religions should approach each other. For him "the correct attitude is one of firm adherence to one's own religion coupled with an equal reverence towards all other religions. It is not simply a question of tolerating other faiths, but of believing that all faiths lead to the same goal."[125] He declared, "I do not believe in the exclusive divinity of the Vedas. I believe the Bible, the Koran, and the Zend Avesta to be as much divinely inspired as the Vedas."[126] Again he said, 'Let Hindus become better Hindus, Muslims and Christians better Muslims and Christians'.[127] His religious concept was known as Sarvadharma Samanatha. He was trained to respect all religions and he respected the best in all religions of the world. He has stated that his God was the God in the heart of millions. He was a unique religious man among politicians and a unique politician among religious men. His concept of unity of religions is gaining ground in other parts of the world.[128] He was one of those political thinkers who believed that religion and politics must go hand in hand. For him, the two could not be separated from each other and, for healthy politics, it was essential that religion must be introduced in it.

Luther was able to stand for the true religious faith and he overcame the evil practices prevailing in the Church that kept the poor people away from the Church and the society. He created awareness among the people through literature, teaching and preaching. He was not afraid of any high official of the Church and the state. He stood up for the biblical truth, had a good fight to eradicate the evils that were suppressing the poor people to enjoy the freedom of religion. Gandhi's concept of religion was based on Truth and Ahimsa. For him religion had practical importance in life. He tried to spiritualize all aspects of human life. His concept of religion is wide, tolerant and comprehensive. Religion is the basic need of a human being. It is instinctive and impulsive. It is rooted in our nature and is as old as weeping or smiling. To him, religion is not pride, pedantry or sophistry. He did not mean this or that religion, a denominational faith, or a creed or a sect. His religion is the science of soul and God. He was of the opinion that religion means recognizing the self, recognition of the cosmic life, recognition of reality, seeing God face to face, attaining moksha through service to man.

Endnotes

[1] T. Aruldoss, *"Martin Luther's reformation; An Evaluation"*, p. 17.

[2] *Luther's Works*, Vol. 48, p.46.

[3] Jared Wicks, *"Martin Luther's Treatise on Indulgences"*, pp. 494 - 497.

[4] M. Charles Jacob. *The Story of the Church*, p. 185.

[5] *Luther's Works*, Vol. 31, pp. 26-27.

[6] *Ibid*, Vol.31, p. 28.

[7] William H. Lazareth, *Luther on the Christian Home*, p. 44.

[8] *Luther's Works* , Vol. 48, p. 338.

[9] E. Robert McNally. *"The ninety Five Theses of Martin Luther:* 1517-1967, p. 450.

[10] *Luther's Works* , Vol. 31, p. 2 08.

[11] *Ibid*, Vol.31, p.207.

[12] *Ibid*, Vol. 31, p. 247.

[13] Gordon Rupp. *"Luther's Ninety-five Theses and the Theology of the Cross"*, p. 2.

[14] Scott H. Hendrix, *Luther and the Papacy Luther and the Papacy*, p. 27.

[15] James Atkinson, *Martin Luther and the Birth of Protestantism*, p. 147 and Ian D. Kingston Siggins, *Luther*, p. 9.

[16] *Luther's Works*, Vol. 31, pp. 29-30.

[17] Heinrich bornkamm, *Luther's World of Thought*, p. 37.

[18] E. Robert Mc Nally, *Op.cit*, p. 40.

[19] Roland H. Bainton. *Here I stand*, p. 69.

[20] Carter Lindberg. *"Theory and Practice: Reformation Models of Ministry as Resource for the Present"*, p. 29.

[21] Carl Arthur Piepkorn, *"A Lutheran Theologian looks at the Ninety— five theses in 1967"* p. 523.

[22] *Luther's Works*, Vol.48, p. 340.

[23] *Ibid*, Vol.48, p.341.

[24] Roland H. Boynton, *The Reformation of the sixteenth Century*, p. 38.

[25] Scott H. Hendrix, *Luther and the Papacy*, p. 28.

[26] *Luther's Works*, Vol.31, p. 30.

[27] *Ibid*, Vol.31, p. 116.

[28] *Ibid*, Vol.31, pp. 29-30.

[29] *Luther's Works*, Vol. 32, p. 64.

[30] *Luther's Works*, Vol. 31, p.25, *Luther's Works*, Vol.48, p. 47 and *Luther's Works*, Vol.31, p. 207.

[31] Gustav Freytag, *Martin Luther*, p.17.

[32] Heinrich Bornkamm, *Op.cit*, p. 49.

[33] *Luther's Works*, Vol.31, p. 204.

[34] Ian D. Kingston Siggins, *Op.cit*, 9.

[35] *Luther's Works*, Vol. 45, p. 285.

[36] Thomas M. Lindsay, *A History of Reformation*, p. 83.

[37] E. Robert McNally, *Op.cit*, p. 448.

[38] Thomas M. Lindsay, *Op.cit*, p. 97.

[39] *Luther's Works*, Vol.45, p. 285.

[40] Kurt Aland, ed., *Martin Luther's 95 theses*, p. 35.

[41] *Luther's Works*, Vol. 31 p.199.

[42] *Ibid*, Vol. 31, p. 180-181.

[43] E. Robert Mc Nally, *Op.cit*, p. 257.

[44] Hans J. Hillerbrand, *Christendom Divided – The protestant Reformation*, p. 7.

[45] Heinrich Bornkamm, *Op.cit* p. 53.

[46] Heinz Bluhm, *Martin Luther: Creative Translator*, p. 7.

[47] *Ibid*, p. 7.

[48] Heinz Bulhm, *"Luther's German Bible"*. Seven Headed Luther, p.148.

[49] E. G. Schwiebert, *Luther and His Times*, p. 527.

[50] Heinz Bluhm, *Martin Luther: Creative Translator*, p. 178.

[51] Roland H. Bainton, *Op.cit*, p. 326.

[52] *Luther's Works* , Vol. 35, p.229.

[53] Roland H. Bainton, *Op.cit*, p. 327.

[54] A.G. Dickens, *Reformation and Society in 16th Century Europe*, p. 85.

[55] *Luther's Works*, Vol.54, p. 408.

[56] Heinz Bluhm, *Martin Luther: Creative Translator*, p. 179.

[57] *Luther's Works* , Vol.35, p. 194.

[58] *Luther's Works*, Vol.37. p. 229.

[59] Heinrich Bronkamm, *Op.cit*, p. 273.

[60] *Luther's Works*, Vol. 48, p. 320.

[61] *Luther's Works*, Vol. 38, p. 320.

[62] J.A. Faulkner, *"Luther and Truth-Telling"*,p. 350.

[63] A.G. Dickens, *Op.cit*, p. 86.

[64] John C. Cooper, *"Some Radical Elements in Luther's Theology"*,p. 200.

[65] Carter Lindberg, *"Theory and practice: Reformation models of Ministry as Resource for the present"*, p. 30.

[66] Ian D. Kniingston Siggins, *Op.cit*, p. 26.

[67] Heinrich Bornkamm, *Op.cit*, p. 283.

[68] Hans J. Hillerbrand, *Op.cit*, p. 31.

[69] Ulrich Michael Kremer, *"Martin Luther in the Perspective of Historiography"*, p. 24.

[70] J.M. Rev. *Luther Research_*, p. 81.

[71] *Ibid*, p. 82.

[72] Walter Altmann, *Luther and Liberation*, p. 50.

[73] *Luther's Works*, Vol. 35, p. 90.

[74] Carter Lindberg, *Op.cit*, p. 30.

[75] R. Pascal, *The Social Basis of the Reformation*, p. 212.

[76] J.M. Rev. *Op.cit*, p. 80.

[77] John C. Cooper, *"Some Radical Elements in Luther's Theology"*, p. 200.

[78] A.G. Dickens, *The German nation and Martin Luther*, London, p. 107.

[79] *Luther's Works*, Vol.35, p. 189.

[80] A.G. Dickens, *The German nation and Martin Luther*, p. 85.

[81] *Ibid*, 86.

[82] Heinrich Bornkamm, *Reformation and Society in 16th Century Europe*, p. 283.

[83] Roland H. Bainton, *The Reformation of the Sixteenth Century*, p. 62.

[84] Karl Holl, *The Cultural Significance of the Reformation*, p. 139.

[85] *Luther's Work*, Vol.35, pp. 190 -191.

[86] *Ibid*, Vol.35, pp.188-189.

[87] Hans J. Hilllerbrand,_Christendom Divided – The protestant Reformation, p.31.

[88] *Luther's Works*, Vol. 48, p. 201.

[89] Roland H. Bainton, *Here I Stand*, p. 320.

[90] Karl holl, *The Cultural Significance of the Reformation*, p. 150.

[91] J. N. Lenker, *trans.*, *Luther's Large Catechism*, p. 6.

[92] J.M. Rev. *Op.cit*, p. 86.

[93] J.N. Lenker, *Luther's Large Catechism*, p.9.

[94] Norma Everist, "Luther on Education: Implications for Today", *Currents in Theology and Mission*, Vol.xii,1985, p.83.

[95] J.N. Lenker, *Op.cit*, p. 27.

[96] *Luther's Works*, Vol. 35, p. 90.

[97] A. Paul Russel., *Lay Theology in the Reformation*, London, p. 48.

[98] J.M . Rev. *Op.cit*, p. 91.

[99] Kyle C. Sessions, " *The source of Luther's Hymns and the Spread of the Reformation*", p. 206.

[100] Eric W. Gritsch, *Martin Luther – God's Court Juster*, p. 46.

[101] D.s. Sharma, *Hinduism Through the Ages*, p. 193.

[102] Nirmal Minz, *Mahatma Gandhi and Hindu-Christian Dialogue*, p. 23.

[103] Mahatma Gandhi, *Fellowship of Faith and Unity of Religions*, (ed.,) Abdul Majid Khan, p. 20.

[104] M.K. Gandhi, *The Story of My Experiments with Truth*, p.449.

[105] M.K. Gandhi, *All Religions are True*, p. 64.

[106] *Harijan*, 22.09.1946.

[107] R. K. Prabhu & H.R.Rao, *The Mind of Mahatma Gandhi*, p.140.

[108] *Ibid*, p. 24.

[109] *Young India*, 04.12.1924.

[110] Mahatma Gandhi, *Fellowship of Faith and Unity of Religions*, p.17.

[111] Nirmal Minz, *Op.cit*, p. 1.

[112] *Harijan*, 26.07.1942.

[113] *Harijan*,01.07.1939.

[114] *Young India*,0.03.1925.

[115] R. K. Prabhu & H.R.Rao, *Op.cit*, p.615.

[116] *Harijan*, 29. 08.1936.

[117] M.K.Gandhi, *The Gospel of Renunciation*, p.4.

[118] *Ibid*.

[119] B.R. Nanda, *Mahatma Gandhi: a Biography*, p.82.

[120] M.K. Gandhi, *My Experiments with Truth*,p.51.

[121] *Ibid*.

[122] Nirmal Minz, *Op.cit*, p. 12.

[123] *Ibid*, p. 50.

[124] *Ibid*, p.1.

[125] D.s. Sharma, *Op.cit*, pp. 193-194.

[126] *Young India*, 06. 12. 1928.

[127] Mahatma Gandhi, *Fellowship of Faith and Unity of Religions*, p. 20.

[128] Cherian Gudalur, *Gandhi's Concept of Truth and Justice*, p. 181.

Chapter 7

Educational Ideology
of Luther and Gandhi

EDUCATIONAL IDEOLOGY OF LUTHER

Martin Luther was not only a great reformer but also a great educator. He was not only a master preacher but also a master teacher. He is said to have written more about education than any other reformer of the sixteenth century.[1] As a great educator and Professor of Theology in Wittenberg University, he was deeply concerned for the education of the children and the youth especially the destitute and the neglected ones. Norma Everist says that Luther made education a function of the Church.[2] Luther had a consistently high regard for children and youth as well. He once commented that youth is the Church's nursery.[3] He also maintained that any social change should begin from the education of children. He thus gave vital importance to education and the preservation of youth for public service both in the Church and the community life. He imparted this idea through his writings, sermons and Table talks. In one of his Table talks he said: I wish nobody would be chosen preacher unless he had first kept in school. Now all young fellows want to become as preachers and flee from school work. But if a young man is kept in school for about one to ten years, he can leave with a good conscience, for it involves much work and is held in low esteem.[4] Likewise, he insisted on the establishment of schools both for boys and girls in every town in order to get well educated and well trained youth to maintain the temporal and the household activities.[5]

Martin Luther also interlinked the education of youth and the prosperity of the Church. He said that the youth are the seed and source of the Church and when the schools prosper, the Church remains righteous and her doctrine pure.[6] He also strongly emphasized on the education of young people in the biblical language so that they might cut through the Catholic maze of commentaries, glossaries, decrials and cannon law. He further maintained that if languages are neglected there may not be people to read the original tongues of the Bible as well as the spirit of its meanings. As a proof and warning, he mentioned the existing universities and monasteries in which men were not only unlearned but also corrupted the languages out of their ignorance.[7] He also felt sad about the deplorable situation of Germany. Although there were good tales and sayings there was no one to impart those things to the common people simply because of ignorance and incapability. But the Romans, for example, had taught their young ones and made them well versed in Latin, Greek and all the liberal arts which ultimately helped them to be capable for every position.[8] Consequently they wrote down all their things so accurately and diligently.[9] Martin Luther was supportive of women education. He encouraged women to come out from celibacy life, to get educated and enter into family life.

While speaking about the significance of the languages, Luther vehemently condemned the Germans who showed much interest in foreign wares such as wine, grain, wool, flax and stone rather than the languages and the arts. He argued that the languages cannot harm us but are actually a greater ornament, profit, glory and benefit both for the understanding of scripture and the conduct of temporal government. But the foreign wares are neither necessary nor useful.[10] Luther also objected to the idea of education at home because, to him it was insufficient. Personal experience was not enough to introduce one to life. Further one needs considerable time to have such experience. On the contrary, education under the guidance of a schoolmaster or school mistress would help the young learn many things.[11] Nonetheless, Luther advocated that formal education need not replace the practical training at home but rather both can be linked and related to each other.[12]

Concern for students

Luther was a student oriented professor. His academic role and his ideas inspired many students. He set a personal example by way of conscientious preparation, lively teaching and humane treatment. As a member of a theological faculty, he showed interest in students even after their graduation. When the students finally received their degrees, he often personally arranged the festive dinner. He continued to correspond with them and even intervened with the authorities concerned on their behalf. For instance, Luther urged the congregation in Zwickau to raise the salary and cancel the debts of a pastor who had six children. Luther warned them that they might not get a pastor if they failed to do so.[13] Besides, his deep concern for his students went well beyond the intellectual sphere and included their social and financial well-being as well. For instance, he wrote 4211 letters and nearly half of them dealt with the physical and social well-being of the students.[14] Lewis W. Spitz says that Luther had written these letters over the course of thirty years.[15] This clearly attests to his astonishing preoccupation with the problem of these students.

Most of his students were poor and some of them were former priests and monks who came to the university with nothing. Luther showed keen interest in these students, because, according to him, they usually proved to be the best students rather than the rich who spent lavishly on unnecessary things instead of learning. Luther most often tried to get financial aid for poor students. He approached the city councils and requested them to support the needy students. Lewis W. Spitz says that Luther even knelt as a suppliant at royal thrones in order to get help for the students.[16] In 1532 he wrote a severe letter to the council of Torgau saying that he would even prefer to do manual work if they fail to assist the poor students to continue their education.[17]

Luther even influenced his friends to plead for the needy ones. For instance, he sent an appeal to the Elector of Saxony through his friend George Spalatin who was the then Secretary of Elector Frederic the Wise. He requested him to help the poverty-stricken students.

During the early middle ages the principal means of obtaining education was the monastic schools staffed by monks and nuns and supported by the endowments of the religions communities. But these schools were poorly maintained and there was a shortage of teachers and the teachers were poorly trained. The curricula too were inadequate.[18] When monks and nuns went over to the evangelical doctrine due to the Reformation movement, the secular authorities confiscated the properties and endowments of the abandoned monasteries and cloisters which eventually paved the way for the fall of the Church-dominated schools. But, to Luther, the reason for the fall was the un-Christian manner in which the educational centers sought temporal welfare and were devoted to men's bellies.[19]

Consequently education was generally held in contempt and derided by the majority of the masses. This negative attitude was further fostered by the rise of materialism which went hand-in-hand with the rapid expansion of the trade and commerce.[20] The citizens of big towns and imperial cities had been primarily concerned with the emerging commercial activities which ultimately created an anti-education attitude among them. The parents did not send their children to the schools because they did not see any value in learning as it was of obviously and directly related to the world of the medieval period and the practice of commerce. The parents as well as their children wanted to spend their time in earning rather than learning. Walter Altman aptly substantiates that many parents did not want to send their children to school because they needed the income which the children could provide by working.[21]

Martin Luther, in his treatise, "To the Councilmen of All Cities in Germany that They Establish and Maintain Christian School", saw five causes for the neglect of children. In the first place, many parents were indifferent to their children's education because they lacked the goodness and decency to do it although their children had the ability. Luther criticized them and referred to them as ostriches (Job 39: 14-16) which lay their eggs and do no more. Likewise the parents, according to Luther, brought the children into the world and did nothing more for them.[22] In the second place, the great majority of parents confined their care to 'food and the stomach' because they themselves were unskilled and uneducated. They did not know how children should be brought up for they themselves had learned nothing except to care for their bellies.[23] In the third place, honest parents who desired to do so had found neither time nor the opportunity for it. Moreover, they could not afford to engage a private tutor due to their poverty.[24] In the fourth place, many parents died leaving their children orphans who were inadequately cared for by their foster parents.[25] In the final place the parents who had no children of their own showed little interest in the education and training of others' children.[26]

The reformation too had a disastrous effect on the Church-dominated schools. The reformers contended that many of the current doctrines and practices of the Church were erroneous and dangerous to salvation. Luther attacked the existing schools in the harshest terms. He referred to the monastic and cathedral schools as 'devil's training centres' and stigmatized their text books as 'asses' dung.[27] Karlstadt and Muntzer were also opposed to learning of any kind and declared it as sinful and devilish.[28] They also argued why one should study Latin, Greek and Hebrew when Luther himself urged the use of the vernacular and published a German translation of the New Testament.[29]

All these presentations reduced the enrolment in the educational centers. Those who took these statements seriously refused to send their children to schools because, according to them, false doctrines were inculcated in the schools.[30] Others went even further holding that God would speak directly to the human heart and, therefore, no form of education is required for the ministerial office. They held that the word prompted by the Holy Spirit was sufficient and there was no need either for academic degrees or formal education which were offensive to God.[31] In general, the spirit of the age was so adverse to formal education and there was a derisive saying 'the learned are daft' which was widespread throughout Germany.[32] Luther too endorsed this fact in the following lines. He lamented as follows: "We are today experiencing in all the German lands how schools are everywhere being left to go to wreck and ruin. The Universities are growing weak, and monasteries are declining"[33] On another occasion he said: "Today schools are not what they once were; a hell and purgatory in which we were tormented with casualibus and temporalibus and yet learned less than nothing despite all the flogging, trembling, anguish and misery".[34]

It was under this situation and anti-education attitude that Luther issued his appeal to the civil authorities and the citizens of Germany about the importance of education. His treatise, 'To the Councilmen of All Cities in Germany that They Establish and Maintain Christian Schools' was published in the year 1524. In it he offered the authorities practical advice to establish schools and also replied to current popular arguments against schooling. In 1530 he published a sermon on keeping children in school in which he explained the use of the schools thus established. These two treatises give a clear conception of Luther's idea on education. Luther's love and passion for the people made him speak in favour of their education. Education, in his view, must be everybody's property and should produce leaders both for the Church and society. The school must be the next thing to the Church, for it is the place where young pastors and preachers are trained and out of which they are drawn to be put in the place of those who die.[35] So he took decisive steps to reform the existing educational system and wanted to broaden the scope. He made education universal and compulsory for all citizens irrespective of sex. He made a breakthrough in the educational system. No longer was education merely for boys but he consistently spoke in favour of education of girls. Furthermore, education was no longer merely for the nobility but it was opened even to the poor. He sought the help of parents, preachers and civil authorities to carry out his educational reforms. He advised them not to treat the matter lightly as it was grave and important. He asked them to give vital concern and priority for the sake of the poor and neglected youth.[36]

Martin Luther exhorted parents to send their children to school. He told them that children were the gift of God and, therefore, they were not entirely our own. God has given them the ability and the talent to study and to learn. So he exhorted the parents to be alert to their children's education and not to seek only their bellies and temporal livelihood.[37] He further questioned them, "where shall we get pastors to administer God's word and sacraments if we fail to send children to school?"[38] When the parents did not like to send their children to school simply because of the income which the children brought by their working, Luther persuaded them with the policy of work and study. Applying this principle, the children could attend the school for one or two hours during the day and spend the remainder of the time either working at home or learning a trade. In this way Luther expected the study and the work to go hand-in-hand while the boys and girls were young and able to do both.[39]

When the parents refused to send their children to school for the reason that their neighbour could send their children, Luther charged them that their neighbour might say the same answer. He further warned them that the spiritual office was decreasing simply because of their fault and negligence. But at the same time Luther encouraged them to produce good pastors, preachers and schoolmasters and schoolmistresses and felt happy for that.[40] When the parents raised doubts about whether their children could become pastors or preachers if they went to school, Luther reassured them and issued them with the statistics of the parishes which required pastors.[41] Luther even blamed the parents when they lacked the earnest desire to train their children but spent so much time in teaching them card-playing, ball playing, racing, tussling, singing and dancing.[42] He advised them to spend their money as well as their time for the education of their children. He even went a step further and asked them to spend their money on education which they earlier spent on superfluous things such as indulgences, relics and pilgrimages. With these exhortations Luther persuaded the parents to send their children to school and to sustain the school.[43]

To sum up, Luther was the most important inspiration in terms of pursuing education and he can be rightly called the father of modern education. Germany has become the land of universities because of his sincere and constant effort. He not only achieved intellectual liberty through his educational policies but also through the school-masters in the cottages. He was the father of the principle 'work and play'. Above all he opened the gates of education to the poor, neglected and hopeless masses.

Admonition to Civil Authorities

The common man and the preachers did not respond and did nothing for the education of the youth or anticipate reforms in the sphere of education. The princes and lords were burdened with the functions in cellar, kitchen and bedroom and did not show any interest in the well – being of the youth. Luther, therefore, approached the councilmen and requested them to establish schools because they had better authority and occasion to carry out such reforms. The property, honor and life of the whole city was committed to their faithful keeping. J.M. Rew declares that it was the most thrilling appeal that was ever made in the interest of higher education and training of youth.[44] Walter Altmann too ascertains that the educational reform is a political task and, therefore, it cannot be done by the ordinary citizens. The princes and the lords too were unable to do it because they had interests and concerns on another level. So Luther finally requested the municipal council which was the local political forum to take up the reformatory task.[45]

Luther kindled the spirit of the civil authorities and persuaded them to establish the schools in order to preserve the spiritual and the temporal estates. It would be a good thing if monasteries and religious foundations were kept for the purpose of teaching young people God's word, the scriptures, Christian morals, so that they might train and prepare fine, capable men to become bishops, pastors and other servants of the Church, as well as competent, learned people for civil government and fine, respectable, learned women capable of keeping house and caring children in a Christian way.[46] Luther believed that these rulers had the right to force their subjects to keep their children in school as they forced them to take up arms for their country.[47] Luther placed before them three strong appeals in terms of the education of children and youth. William H. Lazareth says that the climax of Luther's appeal to the councilmen is a stirring challenge to their preparation of a whole new generation of socially minded young men to establish a better society.[48]

Educational Ideology of Gandhi

In 1937, a National Conference on Education was held at Wardha which gave birth to Basic Education or the Wardha Scheme of Education. By the period 1946-1947, the proportion of educated Adi Dravidars moved upto 0.9%. The teaching of Gandhi against the practice of untouchability in Indian social life brought about a new thinking among the people. As a result of this, intensive efforts were taken by the Congress in implementing Gandhi's plan. This gave moral courage to the Adi Dravidian community to send their children to schools and colleges without any fear. Inspired by the teaching of Gandhi, the educated women of the province condemned the practice of untouchability and worked for the abolition of the evil through their organization. They carried on a vigorous propaganda and fought for equality in institutions. Education is always an infinite enquiry into the world of human consciousness. It is an enquiry that calls forth earnestness of endeavour and purpose.[49]

For Gandhi, education was something more. He was one of those great Indians who systematically applied their minds to the complex problems of Indian education. Besides being a political philosopher and social reformer, he was also a great educationist in his own right. He firmly believed that Indian education was unequal to the task of social change and development. He made many observations on many facets of education. The 'be all and end all' of all ideas of Gandhi on education can be covered in two words, namely, "Basic Education". It is also known as Nai Talim or Wardha Scheme of Education. The idea of Basic Education was conceived and put to test in 1937. It is work-oriented. It gives importance to three Rs i.e., Reading, Writing and Arithmetic, as well as three H s i.e., Hand, Head and Heart. Gandhi's ideas of basic education were comprehensive enough because he looked upon education as an instrument of socio-economic progress, material advancement, political evolution and moral development for individuals in society. To Gandhi "formal literacy did not mean real education. He argued that wholesome education involved the development of the mind and the body.[50] The development of the mind depended upon thorough knowledge of fundamental truths for which a strong conscience was the basic requirement. As for the physical aspect, Gandhi emphasised manual or physical work and also stressed the importance of regular physical exercise in the maintenance of the health of individuals. To Gandhi, therefore, Education means "an all-round drawing out of the best in child and man-body, mind and spirit. Literacy is not the end of education or even the beginning. It is only one of the means whereby men and women can be educated. Literacy in itself is no education".[51]

Gandhi's concept of basic education stressed the four-fold development in human personality, namely, body, mind, heart and spirit. True education stimulates the spiritual, intellectual and physical faculties of the individual. He always emphasized that the goal of education was not merely to produce good individuals, but to turn out individuals who understood their social responsibilities as integral elements of the society in which they lived. Any system of education that ignored these vital aspects was incomplete, ineffective and incapable of creating the conditions of a good society. As a revolutionary in the sphere of education, Gandhi wanted to change the whole system of mechanical, dull and drab education which was the root cause of moral degradation and spiritual bankruptcy. The child must be given a new spirit in utilizing his power of innovation, actualizing his spirit of enquiry and creating with his own unique power of imagination. Gandhi explains: "Our education has to be revolutionaries. The brain should be educated through the hand. If I were a poet, I could write poetry on the possibilities of the five fingers. Mere book knowledge does not interest the child, so as to hold his attention fully. The brain gets weary of mere words, and the child's mind begins to wander.

They are not taught to make the right choice and so their education often proves their ruin".[52]

Gandhi believed that discipline was an important aspect of a sound system of education. Education without discipline was like a boat without a rudder. Discipline is a quality which comes from within one's self, leading to the regulation of one's intellectual, moral and social behaviour. To him, the goals of education included character building, through development of such values as courage in all circumstances, strength and force of personality, the virtue of compassion, magnanimity and fair mindedness and the ability to give all that one has while working towards a noble objective. Gandhi remarked: "I regarded character building as the proper foundation for their education and, if the foundation was firmly laid, I was sure that the children could learn all the other things themselves or with the assistance of friends".[53] Without the qualities of firmness, truthfulness, patience etc., education degenerated like a fully blossomed flower without any fragrance. In fact, Gandhi always stressed the viewpoint that true education is a life - long process. The idea is to stress such values as spirit of co-operation, tolerance, public spirit and a sense of responsibility.

To Gandhi, pre-basic education is from three and half years to six years. The children will be taught music, dance, drama and picture seeing and storytelling. For him, basic education is from seven years to fourteen years and free and compulsory education for both boys and girls. It is self-supporting education, education for life, through life and throughout life and Environment oriented education. Education through mother tongue should be compulsory. It should cover five Hs-Head, Heart, Hand, Health and Habits. Teachers should be good models. There should be a good relationship between teachers and students. The remuneration of the teachers should be met by the school parents and teachers cooperation should be maintained.[54]

For him, post-basic education is from 15 to 17 or 18 years. It is not compulsory. It is only for the interested students. Gandhi established a deemed university, namely Gujarat Vidyapith at Ahmedabad to promote research. To Gandhi, moreover, the origin of basic education in India was closely allied to the Indian villages where the spirit of self-activity, self-service, self-knowledge and self-discipline should have taught a learn-by-means-of-work pattern of education.[55]

Gandhi was a firm believer in the principle of free and compulsory primary education for India and the importance of teaching children a useful vocation and utilizing it as a means for cultivating their mental, physical and spiritual faculties.[56] Gandhi's theory of education was firmly rooted in some of the highest values which constituted the basic philosophy of his life. The moral values of truth and non-violence were the main concerns throughout his life. He believed that truth could be realized only through truth and non-violence.[57] Gandhi held that education should be imparted through crafts like gardening, weaving, spinning, carpentry etc. The realistic scheme of education must be closely integrated with the physical and social environment of the student.

That music as a part of education was neglected in the education of children deeply pained Gandhi. Psychologically the introduction of music side by side with the learning of the basic crafts brought forth a harmony of aesthetic consciousness in the mind of the learner. It also added to the learner's power to have an inner vision of perfection in every work. Gandhi therefore emphasized creating an ideal atmosphere of teaching and learning through music.[58] In Gandhi's scheme of basic education, vocational training or work experience was of the utmost importance. Education was clearly linked with the socio-economic development of the nation. The Kothari Commission also rightly emphasized work experience in education. The Committee recommended that work experience should be introduced as an integral part of the all-India educational system. It defined work experience as participation in productive work in school, in home, in workshop, in farm, in factory or in any other productive situation.[59]

Gandhi's concept of basic education involved the making of education self-supporting. He believed that the student must be trained to become an earning unit after the completion of his studies.

His idea was to make education need-based so that the problem of unemployment could be eradicated at the earliest opportunity. He called upon the state to make use of goods produced by students by providing marketing facilities as and when necessary. Real education to Gandhi meant economic self-sufficiency.[60] His ideas of basic education mainly aimed at the all-round development of human personality. He did not neglect the bread and butter aspects of education. For him the basic education leads to the development of the mind, body and soul. The ordinary system of education cared only for the mind. Nai Talim or Basic Education was not confined to teaching a little spinning. However indispensable these were, they were valueless, unless they promoted the harmonious development referred to.[61]

Basic education or Nai Talim was based on the fundamental principle of "learning by doing". Gandhi was a doer more than a thinker and, therefore, his concept of basic education could be classified as an activity method or practical method. It also insisted on an intimate interaction between the teacher and the student. Values such as co-operation, discipline, sacrifice, integrity, fearlessness etc., were part of such teacher-student relationship.[62] Gandhi always emphasized freedom of the individual and he relied heavily on private initiative for reform and progress in Indian education. The entire body of Gandhian ideas on basic education rested on conformity with certain ethical standards to which he attached the highest importance. It helped the individual to lead a pure personal life. Being concerned with moral issues throughout his life, he laid great stress on religious education.[63] Moral and spiritual development was one of the fundamental aspects of basic education. He saw that spiritual education that may infiltrate in the human heart and may lead to do good for the people of the nation.[64] To purify the body was the primary component of purifying the mind.

Gandhi strongly recommended prayer and reading or recitation of holy scriptures, the Gita for Hindus, Quran for the Muslims and the Bible for the Christian students. Though he argued that prayer was the food of the soul, he felt that spiritual reading was concomitant with the development of a sound character. While explaining the goal of education, Gandhi stated this point of moral education for character building very clearly, "I would try to develop courage, strength, virtue, the ability to forget oneself in working towards great aims. This is more important than literacy".[65]

Even today in India many adults are illiterates. Gandhi worried about adult illiteracy. By adult education, Gandhi meant opening the minds of adults. For him, adult education was true political education. In adult education, we should teach population education, peace education, health and sanitation education and environmental education.[66] To Gandhi, education on health and sanitation was very important to the people. The villagers should be taught how to look after their health and how to keep their surroundings clean. Health is the basis of life.[67] Education, to be true, must always be wide and free in approach. Even sex education, as Gandhi categorically stated, was not at all harmful to pupils studying in schools. Today's education awaits freedom of mind and outlook to dispel the darkness of ignorance related to sex education through earnest endeavour.

Gandhi's ideas on basic education not only prescribed new methods and techniques of education but also a new way of life. Economic advancement, physical improvement, socio-cultural progresses are possible only through reliance on the educational ideas of Gandhi. Side by side with moral education, Gandhi emphasized spiritual education in order to be true to humanity. But it required training in self-realization through self-discipline and self-activity in addition to intellectual training imparted in educational institutions. "Of course, I believed that every student should be acquainted with the elements of his own religion".[68] His educational ideology highlights self-control, one of the essential virtues to be attained through moral and spiritual education. It had a definite contribution towards the fullness of human.

Luther pleaded to devote more time to the education of the poor and the neglected youth. His educational ideology was for the poor. Education and caring for the neighbour may bring a society where we cannot find discrimination among the people. Equality and solidarity may prevail in both the church and the society. Gandhi's whole philosophy of education was based on the principle of Swaraj of human character and personality. He explained the ultimate aim of education very characteristically in the light of service to God and human. Human's ultimate aim is the realization of God, and all his activities, social, political, economic, religious and educational, have to be guided by the ultimate aim of the vision of God. The immediate service of all human beings becomes a necessary part of the endeavor, simply because the only way to find God is to see him in their creation and be one with it. This can only be done by service.

Endnotes

[1] Andrew K.H. Hsiao, *"An Outline of Luther's Concept of Theological Education as It Applies to Asian churches, p. 27.*

[2] Norma Everist, *"Luther on Education : Implication for Today"*. Currents in Theology and Missions, p. 76.

[3] *Luther's Works*, Vol. 54, p. 452.

[4] *Ibid*, Vol.54, p. 403.

[5] *Luther's Works*, Vol. 45, p. 368.

[6] Andrew K.H. Hsiao, *Op.cit*, p. 28.

[7] *Luther's Works*, Vol. 45, p. 360.

[8] *Ibid*, Vol. 45, p. 356.

[9] *Ibid*, Vol. 45, p. 377.

[10] *Ibid*, Vol. 45, p. 358.

[11] *Ibid*, Vol. 45, pp.368-369.

[12] *Ibid*, Vol. 45, p.378.

[13] Lewis. W . Spitz, *"Luther's social concern for students"*, p. 264.

[14] *Ibid*, p. 249.

[15] *Ibid*, p.251.

[16] *Ibid*, p.253.

[17] *Ibid*, p. 253.

[18] Gerta scharffenorth, *Becoming Friends in Christ* , p. 59.

[19] *Luther's Works* , Vol. 45, p. 341.

[20] *Luther's Works* , (On the Evils of Trade and Commerce), Vol. 45, pp.231-310.

[21] Walter Altmann, *"Interpreting the Doctrine of the Two Kingdoms: God's Kingship in the Church and in Politics"*, p. 99.

[22] *Luther's Works*, Vol. 45, p.354.

[23] *Ibid,* Vol.45, p. 355.

[24] *Ibid.*

[25] *Ibid.*

[26] *Ibid.*

[27] *Ibid,* Vol. 45, p.342.

[28] *Ibid,* Vol. 45, p. 343.

[29] *Ibid.*

[30] *Ibid,* Vol. 45, p. 342.

[31] *Luther's Works,* Vol.47, p. 209.

[32] *Ibid.*

[33] *Luther's Wor ,* Vol. 45, p. 348.

[34] *Ibid,* Vol.45, p. 369.

[35] *Luther's Works,* Vol. 41, p. 176.

[36] *Luther's Works ,* Vol. 45, p. 350.

[37] *Luther's Works,* Vol. 46, p.229.

[38] *Luther's Works,* Vol. 45, p. 371.

[39] *Ibid,* Vol. 45, p.370.

[40] *Luther's Works,* Vol. 46 pp. 222-223.

[41] Walter Altmann, *Op.cit,* p. 98.

[42] *Luther's Works,* Vol. 45, p.369.

[43] *Luther's Works,* Vol. 54, p. 452.

[44] J.M . Rev. *Op.cit,* p. 90.

[45] Walter Altmann, *Op.cit,* p. 97.

[46] *Luther's Works,* Vol. 37, p.364.

[47] *Luther's Works,* Vol. 46, pp. 256-257.

[48] William H. Lazareth, *Luther on the Chrisitian home,* p. 157.

[49] Cherian Gudalur, *Gandhi's Concept of Truth and Justice,* p.182.

[50] *Harijan,*09.10.1937.

[51] *Harijan,*31.07.1937

[52] D.G. Tendulkar, *Mahatma,* Vol.V, p. 43.

[53] M. K. Gandhi, *An Autobiography,* p. 246.

[54] Humayan Kabir, *Education in New India,* p.23.

[55] D.G. Tendulkar, *Mahatma,* Vol.VIII, p.166.

[56] *Harijan,*09.10.1937.

[57] *Harijan,*30.05.1936.

[58] *Harijan,* 11.09.1937.

[59] *Report of the Educational Commission* 1946-1966 (Kothari Commission), p.7.

[60] *Harijan*, 18. 09.1937.

[61] D.G. Tendulkar, *Mahatma*, Vol. VII, p.381.

[62] *Young India*, 21. 02. 1929.

[63] *Harijan*, 23. 03. 1947.

[64] *Harijan*, 08.05. 1937.

[65] *Harijan*, 31.07.1937.

[66] M. K. Gandhi, *Consructive Programme: Its Meaning and Place*, p.17.

[67] *Ibid*, p.19.

[68] M. K. Gandhi, *The Story of My Experiments with Truth*, p.249.

Chapter 8

Comparison of Luther and Gandhi: Convergence and Divergence

Some similarities in the life, work and the ideologies of Martin Luther and Mahatma Gandhi in liberating the people from religious and political destruction prevailing in both the Church and the Society. Both were highly religious and got sufficient education. They objected to a society in which there was oppression, exploitation, ignorance and disparity. What they said, what they meant and what they did are even now significant for the emancipation and upward mobility of the oppressed. Having felt the social and religious responsibility, they advocated transformation for social, political, economic, religious and educational orders. Their teachings and treatment can be juxtaposed with the challenges that the oppressed are facing today. Since their understanding was always existential and anthropocentric, they became companions of the oppressed and helped them to see how and where they stand. They also inspired the people to renew their commitment and to expedite their participation in the struggle for justice.

The absence of unity is a common phenomenon among the people because, in a country like India, they are religiously and geographically divided and separated, and they speak different dialects. As people belong to various sub-castes they do not have proper integration and coordination. In this situation Luther and Gandhi indicate the concept of solidarity as a code word for their liberation because solidarity was one of the elements of the success of Luther's reformatory deeds. When they wanted to rebuild and reconstruct the socio-economic, political and religious systems, they created a sense of solidarity. They especially established solidarity with the exploited mass and called them to the united struggle against all sorts of injustice. They put an end to the divisions based on various dialects and awakened the national consciousness to unity. In short, their idea of Solidarity served as an instrument in the process of reformation and revolution in bringing changes in the society. Therefore, the concept of solidarity is recommended for the liberation of the oppressed and depressed. When they are united they will surely succeed in their struggle for liberation because united they succeed, divided they fall is the message that was imparted by them.

Luther and Gandhi's *social ideology* was based mainly on the protest against exploitation and demanding equality. They were against inequality, ill-treatment, narrow mindedness and oppressive culture. They challenged the dominant consciousness of their day and objected to the inhuman treatment and inequalities which were threats to building up human relationship. They asserted the dignity and the rights of all human beings in all walks of life and declared that everyone should live a dignified life because it is disgraceful for anyone to live without self-respect. They became sharper and said that no one should live at the mercy of others. In other words, their chief aim was to raise the marginalized to a higher and dignified level. Gandhiji took interest to work for the welfare of all (Sarvodaya) with emphasis on the welfare of the last (Antyodaya). They advocated the dignity of neighbours as human beings and their rights as full citizens and full members of the community. Luther had a deep concern for the welfare of neighbour. Gandhi also advocated the spirit of neighbourliness through his concept of Swadeshi. In doing so, they sought to abolish the differences that result from wealth, power supremacy etc.

Luther vehemently opposed the priests when they withheld the cup from the laity. He said that the priests should not erect fences which affirmed inequality since every baptized member has equal rights. Thus he broke down the master-slave relationship of the time. Gandhi through his ideas of casteless and classless society and trusteeship worked for social and economic equality in the society. Luther and Gandhi did not remain silent in the midst of injustice but they had a bigger voice and stronger disapproval on injustice. They did the maximum to change the unjust institutions and sinful structures wherein injustice exists. In other words, they opposed the unjust structures which had their roots and tenacity in injustice and wanted to reconstruct the structures and preserve justice. They were of the opinion that changes would take place only when the unjust structures were changed. Luther and Gandhi opposed capitalism when it guarded and defended inequality, that is, inequality in treatment and opportunity. They condemned social structures and economic organizations which led people to humiliation and degradation.

They encounter inequalities in leadership roles as it continues to be the monopoly of upper castes in the realm of the economic as many live below the poverty line; in residential status as they live in huts in the segregated areas; in occupation as they have no option to choose their own occupation; in profession as they are always pushed to do low paid jobs; and in education as most of them are illiterates. Owing to these inequalities the people of the nation are pushed into the state of poverty, illiteracy, untouchability and so on. At this juncture they inspire as well as instigate the poor to organize legitimate struggles in order to be released from rejection and segregation. Luther exhorts them further that they should continue their struggles till the unequal vertical social order is transformed to the horizontal social order where all are equals. Thus they become more relevant for the exploited who aspire for more recognition, love, dignity and equality.

Luther and Gandhi were differing in achieving the just social implications which were denied by the dominated groups in the society. To gain the natural justice Luther allowed war with the opponents. He justified war and he allowed rulers to go to war in order to protect their subjects not only against internal violence but also against external attack. In other words, a prince may go to war in defense of his people if they are invaded by another power. He thought that a war of self-defense was a form of punishment on the invader. In other words, Luther justified war only when it was lawful and in self-defense. He also distinguished wars into wars of desire, and wars of necessity. Gandhi never went or encouraged war or any untoward incidents to gain the natural justice which was denied in the community life. Gandhi always expected people only to use non-violent methods even though achievement of goal may be delayed. Even today Luther and Gandhi's teachings were more significant and relevant for the oppressed people who have experienced inequalities for centuries in various fields.

In *politics,* Luther and Gandhi's nationalism and promotion of solidarity were deeply rooted in their life and work. In his writings and speeches, Luther always insisted on the inter-relation and the integration of the Germans. And Luther and Gandhi never encouraged and allowed politics in the religious and educational systems. For a period of forty years, from birth till the writing of Indian Home Rule, Gandhi was in the making, or in the process of evolution. He was preparing himself and others during this period for the final battle in India for India's liberation. This is evident from Gandhi's statement and actions and contacts during this period of forty years especially when he was in South Africa. That is why he came to India five times and went to England three times during his tenure in South Africa and met innumerable persons high and low and made the South African question and India's freedom a burning issue of the first order and priority. Gandhi put into practice the ideas couched in *Hind Swaraj* for the next forty years of his life. In other words, Gandhi combined in himself Karl Marx and Lenin. He has succeeded more than any other leader or social reformer of the world in this respect, holding truth as the goal, love as the means, and justice as the result. Gandhi was able to transplant truth, love and justice to innumerable unknown activists and a number of outstanding known activists like Rajendra Prasad, Sardar Patel, Vinoba Bhave, Jayaprakash Narayan, Martin Luther

King, Nelson Mandela and the like. What is summarized above is a sketch of Gandhi's revolution in the realm of 'War without violence' for social welfare and justice. Gandhi was not a mere political thinker and freedom fighter but he aimed at constructing a new social order called Sarvodaya.

In *political ideology* Luther and Gandhi differ. Luther classifies the difference and distance between the secular government and the spiritual government. For him the spiritual head should not involve in politics and politics is purely for the secular people. He never allowed the religious head to be the part of the secular government. This ideology was not accepted by many of the Popes and they were waiting for a time to send Luther out of the Church. Gandhi was supportive that every one or all the citizens of India should participate in politics. But he never encouraged politics in the field of education and other constructive programmes. Luther was the man of the masses. Gandhi was supportive that every one or all the citizens of India should participate in politics.

The economic ideology of Luther and Gandhi disclosed constructive criticism and protest against the dehumanizing process and unethical exploitation. They opposed the evil and unfair trading practices and strongly denounced greedy and avaricious behaviour and the unjust advantages taken by the capitalists and the merchants because they exploited the poorer class and converted them to beggars. They also objected to those who monopolized trade because they did not like the economic strength of the community resting in the hands of a few powerful capitalists which in turn would make them exploiters. When the goods were sold for the highest prices and the poorer classes were exploited, Luther vehemently protested against the greed for excessive profit. On the contrary he asserted that the true purpose of selling ought to be to satisfy the needs of the masses rather than gaining enormous profits. When the practices of commerce became shameful, unjust and illegal, he categorically says that the concern must be directed more towards doing no injury to the poor customers than towards taking unjust advantage of a specific situation. In setting prices, account must be taken of the common good and, above all, prices must express distributive justice. The poor customers must not be made into paupers but enabled to live with dignity and decency.

Luther and Gandhi struggled against the unjust economic system and regularly fueled the search for more just and equal distribution. When there were widespread abuses in the financial exactions and when the Church authorities robbed the common people by way of indulgences, dispensations, tithes, pilgrimages, and so on, their indignation went to the extreme because they were no longer concerned with people but with money. The purpose of money ought to be to help the needy and not to make enormous and excessive profit. Thus they attacked those who made heavy profit without doing any work and without showing any concern for the needy. During their entire life, they involved in the quest for justice and never got tired of social activities. Luther powerfully protested against the indulgence system as it was, according to him a clear fraud. It devoured and impoverished the masses and widened the disparity between the haves and have-nots. Luther was highly against selling indulgence and also forcing the people to buy the ticket of indulgence as a pass to the entry in heaven. He protested against this because as per the papal indication economically backward who was not buying indulgence will go to purgatory. Gandhi was critical of capitalism and he boldly protested against the capitalist system because he found it irrational, inhuman and unscientific. It helped only a minority of people to enjoy all the power and privileges. In other words, it helped only the moneyed people to accumulate their wealth further but destroyed the human values of the masses.

Luther and Gandhi protested against luxury in the midst of poverty and argued that no one has any right to hold large property or to accumulate it. Property ought to be used redemptively and creatively to help the needy and to develop the social and economic order so that it can be a help rather than a hindrance, particularly to the weaker sections. He added that all things are common property and, therefore, to be used humbly in the services of the needy and their welfare. The economically backward who are exploited in so many ways should learn from Luther and Gandhi to show their protest against any sort of exploitation which affects their growth and they should do it then and there without caring about the power or the status of the exploiter. Thus, within a highly unequal and hierarchical social order, they expressed a concern for the poor and an opposition to ostentation and luxury. In other words, they questioned the unquestioned hierarchical social order for the sake of justice.

They should be a critical force and should make a strong element of protest and revolution. Resistance ought to be a legitimate part of their struggle. With their antagonistic voice, they showed that there is a force to protest, condemn and denounce exploitation. If the poor people keep quiet, the exploiters and their exploitation should continue and increase. Hence, whenever exploitation is evident to their notice, they should protest because protest should be a part of their struggle for liberation through which they can achieve their goal.

Luther and Gandhi spoke highly of the poor and pledged to eliminate the practice of begging. They vehemently attacked the idea that by encouraging begging one can obtain merit by way of giving alms to beggars. They added that charity is not at all enough because it does not go to the root of the matter but rescues temporarily the victim without doing anything to remove begging completely. In reaction, they worked out a structural means that is a 'common chest' to put an end to begging to remove the perpetual dependency of the poor. They dedicated themselves to the cause of the marginalized and gave special attention to those without a voice. They identified with them and their aim was to regain justice for them. They fought for their rights, that is, fraternity for their minds and equality and liberty for their spirit. When human values were consistently ignored due to the spread of capitalism and when profit came before the lives of human beings and when money became the measure of value and disregarded the value of poor people, they challenged this and strongly endorsed that human beings are more important than material things and ought to be the first consideration and never be sacrificed to the claims of materialism. To eradicate poverty they went for self-employment that may benefit the daily need of the poor people.

Luther and Gandhi's *religious ideology* come from their rich religious background. Their parents taught them how to respect and follow religion in their personal life. Gandhi was a lover of religions and never went against the other religious faiths. He was always after to purify the religion within. Both were not in favour of blindly supporting the interpretations and practice comes from the religious head in the name of religion. They stood as a motivating factor for the eradication of evil practices that were happening in the name of religion. It is obvious that the reformatory and revolutionary works of Luther and Gandhi inaugurated cut across the entire spectrum of society and stimulated the creative process, facilitating strong reaction towards change. It also added a new dimension to the process. It gave the masses an insight into the socio-political, economic and religious situations in which they lived so that they could be aware of the root causes of their oppression. In other words, the writings of Luther and Gandhi gave awareness to those who were not conscious of their own life, self-confidence and courage to alter it. The common inspiration and sense of responsibility gave the power to shape their future. They involved themselves with courage and fearlessness to abolish injustice. With this experience they resorted to the potentiality and the dynamic role of literature to liberate from poverty. Gandhi condemned the unwanted occurrences happening in the name of religion. He stood with Raja Ram Mohan Roy and Christian missionaries for the eradication of caste system, sati, female infanticide, child marriage, *devadhasi* system etc. And he emphasized on the truthful religious practices that may empower the ordinary people to have a real faith in God. Gandhi to a great extent wanted to see 'Truth' in the centre part of all religious practices.

Luther advocated abolishing *forced celibacy*. The emperors, Arch-bishops and Popes were disturbed by the great Luther. The authorities were not able to punish this man because he wanted to reform the church and the society in accordance to the word of God. The early influence of Luther enabled him to stand for the truth. Finally he was able to advocate the abolition of celibacy in the new religious order. Luther consistently stood for freedom and studiously avoided doing anything which would coerce the minds of people. His idea of freedom was opposed to all attempts to dominate the minds of people. He stood with the afflicted and despised and defended their liberty and created among them the awareness that all have the same dignity and equal standing. With his doctrine of justification by faith alone he affirmed the dignity of every person by way of imparting the truth that God accepts everyone even the sinner unconditionally. In other words, he ruled out the idea of merit and ranking with his emphasis on the priesthood of all believers and he destroyed the prerogative power of the clergy and declared spiritual democracy. Gandhi entered in the family life, later found it difficult to give time to his family affairs. He was not negative or supportive to celibacy life. However, Gandhi leaves it to the freedom of individuals.

In religious contribution Luther and Gandhi stood as purifiers of religious faith. As per them religion has to create or provide a common platform to the people for worship without any discrimination in the name of caste, colour and creed. The 16th century reformation of Luther in Germany was among the Christians and therefore concentration on reformation was mostly related to the sphere of religious activities and the reformation mostly benefitted the people of a particular faith. Since India is secular, democratic and religiously pluralistic Gandhi's reformatory and revolutionary action was not limited to a particular community or religious group. His work was mostly allied with freedom and development, and he never allowed any division among the people in the name of religion, caste, colour and creed. Luther stood for religious freedom. By doing this he was able to fight for the social, economic, educational and political development of the deprived people of the society. Gandhi stood strongly for national freedom. While doing this he was able to fight for the eradication of poverty and the evil practices prevailing in the society in the name of religion.

Luther and Gandhi's *educational ideology* had a unifying effect on the people. From their childhood onwards they gave importance for learning.

They were equipped well with school and college education. They were convinced with the fact the education is an effective instrument to bring far-reaching changes because it helps to acquire knowledge and creates awareness. It assists to build up an egalitarian society. In other words, it develops the total personality and aids to elevate the socio-economic growth of the underprivileged. But unfortunately most of the people are denied and prevented from having access to the field of education. The poor have only a few years of schooling. As a result, they face enormous disabilities and experience unending crises because they cannot obtain employment and higher salaried posts are unimaginable for them. Owing to their poor education they fail to know the legal provisions or the educational privileges. In short their illiteracy itself is a stumbling-block for their development and betterment.

To educate and instruct the people Luther and Gandhi involved in literary contribution that may enable the people to think the importance of education needed for a meaningful life in society. Luther's German Bible had a unifying effect on the people, when he made the translation of it in the language of the masses. His order of worship in the vernacular language created a spirit of nationalism among the Germans. It became the most powerful agent for raising the consciousness of the suffering mass. It may be recalled here that Gandhi when he was imprisoned in Yeravda prison in 1930 he translated 18 chapters of Gita in Gujarati language and sent them in his weekly letters to the members of Sabarmati ashram who found it difficult to follow Sanskrit. Similarly he also published Indian opinion in four languages viz., Gujarati, Hindi, Tamil, and English to take the message of non-violence to the Indians in South Africa. Also he propagated the importance of education through mother-tongue through his Basic Education Scheme (Nai Talim).

Luther and Gandhi guided the poor to realize the power of education which is the foremost phenomenon of their liberation. They applied this criterion when they wanted to reform religion and society. They envisioned a just society by way of educating the common people. They decided to make them conscious of their situation and the exploitation to which they were subjected and their rights and their capability for action. They thought that the prevailing injustices were the result of their ignorance and that when they were equipped with knowledge they could enjoy freedom and liberty. They therefore published a variety of books and pamphlets and created hope and confidence to fight against violation, abuses and injustice. When education was a monopoly of the elite, they made a breakthrough and made it everybody's property. When education was meant only for men, they made it accessible to both the sexes. When education was held in contempt by the masses owing to the rise of materialism and commercial activities, and when the parents wanted their children to spend time in earning rather than learning, Luther fervently appealed to them to educate their children. When they failed to respond positively, he appealed to the priestly community as well as the civil authorities to induce and persuade the parents to turn towards education. To convince the parents, Luther himself offered a new educational policy, that is, study and work simultaneously.

Above all, Luther and Gandhi themselves helped and encouraged students to continue and complete their studies. For example, Luther's ninety five theses were released in order to make a direct protest against malpractices and to make the masses to be aware of their abuses. His German translation of the Bible was published to meet an emergency. He released it in the tongue of the people in order to bridge the gap between the hierarchy and the common people. He also put an end to the feeling that the scripture belongs to one particular priestly community. Though the people were released from the heretical teachings the activities of the hierarchy kept the masses in a state of oppression. During the Peasant's War Luther wrote frequently and transmitted his ideas and views in order to advise as well as condemn both the rulers and the peasants. He released his tracts to avert strife, bloodshed and civil war. His tracts on trade and usury threatened and condemned the trading community and brought to light the unjust and avaricious behaviour of the merchants. Luther published such documents to make the masses conscious of the evil and tricky practices of the merchants. With his treatise on education he impressed the values and importance of education on both the civil authorities and parents and protected the children from illiteracy. Again it was their treatise on education that helped to produce good and able leaders both for the Church and the society.

To overcome such evil practices they felt the need of education. Luther and Gandhi did their utmost and took diligence and care to help the common people to gain intellectual liberty which is a must for the transformation of the social order. In other words, Luther firmly believed that any change would begin only with the education. Hence, formal and informal education are highly essential for the poor to liberate themselves from their age-old oppression and this is the thing that they imparted to the poor who are educationally backward. One of the very important services that they did for society was their writings. They powerfully utilized the media of printing and published voluminous literature, made liberal use of the information explosion and a flood of reformatory writings emerged from their pen and they became the popular literature of the people. Their documents were designed to meet the need of the hour. They were a conscious attempt to influence people and to prepare them for transformation. With their writings, they made people, especially those who belonged to the weaker sections, understand the real situation critically. Their works created an atmosphere wherein people began to carry on the struggle for their liberation and social transformation. They also gave them great confidence and created a spirit of responsibility to get involved and to liberate themselves from the clutches and chains surrounding them. Through their treatises on education Luther and Gandhi impressed the values and importance of education on both the civil authorities and parents and protected the children from illiteracy. The common people got new vision, new courage, new impulses, new perception, a new kind of inspiration and the sense of responsibility and also the power to shape their fortune. They involved themselves in courage and fearless attempts to abolish injustice.

Luther and Gandhi struggled hard to regain the denied natural justice in the society. These revolutionaries were not appreciated by many therefore the end of their life was not peaceful. Luther was excommunicated from the parent Church and Gandhi was shot to death by one of his fellow travellers. People of the nations were not able to access the value of their ideology and service to the nations. In our contemporary context the poor are facing and experiencing different kinds of injustices. They are debarred and restricted from using public roads; from drawing water from public wells; from entering into temples; from staying in lodges; from leading marriage procession through the main streets of the villages; from walking in the areas of touchable with open umbrellas or footwear; from wearing decent dresses and ornaments; from cremating the dead bodies in the public cremation ground; from utilizing the services of barbers and washer men; from giving high sounding names to their children and from speaking the classical language. To the poor who are experiencing such injustices, Luther and Gandhi suggest 'struggle' to be the means of winning, because without struggle there can be neither liberation nor transformation and renewal. Change is possible only through human struggle. In the context of religious riots and community clashes, Luther and Gandhi's ideologies are more relevant and applicable to impart religious tolerance, peace and harmony in the society. There are more similarities than instances of divergence in the life and work of Luther and Gandhi. Their social, political, economic, religious and educational contribution towards the freedom of individuals is noteworthy in our religious pluralistic context. In other words, the liberation of the poor, according to Luther and Gandhi, purely and simply depends on the constant and constructive struggle for justice.

Conclusion

It is enormously exciting to know about Martin Luther and Mahatma Gandhi, the remarkable leaders who opened a new era in the history of the Christian Church and Indian politics, and were known as great heroes in world history. Both the leaders were the architects of the destiny of their own lives and that of their nations at different periods. Both of them were rare and remarkable men of history and they inspired and led so successfully the reformation and revolution in the 16th and 20th century in Germany and India respectively.

Luther is a great example of a man of brilliant and varied gifts of intellect and heart, who used his gifts and talents to reform the Church. His reformatory zeal and goals strengthened both the Church and society. He lived in the 16th century in Germany and stood for eradicating the evil forces that prevailed both in the religion and in the society, particularly in Christian religion. The religious, social and political context of the 16th century also pushed him into the storm of reform. He stood strongly and challenged boldly the highest constituted powers of heaven and earth, Pope and Emperor. He discovered the evangelical faith and truth. He began to fight for the truth which was taught by Jesus and the Apostles.

Luther challenged the authority of the Church in matters of faith, doctrine and practices. He shook the very foundation of the Roman Church. He said salvation should not be viewed as something earned or bought by prayers and money and there should not be a sense of the mechanical about the very life of the Church. He did the maximum to the Church and the society. He was the man behind the right changes in the teachings and practices of the Church. He is remembered as the ecumenical figure and hero for the invention of a new Church called Protestantism. He brought freedom to the people in worship. Hierarchy in the structure of worship was highly condemned and the word of God was given prominence in the services. He stood for the religious and political liberation of the German people.

Luther was condemned by the Catholic Church. The great reformer was highly disturbed by the religious head of the Church and was excommunicated from the mainline Church. He stood strong in his conviction, broke the celibacy life and also provided a life for a nun in a monastery. His intention was not to have a new Church. Due to the excommunication, the Catholic Church was divided into two streams, namely Roman Catholic and Protestantism. He was condemned as a heretic by the Roman Church and also declared an outlaw by the Holy Roman Emperor. Yet, he became a successful Reformer and champion of evangelical faith.

It is indeed hard to believe that Gandhi is no more in our midst to-day. His powerful personality has left such an indelible influence on every aspect of our individual and national life. He embodied in his own person, all those great and lofty principles which have throughout the ages governed and given sustenance to the life and thought of the millions of this country. The inspiration of his leadership has helped many a perplexed soul to find the path of peace and truth. In the early 19th century slavery and bondage prevailed in many parts of the country. People were suffering from different kinds of epidemics and medical facilities were not accessible to all. Economically, religiously and politically high class people enjoyed all the privileges. In this context, he stood for the freedom of the people from British domination and freed the nation from the hands of the white people. He worked for the people by responding to the issues of the people. He stood with the ordinary people and fought for their political freedom.

The hierarchy of the British management kept the Indians as slaves and they were not able to raise their voice for the betterment of the country. Gandhi was able to realize the need of freedom. Therefore he stood for the unity of the nation by keeping the Indians under one umbrella. He respected all the religions and was friendly with the all caste people. He lived as a model figure of his age. The speciality in him was that he lived for the people. He loved the country, wanted to see the country without any division in the name of caste, colour and creed. The spirit of nationalism was deeply rooted in him. He called the people to use things made by the people of our country (Be Indian and buy Indian in spirit).

The people of the country suffered from various common and contagious diseases. Outbreaks of epidemics became regular and seasonal. Health care and education were the other areas in which he involved himself to lift the people from their ignorance. He knew very well that through education and health care he would be able to save the life of the people. Gandhi served the country as a nation builder, emancipator and educationist to free the people from the hands of the white people. He stood as a role model of leadership and also showed a way of life for India to survive as a free nation. His message, however, is not only for India but for the entire world. He expected that man can live in peace with his fellowman and they can promote each other's welfare.

Luther and Gandhi were not born great but in middle class families. But they trained themselves to face all risks cheerfully and undergo sufferings gracefully. Though they came from different environments, their devotion and dedication to social progress in all spheres and selfless service to the poor brought them close to each other. They coveted no power, no position, and no wealth. And yet they were able to command the respectful obedience of millions in Germany and India. Insults and injuries could not daunt their spirit. It was this fearlessness which they instilled in the hearts of their countrymen and which ultimately led to the success of the struggle for freedom. They touched all the spheres of life--social, political, economic, religious, educational etc.

Luther and Gandhi were good administrators, good scholars, writers and teachers of mankind. They were men of simple living and high thinking. Their lives were unique examples of unity of thought, word and action. They would not lay down one policy for the leaders and another for the masses. What they preached, they practised. That was one of the secrets of their success. They lived like poor people and worked for their welfare. It was this self-imposed poverty which endeared them to the people, who learnt from them self-reliance and self-respect. Their emphasis was on spirituality and moral life. Both of them wrote for the specific causes they were working for. The supreme importance of both of them lies in their effort to build up practicable and workable alternatives in the midst of the encircling gloom of growing economic disparity, political turmoil and social anarchy in Germany and India.

Luther and Gandhi's life and backgrounds were helpful for them to strive hard to accomplish the task of what was required in the religion and society. Both of them stood for Truth and brought reformation and revolution for the benefit of the people. They suffered for the people and their contributions remain as a living dictionary. Gandhi was not properly understood or rightly respected by the people of this nation. The end of his life was not peaceful: He was gunned down by a man in an unexpected situation. Both these leaders were men of action. They were great social scientists. There was no gap between their words and actions. Their thoughts were powerful. They tried to translate their thoughts into action rather than put them in flowery and attractive language.

Today, we are living in a religious pluralistic context. Globalization, tremendous scientific growth, technological culture, market forces, religious fundamentalism, terrorism and media explosion have shaped the new millennium world context. These forces tend to make a new community with less human values and accelerate dehumanization. Increasing rates of crime, sexual exploitation, suicide and ecological crises challenge humanity at various levels. Moral life is being threatened tremendously. The genuine spirit of human relationship is disturbed and distorted in the postmodern context due to the competitive culture. Inequality, imbalances and disparities in the field of education and employment have created a complex and unhealthy competitive situation and reduced opportunities of life among the people. All the human potential is seen only as the ability to generate profit.

Violence and terrorism are the breaking and flash news of the media, disturbing the normal life of the people. The developed countries justify war as an instrument to eradicate terrorism. In this prevailing context the people of this country are longing for a change in all dimensions of human life. To change the life situation of the people, it is a must to know the role played by the historical heroes who lived in Germany and India. Their differences were few and their similarities were many, which bound them together and so the people affectionately called Martin Luther, the Father of Protestant Christianity and Mahatma Gandhi, the Father of the nation. It is the duty of the younger generation to study the life history of the two historical heroes who lived in different political, religious contexts in Germany and India. Their work and contribution can be researched separately by giving more time and space to their literary contributions. The work and teaching of Luther and Gandhi may be studied systematically, interpreted rightly to the younger generation to involve actively in bringing life to the people who are longing for it and deprived in society.

Bibliography

(i) Martin Luther

Primary Sources

Jaroslav Pelikan and Helmut Lehmann, (ed.,) *'Luther's Works', Vols.* 1-55, (1955-1975): (The American edition of *Luther's works* in English Translation), St Louis/ Philadelphia, New York.

Secondary Sources

(i) Books

Alagodi S.D.L. (1986): *God Help Me*, Banerjee Printers, Serampore, North India.

Aland Kurt (ed.,) (1967): *Martin Luther's 95 Theses* , St. Louis, Concordia.

Andor Muntag (1977): *Theory and practice of the Doctrine of the Two kingdoms in the Lutheran Church in Hungary*, LWF, Geneva.

Andrew, K.H. Hsiao, (1979): *An Outline of Luther's Concept of Theological Education as It Applies to Asian churches*, The Gospel and Asian Traditions, LWF, Geneva.

Anza Lemo, (1987): *The Doctrine of the Two Kingdoms – Its Socio Economic Implications in our Societies*, The Gospel and Asian Traditions, Bangalore.

Atkinson J.(1968): *Martin Luther and Birth of Protestantism*, Harmondsworth, London.

Bainton Ronald,H. (1950): *Here I Stand*, Nashville, Abingdon.

-Do- (1952):*The Reformation of the Sixteenth Century*, The Beacon Press, Boston.

Bernard Reardon, M.G. (1981): *Religious Thought in the Reformation*, Longman, London.

Brown Robert MC Afee. (1961): *The Spirit of Protestantism*, Oxford University, London.

Cargill Thompson, W.D.J. (1987): *The Political Thought of Martin Luther*, Harvester, Sussex.

Carter Lindberg, (1993): *Beyond Charity: Reformation Initiatives for the Poor*, Minneapolis, Fortress, Augsburg.

-Do- (ed.,) (1985): *Property and poverty in the History of the Chruch- Christian Ethics,* LWF, Geneva.

Charles Jacob, M. (1925): *The Story of the Church,* The United Lutheran Publication House, Philadelphia.

Dickens, A.G. (1974): *The German nation and Martin Luther,* William Clowes and Sons, London.

-Do- (1966): *Reformation and Society in Sixteenth Century Europe,* Thames and Hudson, London.

Edward D. Schnieder. (1990): *Lutheran Theological Foundations for Social Ethics,* LWF, Geneva.

Eric W. Grietch.(1976): *Martin Luther- 0' God's Curt jester,* Fortress, Philadelphia.

Eric. W. Grietch and Robert W. Jenson.(1976):*Lutheranism,* Fortress, Philadelphia.

Fife R.H. (1959): *The Revolt of Martin Luther,* Concordia, New York.

George P. Fisher. (1875): *The Reformation,* Charles Scribner's, New York.

Gerhard Ritter. (1968): *Why the Reformation occurred in Germany- Reformation Material or Spiritual,* Lexington.

Gerta scharffenorth. (1983): *Becoming Friends in Christ,* LWF, Geneva.

Gord on Rupp (ed.,), (1973): *Luther and government, Luther A Profile,* Macmillan, London.

Gordon Rupp. (1967): *Luther's Ninety-five Theses and the Theology of the Cross,* ST. Louis, Concordia.

Gustav Freytag. (1897): *Martin Luther,* AMS, New York.

Hans J. Hillerbrand. (1971): *Christendom Divided – The protestant Reformation,* Hutchinson & Co, London.

Hans Schwartz. (1985): *True Faith in the True God, An introduction to Luther's Life and Thought,* Minneapolis, Fortress, Augsburg.

-Do- *Luther's Doctrine of Two kingdoms – Help or Hindrance for Social Changes,* Minneapolis, Fortress, Augsburg.

Hegel G.W.F, (1953): *Philosophy of Right,* (Eng.tr) T.M. Knox, Oxford University Press, London.

Heinrich Bornkamm. (1958): *Luther's World of Thought,* St. Louis, Concordia.

-Do- (1962): *Reformation and Society in 16th Century Europe,* St. Louis, Concordia.

Heinz Bluhm. (1965): *Luther's German Bible - Seven Headed Luther,* St.Louis, Concordia.

-Do- (1965): *Martin Luther: Creative Translator,* St. Louis, Concordia.

Hendrix Scott H. (1981): *Luther and the Papacy,* Fortress, Philadelphia.

Holy Bible- Kings James Version, Proverbs 13:23

Hugh Tomson Kerr. (ed.,), (1943): *A compend of Luther's Theology,* The Westminister, Philadelphia.

Ian D. Kingston Siggins. (1972): *Luther,* Oliver & Boyd, Edinburg.

Jacobs, H.E. (1898): *Martin Luther: The Hero of the Reformation,* New York.

James Atkinson. (1968): *Martin Luther and the Birth of Protestantism,* John Knox, Atlanta.

John T. Noonan. (1959): *The Scholastic Analysis of Usury*, Harward University, Cambridge.

John Tonkin. (1971): *The Church and the Secular Order in Reformation Thought*, Columbia University, New York.

Jurgen Moltmann. (1984): *On Human Dignity: Political Theology and Ethics*, SCM, London.

Karl Holl. (1938): *The Cultural Significance of the Reformation*, Living Age Book, New York.

Koenigsberger, H. G. (ed.,), (1973):*Luther:A Profile*, Macmillan, London.

Koestlin, J. (1893): *Life of Luther*, Awingon Press, NewYork.

Latourette, Kenneth Scott. (1953): *History of Christianity*, Harper and Brothers, New York.

Lawrence P. Buch and Jonathan W.(1972) *The Social History of the Reformation*, Ohio State University, Columbus.

Lefever, H.C. (1954): *The history of the Reformation*, CLS, Madras.

Lenker, J. N. (1967) : *Luther's Large Catechism*, Minnesota, Augsburg.

Lewis W. Spitz. (1972): *Luther's Social Concern for Students,* Ohio State University, Columbus.

-Do- (ed.,) (1968): *Spiritual Lexington*, D.C. Heath, Lexington.

Lindberg Carter, Piety. (1984): *Politics and Ethics: Reformation Studies* in *Honour of George Wolfgang Forell,* 16th Century Journal Publishers, Kirksville.

Martin Brecht, (1994): *Marthin Lutehr: Shaping and Defining the Reformation* - 1521-1532, Minneapolis, Fortress, Augsburg.

Manickam Kampar& groups, (ed.,), (1988): *Selected Works of Martin Luther*, Tamil Nadu Theological Club, Madurai.

Mc Grath, Alister E. (1985): *Luther's Theology of the Cross,* Basil Blackwell, Oxford. (1988): *Reformation Thought*, Basil Blackwell, Oxford.

Mondal.K. Ashis. (1976): *New Movements*, ISPCK, Calcutta.

Pascal, R. (1933): *The Social Basis of the Reformation*, Watts, London.

Paul Russel. (1986) : *Lay Theology in The Reformation*, Cambridge University, London.

Per Frostin. *God versus Capitalism: Would Luther have Enjoyed Mars?* Tugon. 8. Cf. WA 51: 331-424.

Rev, J.M. (1917): *Luther Research* AMS, New York.

Robert Kolf. (2006): *Luther's Way of Thinking*, Luther Academy of India, Trivandram.

Schwiebert, E.G. (1950): *Luther and His time*, St. Louis, New York.

Searle, G.W. (1974): *The Counter Reformation*, Oxford University Press, London.

Timothy George. (1988):*Theology of the Reformers*, Hashville, Broadman.

Thomas M. Lindsay. (1950): *A History of Reformation*, Charles Scribner's, New York.

Ulrich Duchbrow. (1977):*Two Kingdoms – The use and Misuse of a Lutheran Theological Concept*, LWF, Geneva.

Ulrich Michael Kremer. (1990): *Martin Luther in the Perspective of Historiography, Seven Headed Luther*, Peter Newman brooks, Clarendon, oxford.

Walker Williston. (1985): *A history of the Christian Church*, Charles Scribner's Sons, New York.

Walter Altmann.(1992): *Luther and Liberation*, Fortress, Minneapolis.

William H. Lazareth. (1960): *Luther on the Christian Home*, Muhlenberg, Philadelphia.

(ii) Journal Articles

Armas k. E. Holmio, 'Luther and War', *Lutheran Quarterly*, No: 4,1952.

Cargill Thompson, W.D.J. 'The Two Kingdoms and The Two Regiments: Some problem of Luther's Zwei-Reihe-lehre', *Journal of Theological Studies*, Vol.20, Bangalore,1969.

Carl Arthur Piepkorn, 'A Lutheran Theologian looks at the Ninety-five theses', *Journal of Theological Studies*, No: 28, Bangalore, 1967.

Carter Lindberg, 'Theory and practice: Reformation models of Ministry as Resource for the present', *Lutheran Quarterly*, No: 27, Madras, 1975.

_____ 'There shall be No Beggars among Christians: Karlstate, Luther and Origin of Protestant Poor relief', *Church History*, No:16, CHAI, Bangalore,1977.

_____ 'Beyond Charity: Reformation Initiatives for the poor', *Church History*, No: 1, CHAI, Bangalore, 1977.

_____ 'Theory and practice: Reformation models of ministry as Resource for the present', *Lutheran Quarterly*, No: 27, Madras, 1975.

_____ 'Thorough a Glass Darkly', *The Ecumenical Review,33*, CHAI, Bangalore, 1981.

Craig L. Nessan. 'Liberation Theology's Critique of Luther's Two kingdoms Doctrine', *Currents in Theology and Mission*, No: 16, Bangalore,1968.

Eivind Berggrav. 'State and Chruch – The Lutheran View', *Lutheran Quarterly* No: 4, Madras, 1942.

Faulkner, J.A. 'Luther and Truth-Telling', *Lutheran Quarterly*, No: 54, Madras, 1924.

Haje Holborn, 'The Social Basis of the German Reformation', *Church History*, No: 5, CHAI, Bangalore, 1936.

Hans Schwarz. 'Luther's Doctrine of the Two Kingdoms – Help or Hindrance for Social Change', *Lutheran Quarterly*, No: 27, Madras, 1975.

Harold, J. Grimm. 'Luther's Conception of Territorial and National Loyalty', *Church History*, No: 17, CHAI, Bangalore, 1948.

_____ 'Luther's Contribution to Sixteenth Century Organization for Poor Relif', *Archive for Reformation History*, No:61, CHAI, Bangalore, 1970.

_____ 'Luther's Conception of Territorial and National Loyalty', *Church History*, No: 17, CHAI, Bangalore, 1948.

Jared Wicks. 'Martin Luther's Treatise on Indulgences', *Theological Studies*, No:28, Bangalore, 1967.

John C. Cooper, 'Some Radical Elements in Luther's Theology', *Lutheran Quarterly* No: 20, Madras, 1968.

Kyle C. Sessions. 'The source of Luther's Hymns and the Spread of the Reformation', *Lutheran Quarterly*, No: 17, Madras, 1965.

Lowell C. Gree. 'Resistance to Authority and Luther', *Lutheran Quarterly*, No:6, Madras, 1954.

Norma Everist, 'Luther on Education: Implications for Today', *Currents in Theology and Mission*, Vol. 7, Bangalore, 1965.

_____ 'Luther on Education: Implication for Today', *Currents in Theology and Missions*, No:12, Bangalore, 1985.

_____ 'Luther on Education: Implications for Today', *Currents in Theology and Mission*, Vol.7, Bangalore, 1985.

Patro .S. Subhasot, 'What does Luther Mean to India? Martin Luther's Obedience to God's glory', *The Indian Lutheran*, Vol.3, November, 1983.

Richard Kroner. '*The Meaning of the Reformation Today*', *Lutheran Quarterly*, Madras, 1951.

Robert McNally E. 'The ninety Five Theses of Martin Luther', 1517-1967', *Theological Studies*, No: 28, Bangalore, 1967.

Trutz Rendorff. 'The Doctrine of Two Kingdoms, or the Art of Drawing Distinctions Research concerning the Theological Interpretation of political Affairs', *Lutheran Churches —Salt or Mirror of Society*, Bangalore, 1984.

Walter Altmann. 'Interpreting the Doctrine of the Two Kingdoms: God's Kingship in the Church and in Politics', *Word and World*, Vol.7, 1987.

William A. Johnson. 'Luther's Doctrine of the Two Kingdoms', *Lutheran Quarterly*, No: 15, Madras, 1963.

(ii) Mahatma Gandhi

Primary Sources

The Collected Works of Mahatma Gandhi, Vols.1-100, (1958-1993). The Publication Division, Ministry of Information and Broadcasting, Government of India, New Delhi.

Shriman Narayan, (ed.,) (1986), *The Selected Works of Mahathma Gandhi*, Vol. 1-VI, Navajivan Publishing House, Ahmedabad.

Secondary Sources

(i) Books

Ahluwalia, B.K. and ShashiAhluwalia. (1978): *Facets of Gandhi*, Indian Academic Publishers, New Delhi.

-Do- (1982): *Netaji and Gandhi*, Indian Academic Publishers, New Delhi.

Andrews, C. F. (1987): *Mahatma Gandhi, His life and Ideas*, Anmol Publications, Delhi.

Bhatt, B.D. & Sharma, S.R., (1989): *Women's Education and Social Development*, Bharatiya vidya Bhavan, Bombay.

Bose, Subas chandra. (1964): *Selections from Gandhi*, Asia Publishing House, Bombay.

Charles J. Koilpillai. (1990): *How to Write a Research Essay*, Nalanda House Publications, Madras.

Cherian Gudalur. (1999): *Gandhi's Concept of Truth and Justice*, Poornodaya Book Trust, Kochi.

Cohen R. Morris and Nagel Ernest. (1989): *An Introduction to Logic and Scientific Method*, Allied Publishers Private Limited, New Delhi.

Das, B.C. (1979): *Gandhi in Today's India*, Ashish Publishing House, New Delhi.

Dastur Aloo, J. Usha Mehta. (1991): *Gandhi's Contribution to Emancipation of Women*, Popular prakashan, Bombay.

Desai Morarji. (1978): *The Story of My life*, Volume 1, S. Chand and Co. Ltd. New Delhi.

Dhananjay Keer, (1973): *Mahatma Gandhi, Political Saint and unarmed Prophet*, Bombay.

Elizabeth T. Mclaughlin. (1974): *Ruskin and Gandhi*, Associated University Press, England.

Gandhi, M.K. (1920): *Fellowship of Faith and Unity of Religions*, (e.d.,) By Abdul Majid Khan, G.A. Natesan &Co, Madras.

_____ (1926): *Hind Swaraj or Indian Home Rule*, Ahmedabad, Navajeevan Publishing House, Ahmedabad.

_____ (1928): *Satyagraha in South Africa*, S. Ganesan Publisher, Madras.

_____ (1941): *Constructive Programme: Its Meaning and Place*, Navajivan Publishing House, Ahmedabad.

_____ (1948): *My Philosophy of Life*, Bombay.

_____ (1955): *Truth is God*, Navajivian Publishing House, Ahmedabad.

_____ (1959): *Economic and Industrial life and Relations*, Vol.1, Ahmedabad.

_____ (1968): *My God*, Navajivian Publishing House, Ahmedabad.

_____ (1989): *The Story of My Experiments with Truth*, Mahadev Desai (Tr.), Navajivian Publishing House, Ahmedabad.

Gray, R.M. & Parekh, M.C. (1924): *Mahatma Gandhi*, Navajivan Publishing House, Ahmedabad.

Gousalya, S. (2002): *Gandhi and Kamaraj*, Bestsy Institute of Non- violence and Women Studies, Madurai.

Homer A. Jack. (1983): *The Gandhi Reader*, Indiana University Press, Madras.

Jawaharlal Nehru, (1989): *Discovery of India*, Oxford University Press, New Delhi.

Kripalani, J.B. (1991): *Gandhi: His Life and Thought*, (II-Edition), Publication Division, Government of India, New Delhi.

Kumarappa Barathan, (1968): *Why Prohibition?* Shri Gandhi Seva Ashram, Himachal Pradesh.

Louis Fischer. (1983): *The life of Mahatma Gandhi*, Herper & Row Publishers, New York.

Mallammal, M. (1992): *St. Ramalingam and Mahatma Gandhi*, Valliammal Institution, Madurai.

Mohit Chakarabarti, (1990): *The Gandhian Dimensions of Education*, Daya Publishing House, Delhi.

Muthanna, I.M. (1986): *Mother Besant and Mahatma Gandhi*, Thenpulam Publishers, Vellore.

Nanda, B.R. (1965): *Mahatma Gandhi: A Biography*, University Press, Delhi.

Nirmal Minz,(1970): *Mahatma Gandhi and Hindu-Christian Dialogue*, CLS, Madras.

Pyarelal, (1965): *Mahatma Gandhi - The Last Phase*, Volume- I, Navajivan Publishing House, Ahmedabad .

Paradhan H. Prasad, (1994): *Gandhi, Marx and India*, Association book agencies Pvt. Ltd, Delhi.

Patel, J.P. and Marjorie Sykes, (1987): *Gandhi- His Gift of the Fight*, Rasulia, Hoshagabad, Madhya pradesh.

Patil, V.T. (1983): *Studies on Gandhi*, Sterling Publishers Pvt.Ltd, New Delhi.

Patil, V.T. and Lokapur I.A. (1981): *In Gandhi's Concept of Decentralization: An Analysis*, Gandhi Marg, Vol-III, New Delhi.

Prabu, R.K. and Rao, U.R. (ed.,) (1967): *The Mind of Mahatma Gandhi*, Navajivan Publishing House, Ahmedabad.

Radhakrishnan, S. & Muirhead. (1966): *Contemporary Indian Philosophy*, Unwin Limited, London.

Radhakrishanan Sarvapalli. (1977): *Mahatma Gandhi: Reflection of his Life and Work*, (V Ed.), Jaico Publishing House, Delhi.

Romain Rolland. (1924): *Mahatma Gandhi*, The Century Company, New York.

Samar Guha. (1986): *The Mahatma and Netaji :Two Men of Destiny of India*, Sterling Publishers Private Limited, New Delhi.

Sethi, J.D. (1990): *Gandhi Today*, Vikas Publishing House, Uthar pradesh.

Sharma, D.S. (1967): *Hinduism Through the Ages*, Bharatiya Vidya Bhavan, Bombay.

Sindhu Kulbir Singh. (1985): *Methodology of Research Education*, Sterling Publishers Private Limited, New Delhi.

Singh, K.N. (1979): *Gandhi & Marx* Associated Book Agency, Patna.

Singh, V.P. (1920-1947): *History of Freedom Movement*, Asia Publishing House, Bombay.

Stanly Jones E. (1927): *Mahatma Gandhi - An Interpretation*, Free Press, New York.

Sykes Majorie, J.P. (1986):*Gandhi – His Fight of the Fight*, Hoshagabad, Madhya Pradesh.

Tandon, R.K. (1990): *Women in Modern India*, Indian Publication & Distributers, Delhi.

Tendulkar, D.G. (1960): *Mahatma: Life of Mohandas Karamchand Gandhi*, (Vol.8) (II Ed.), Publication Division, Government of India, New Delhi.

Zaidi, A.M. & Zaidi, S.G. (1885-1947 &1976-1981): *The Encyclopedia of Indian National Congress*, (Vol.12), New Delhi.

Journals and Reports

Fortnightly Reports, II Half of April, 1919, *Tamilnadu Archives,* The Government Press, Madras.

-Do- II Half of November, 1921, *Tamilnadu Archives,* The Government Press, Madras.

Kothari Commission, *The Report of the Educational Commission,* 1946 – 1966.

Rajagopal, P.V. & Jeyaprgasam, S. (ed.,) *Non – Violence,* CESCI, Madurai, 2007-2009.

Sinha, V.C. (ed.,) *Khadi Gramodyog, 'The Journal of Rural Economy',* November, 1982.

(iii) Unpublished Ph.D Thesis

Kulanthaivel, K. **(1965):** *Comparative Study of Educational Philosophies of John Dewey and Mahatma Gandhi,* University of Madras, Madras.

Vellaiammal, R. (2009): *A Comparative Study of Gandhiji and Rajaji,* Gandhigram Rural Institute – Deemed University, Gandhigram.